"Do you regret n[ ] what you did?"

"No, I don't, but I know I ought to!" Julia turned to Raphael, her eyes wide with consternation. "Not for my own sake, but for Christina's. But I don't want you to go to prison. Raphael— oh don't you see? You must let her go. The fuss will all die down—in a month or two you can let me go back. I'll never say anything. I promise you!"

"There is one way of assuring that," Raphael said.

"You mean—kill me?" Her voice broke slightly, and he turned to her with angry disbelief in his eyes.

"Are you insane? Do you take me for a murderer?" He put his arms around her and raised her face to his, gently stroking her cheek.

"Marry me," he said.

VANESSA JAMES began a successful career in London as a critic and journalist and worked as an editor and writer for *Vogue, Harper's Bazaar* and the fashionable magazine *Queen*. She began writing books after her son was born, nonfiction as well as romance novels, which combine winning characters and a fast-paced style. She holds a master's degree in English and is a busy and most versatile writer.

Books by Vanessa James

VANESSA JAMES

prisoner

Harlequin Books

TORONTO • NEW YORK • LONDON
AMSTERDAM • PARIS • SYDNEY • HAMBURG
STOCKHOLM • ATHENS • TOKYO • MILAN

Harlequin Presents first edition December 1986
ISBN 0-373-10937-7

Original hardcover edition published in 1986
by Mills & Boon Limited

CHAPTER ONE

JULIA was late, and she began to run. Partly out of anxiety—there was no knowing what Christina might get up to given fifteen minutes on her own—and partly for the sheer pleasure of it. Because she was in Rome, and she loved the city; because it was the most beautiful day, the first really warm day of spring; but mainly just for the hell of it. Every day in Rome felt special, the very air felt intoxicating. She was twenty-two, and that day she just felt as if anything were possible, and there was nothing, but nothing, that she couldn't do.

She passed the elegant doors of the Hassler hotel, reached the top of the Spanish Steps, paused for a moment to take in her favourite view—the flower-sellers at the foot of the steps, the balcony and wisteria of the house where Keats had died, the streets beyond—and then began to race down the steps.

It was early afternoon, and although there were as yet few tourists in Rome, the Spanish Steps, as always, had a respectable number of visitors. A group of American students; a young man with shoulder-length hair playing the guitar. Several of the men looked up as she raced past, and then turned to watch her with more than passing interest: a tall, slender girl, with a riot of copper-coloured hair. She was wearing the most ordinary clothes—blue jeans, a white T-shirt, flat sandals—but Julia never looked ordinary, no matter what she wore. As one of the students called after her, she turned and acknowledged him with a quick wry grin, the wide full lips lifting at the corners. He rose to his feet in a hopeful manner; Julia's eyes flashed—one quick dismissive glance and he hesitated, then sat down again ruefully. Julia had extraordinary eyes, almost topaz in colour, fringed by lashes that were black and thick. *Don't try it*, said the eyes; even the most persistent of Italians quailed before that glance, and the student was certainly not about to risk their anger.

5

Julia grinned to herself. The look was useful, and she was glad it worked. When she had first come to Rome, and had been less practised, every trip to the shops had ended up a parade—Julia, followed by a gesticulating, eager crowd of love-lorn males, each trying in a multitude of tongues to persuade her that she was the object of his undying affection, and that she ought to have dinner with him forthwith. Julia found it flattering to begin with, and then tiresome. These days she got about the city much more quickly.

She paused at the bottom of the steps and then, on impulse, bought a small bunch of violets from one of the flower-sellers, asking for them, and paying, her distinctive voice slightly husky, in an Italian which was now almost unaccented and perfect. She stood there for a moment, holding the flowers to her face. They smelled glorious: of earth newly washed by rain, of the spring, of the country—of home. For a moment she stood still, forgetting the traffic, the hustle of people, forgetting Rome itself. Then she lowered the flowers, looked up and froze.

The man was there again. It was the same one—she was certain of it. Today he was standing at the foot of the steps, leaning negligently against the wall, regarding her intently and without embarrassment. For a second, no more, their gaze interlocked, and Julia felt colour quicken in her cheeks. It wasn't likely she'd made a mistake. Most definitely, this was not the kind of man you forgot.

He was Italian, she judged, but very tall, well over six foot, aged—she couldn't be sure, but somewhere in his early thirties, she would judge. He was powerfully built, with wide shoulders, not the kind of man you'd like to face in a fight. Exceptionally dark, even for an Italian and his black hair was brushed carelessly back from his tanned forehead, and worn slightly long. Today he was wearing dark glasses which obscured his eyes completely, and gave him a sinister and predatory look, but she had glimpsed his eyes the previous day, and they too were black, deeply set under straight brows—they looked straight through you. He was wearing an open-necked shirt and a pale linen suit that could only have come from a very expensive

tailor. None of the jewellery some Italians affected—no gold
chains, no sub-Hollywood histrionics ... He looked handsome—very. And rich, and bored, and dangerous, and he was
watching her, there was no doubt of it.

She could not understand it. It was four days running now.
She'd first glimpsed him when she'd been guiding a reluctant
and bolshie Christina around the Forum. The next day, in the
museum. The previous day at the café where she and
Christina had lunched in Trastevere. And here he was again
... It could have been coincidence, but she doubted it. On the
other hand, his motives, for an Italian, were obscure. No
attempt had been made to speak to her, to draw her into
conversation.

He was simply there, just as he was now, and Julia wished
heartily that he wasn't. He made her feel nervous and unsure.
She had half a mind to go straight up to him, and ask him—
Are you following me? Because if so, please stop. But she
didn't. She might have been wrong, and then she would have
felt very foolish. And besides she had to be careful, not for her
own sake, but for Christina's.

This was Italy, after all. When she had taken on this job she
had been specifically warned about kidnappers, and the words
of Christina's father, Giovanni, said to be the second richest
industrialist in the country, still rang in her ears. So now
she gave the man a brief, searching glance, consciously
memorising his face. And then turned quickly away, though
not before she saw his lips lift a little at the corners, as if to
mock her. Damn him, she thought. He was probably just an
Italian philanderer with a very un-Italian slow-burn tech-
nique—but she'd mention it to Christina's family, just in case.

She glanced back over her shoulder and heaved a sigh of
relief. It was OK; he wasn't following her ... All the same,
just to be sure, she took a roundabout route, which made her
later, of course. When she finally reached the café where she
and Christina had agreed to meet, she was nearly half-an-hour
late. It was a famous place, and Julia had chosen it as their
regular meeting place carefully, for its clientele were, for the
most part, rich, respectable and elderly.

She wasn't about to risk meeting Christina in the kind of places *she* favoured—somewhere conspicuous, outdoors and fashionable. Christina might only be fifteen, but she looked eighteen, and her ability to pick up unsuitable men had astonished even Julia.

She could see her now, sitting at the back of the inner room—and, thank goodness, it was all right. The bodyguard was still with her, and he was even more practised at fending off unsuitable pick-ups than Julia now was. And beside him, Christina. Plump, heavily made-up, her full mouth turned down at the corners in its habitual sulky pout.

Much to her father's distress, she had cut her hair: it now stuck out in short, punky spikes round her pale face. The eyes were heavily outlined in black, the lips were shiny scarlet. She was wearing, as usual, a skin-tight short skirt, bare legs, spiky-heeled shoes, and a low-cut blouse that left absolutely nothing to the imagination. Eighteen? Julia sighed. Today she looked twenty-five going on forty ... Christina Contadelli, aged fifteen, only daughter of Giovanni and heir, with her elder brother, to a fortune conservatively estimated at some two hundred million dollars. ...

Christina looked up and acknowledged her arrival with an irritable sigh, stubbed out one cigarette and promptly lit another. Julia gave an inward groan. Sometimes she wondered what on earth had possessed her to take on this job. Christina wasn't supposed to smoke. She wasn't supposed to dress like that. She wasn't supposed to ogle waiters, the way she was doing now. She was supposed to be on temporary leave from Le Rosey in Switzerland, which, like five previous schools, had threatened expulsion. The headmistress had been persuaded by Giovanni that a few months away would bring Christina, belatedly, to her senses. She was supposed to be improving her English and her French, with Julia's assistance. She was supposed to be assimilating the culture of her native city, escorted by Julia to its sites and museums, guide book in hand; and exposed by night to irreproachable culture in the shape of concerts, opera performances, and theatre. She was supposed, actually, to stay out of trouble, and start to grow up, and after five months Julia saw little prospect of success.

Julia had been given the job because her father, now retired, had been a student friend of Giovanni years before. Giovanni, with typical impulsiveness, had met Julia once and decided she was just the kind of young woman he needed to take his rebellious daughter under her wing. He offered the job and Julia, who was broke, accepted it. Not long after, Giovanni took off on a business trip to South America, and she hadn't seen him since.

She smiled as she reached Christina's table, held out her hand, and Christina ignored it.

Julia sighed. It was going to be one of the more difficult days—she could see it coming. She might have accepted this job because she needed the money—the translations she did, which she had hoped would finance her stay in Rome, had proved to bring in painfully little. But she had stuck to it for very different motives. Christina often exasperated her and occasionally made her very angry, but Julia also felt sorry for her. In her more optimistic moments she still occasionally hoped that she might be of help to Christina, poor little rich girl that she was ... But that was in the optimistic moments. At other times, and this looked like being one of them, Julia wanted nothing more than to throw in the towel.

As she drew out a chair and sat down Luigi rose quickly to his feet, obviously only too anxious to get away from Christina. He muttered a few quick excuses. They would be back around five? He would inform the servants. There was nothing *Signorina* Hamilton needed? Good, then, if Christina and she would excuse him ...

Christina stopped him with an oddly imperious gesture. She lifted one plump hand from the table; her nails, painted crimson, were bitten almost down to the quick. In spite of her father's instructions not to wear jewellery on these expeditions with Julia, she was wearing a gold bracelet round her wrist that was an inch wide and an inch thick.

'I need some things picking up. Just a few packages. I might need them tonight ...' She enumerated them, insolently, and

Luigi listened impassively. All three knew it was not Luigi's job to fetch and carry for Christina, and all three knew he'd do it just the same.

When he had gone, Julia met Christina's eyes. The girl gave a triumphant little smile.

'Don't say it. I know.' She pulled a face. 'It's not his job. So—why should I care? Daddy pays him well enough. Why should he laze about all afternoon? And anyway ...' she shrugged, 'it amuses me. He wants to tell me to go to hell and he doesn't dare.'

'You're quite right,' Julia interrupted her crisply. 'And it's a great pity he doesn't—it would do you good. But you underestimate him, you know, Christina. He doesn't keep quiet because he's afraid of you, he keeps quiet because he needs his job.'

'Like you, I suppose?' Christina lit another cigarette. 'Why pretend? You're the same as him. You only put up with me because you need the money.'

Julia sighed. She had heard this before. 'We could enjoy ourselves. It doesn't have to be a penance, you know, Christina ...'

'It doesn't have to be, but it is.' Christina's mouth turned down sulkily. 'You don't want to be here, and I don't want to be here. So—what's the point?'

Julia bit back the answer she wanted to give. It was difficult indeed to see what the point was. Christina's English, which she spoke with an affected American accent picked up from rich friends at Le Rosey, had been good when Julia started the job. It had improved minimally; she refused to speak French. She regarded Julia's attempts to interest her in history and culture as a total bore. Her manners, if that were possible, had got worse, not better. What *was* the point?

The point, as Julia had finally convinced herself, was that Christina was actually a clever and talented girl, who happened to have been spoiled rotten and simultaneously neglected for most of her fifteen years. Her mother was dead, her father was constantly away on business, she was now parked with Julia as she had been parked with a succession of nannies and servants since birth. She had everything she wanted and nothing that she wanted, and she pretended to hate others, because, Julia suspected, she hated herself. However, this was amateur psychology, and Julia was too sharp to say what she thought and felt. One hint of the pity she felt and the relationship with Christina, tenuous as it was, would break down completely. So now she shrugged off the girl's rudeness.

'The point is—I'm here now, and it's a beautiful day. What would you like to do?'

'Who cares? I can tell you what I *don't* want to do. I don't want to go trekking around some boring old museum, that's for sure. And I don't want to go to some dusty old picture gallery either. Honestly . . .' Her eyes met Julia's. 'I wonder about you sometimes. I mean—you're not old. You're not bad looking—in fact,' her tone became grudging, 'you can look quite pretty. Yet all you want to do is trek round with a bloody guide book like some ancient American tourist. What's the matter with you, Julia?'

'Just doing what your father wanted, that's all,' Julia said, more cheerfully than she felt. 'He thinks you need educating, and I don't entirely disagree. *I* need educating, come to that— and some people would give anything to be able to do what we've been doing these past months.'

'Well, I'm not one of them.' Christina leaned forward across the table. 'Why don't we go to a movie or something? Or just go and sit outdoors in a café? Somewhere with a bit of life . . .'

Somewhere with men, Julia thought, and Christina, reading her mind, suddenly smiled.

'Yes, why not?' she said slyly. 'After all, it must be boring for you too. Wouldn't you like to meet a nice Italian boy? Someone who'll look in your eyes and tell you you're beautiful?'

'Not a lot,' Julia said truthfully. 'I had enough of that my first week. The charm wears off after a bit.'

'Does it?' Christina gave her a withering look, and with difficulty Julia reminded herself of her age. 'I wouldn't know. .

I might as well be a nun, the way I live.' She paused. 'Look, I really do have a headache, Julia, honestly I do. If you won't go to a movie or a café, why don't we go home just for once? We could swim in the pool—just sit and talk. I'll even practise my French. Promise—go on, Julia, say yes.'

Julia felt herself relent somewhat. Come to that, she didn't feel like dragging a reluctant Christina round yet another classical site either.

'Will your brother be there?' she said, attempting to make her voice casual. But Christina was quick; she smiled slyly.

'Absolutely not, I swear it. Carlo's at work. He won't be back till—oh, seven or eight. Really, Julia, you needn't worry. Though he'll be very cross if he finds out he's missed you. Odd, isn't it? You want to avoid him and he wants to see you. He must be nuts . . .'

'Thanks a lot,' Julia gave a wry smile. 'I'll ignore the insult, since I'm sure you're wrong anyway . . .'

'Oh no, I'm not.' Christina gave her a coy glance. 'He never stops asking me about you. He goes on and on about you. Your hair, your eyes. The time he took you out to dinner. All the times you've refused to have dinner with him since . . .'

'Yes, well.' Julia stood up quickly. She didn't want to be reminded of that dinner, an experience she certainly didn't intend to repeat. 'Carlo's engaged, and you've got a vivid imagination . . .'

'Engaged?' Christina took her time gathering her things together and getting to her feet. 'Oh, sure. Dynastically suitable, carefully arranged from the cradle. Union of two of the biggest companies in the country, the Contadellis and the Ricionis. Very suitable. Everyone thinks so, except Carlo. Since he met you . . .'

'Look, Christina, stop this.' Julia met her eyes. She had met Carlo's fiancée, Lucretia—Lucky as she was always called—and she had instantly liked her. Her adoration for Carlo had been transparent and touching, and Julia thought that Carlo, who like Christina was still young and still spoiled, was exceptionally fortunate to be engaged to such a girl, whether the reasons were dynastic or not. 'Carlo's engaged, he's getting married in a couple of months . . .'

'And he fancies you like mad,' Christina interrupted her quickly. 'And don't say it's my imagination, either, because he told me so himself. And if you ask me, he's going to pull out of the marriage. He's just waiting for Daddy to come home, and then he'll tell him. Look at it this way, why don't you, Julia? Play your cards right, and you could be *Signora* Contadelli. Think of it! Millions to play with, clothes from Paris, houses all over the world. A handsome devoted husband doting on you shamelessly. And me as your sister-in-law! Honestly, Julia, don't tell me you're not tempted.'

'Surprising as it may seem, not at all.' Julia turned and began to lead the way out of the café. She passed it off—she had no intention of letting Christina see that she was rattled, for the girl liked nothing better than to shock. But all the same, she was. She had given Carlo no encouragement whatsoever, and she wasn't remotely attracted to him or his wealth, but he was stubborn, like his sister. And she knew that at least part of what Christina had said was true. Carlo was showing alarming signs of infatuation, and her coldness to him only seemed to heighten his emotions. Yesterday he had sent her a pleading, impassioned letter, declaring his love, his adoration, his undying respect for her. Pleading for a meeting. Julia hadn't answered it, she had put it aside. But it would have to be answered—and firmly—very soon.

They came out into the warmth and sunshine, Christina still with a sly little grin on her face, and Julia turned to her with a sigh.

'Okay,' she said, 'you win. I don't feel much like trekking round with a guide book today. We'll go back to the house and swim—just this once, all right?'

'Terrific! Oh good.' Christina's face immediately lit up. 'I've bought the most terrific new bikini, Julia—just wait till you see it . . .'

She chatted on as they walked up the street, and continued once they were in the back of the taxi. Her bikini, her sun-tan, the party she and Carlo were going to the following week at the castle Lucretia's parents owned in Tuscany. What she would wear, whom she hoped to meet . . . Julia listened,

thinking how normal Christina could be when she forgot to
sulk and to be unpleasant. So—all her plans were frivolous,
who could blame her? She was a young girl after all, and of
course she wanted to go out and have fun. It wasn't really
fair, this plan of Giovanni, condemning her to a round of
educational sightseeing . . .

By the time they reached the gates of the Contadelli
palazzo, some kilometres outside the city, Julia felt quite well
disposed towards her. They had agreed to go shopping the
following day so that Christina could buy a new dress for the
party. They were both relaxed, full of plans, and excited. Then
they drew up outside the flight of steps that led up to the
portico, and Christina gave a little laugh.

'Oh dear,' she said, in tones of mock repentance, 'I must
have made a mistake. Look who's here, after all! It's
Carlo . . .'

The Contadelli pool was Olympic-sized, like everything else in
the Contadelli mansion. It was also very beautiful—a pale
sheet of water, surrounded by flagstones of white marble. And
at one end, outside the changing pavilion built in the style of a
small temple, was a shaded loggia, heady with the smell of
roses, cool from the plants that interwove across its pergola.
In the water Christina splashed about happily in a bikini at
least one size too small. On a supremely comfortable wicker
chaise-longue, Julia sat in the shade and fumed.

Carlo was at her side. He had not left her side since the
moment she had arrived, and it was now perfectly obvious to
Julia that she had been set up. This was a plot, hatched by
brother and sister, and she had fallen for it. Carlo had offered
champagne. That refused, he had offered fresh lemonade,
cigarettes, conversation. And now, having made little
headway with the other efforts, silent adoration. He was lying
next to Julia, his chair drawn as close to hers as he dared, his
handsome face regarding hers unrepentantly.

Julia stared fixedly straight in front of her, and wondered
how to escape. If she went in the water—she had already tried
that—Carlo went too, and Christina promptly got out and

left them together. If she sat here Carlo followed her, like a spaniel. She'd be able to leave eventually, it was true, but not before five—until then Christina was technically in her charge. And then Carlo was certain to offer her a lift, and she'd have to find a way of refusing it politely but definitely.

Carlo gave a gusty sigh, and Julia regarded him under her lashes, cautiously. He was twenty-one, and undeniably handsome. Well-built, tanned, with short curly brown hair, and the eager face of a little boy who was as used to getting his own way as his sister was.

'Ah, Julia . . . today you are looking so lovely.' He fixed her with a gaze of blind admiration.

Julia said nothing. She kept her eyes on Christina, who was in the process of hauling herself out of the pool. She eventually managed it, nearly losing the top half of her bikini in the process, and padded wetly across to them. Julia saw brother and sister exchange a brief glance, then Christina indicated her bikini.

'I'm going to change,' she announced, as Julia sat up hurriedly. 'This stupid thing's too tight—I must have grown or something. I'm going to get another one—but it's up at the house. I won't be a minute . . .'

'Christina, wait!' Julia half rose to her feet, but Christina had already gone. Julia sat down again, feeling crosser than ever. Christina never fetched anything for herself—a servant was always sent for. It was perfectly obvious that this was the next step in a planned operation.

Carlo wasted no time. Before Christina was out of sight he was reaching for Julia's hand, and she was snatching it away.

'Oh, Julia! But you are so cruel.' He laid his hand on the arm of her chair instead. 'Why are you so cruel? You know what I am feeling. I cannot hide it . . . you received my letter?'

'Yes, I received your letter.'

'Then why have you not answered it?' He regarded her anxiously. 'You must know, then, how I feel. What I think. How much I love you. Oh, Julia, don't you understand, the moment I saw you, I . . .'

'Look, Carlo, stop this.' Julia rounded on him quickly. 'I

don't know if this is some joke you and Christina have dreamed up, but if so, it's a very bad one.'

'A joke?' Carlo looked deeply wounded. 'But how can you say this? How can you even think it? It is true, everything I wrote. Julia, please . . .'

'It isn't true,' Julia interrupted him, and then, seeing the colour wash up over his cheeks, she softened her tone. 'Look, Carlo, you're arguing yourself into this, don't you see? You don't love me. You hardly know me. And you're engaged, you're getting married in two months' time—aren't you forgetting that?'

'You are wrong. I am not getting married.' Carlo's mouth set in an obstinate line. 'It was all stupid, that plan. I see it now. To marry—because our fathers want it—for business reasons . . . what kind of marriage is that? I shall marry for love, and I shall tell my father that when he gets back. I love you, Julia. You are so beautiful. So clever. So good. I am Italian—not one of your cold Englishmen with no imagination. I fell in love with you the moment I saw you. With your beautiful hair, and your golden eyes, and your . . . your . . .' He hesitated, his eyes falling in the direction of Julia's breasts. She promptly covered them with her hands and hitched the neck of her plain black swimming costume a little higher. Then she stood up, and Carlo did the same.

'Look, Carlo, please . . . this is silly. I didn't answer your letter straight away because I wanted to think what to say. Because I want you to understand. It's not just that I don't love you, Carlo, it's that you don't love me either. You're imagining it. It's natural enough. You're getting married soon, and maybe you feel that you want to . . . to—oh, I don't know, experiment a little first, but . . .'

'You are wrong.' Carlo stepped forward purposefully. 'You should not talk like that. I am not a little boy, I am a man. I know my own mind. You forget that maybe . . .'

Before Julia could move he reached out, grabbed her arm, and pulled her tightly against him. He clearly intended to assert the manliness of his feelings, and indeed, Julia realised with shock, there was no mistaking his arousal. Before she could struggle away he pulled her round, kissing her on the lips. It was neither a boyish nor a chaste kiss. Carlo did not waste time, nor opportunity. With a deep sigh, he moved one hand purposefully up over the swell of her breast and attempted to part her lips with his tongue. He kissed her with mounting urgency and passion, and then, when she eventually managed to push him away, stood regarding her smugly, as if thoroughly pleased with himself, and quite sure that Julia would now melt into instant subservience.

Julia's eyes flashed, and Carlo's look became less confident.

'Julia. My beautiful Julia. Please! I am sorry . . . But I could not help myself. You are so lovely. I want you so much. Please . . .'

'Look, Carlo.' With difficulty Julia managed to control her rising anger. 'Just don't do that again. Ever, do you understand? And stop all this. Stop it now! If you or Christina ever attempt to trick me into this kind of situation again, I shall quit this job straight away. It's just stupid. I've told you what I think and what I feel—I'm not going out with you again, and I never would have the first time if I'd realised what was going to happen. You told me it was to talk about your sister, and that's the only reason I agreed. And that's that. No more dates. No more declarations, and no more kisses, OK? In fact, it would be a whole lot better if you and I didn't meet at all—maybe then you'd come to your senses.'

'Don't do this to me!' Carlo gave a wail of distress which sounded genuine, even to Julia. 'Please—I meant everything I said. It's true. I need you, Julia. I want you, and I'm not going to change my mind. Even if you won't meet me it won't make any difference—I shall still love you. I shall still think of you. I . . .'

He broke off. There was a discreet cough from the other side of the pool, and Christina hove into view, clad in a new violet silk bikini, with a smirk of amusement on her face. Julia looked from one to the other, from brother to sister, and gave a gesture of exasperation. Maybe if you'd had everything you'd ever asked for since the age of two, it would be difficult to believe there was something you couldn't have. Well, Carlo and Christina would just have to learn for once. Her heart lifted; it was—at last—five o'clock.

'Carlo, Christina, I'm going.'

She turned into the little changing room without a backward glance, and when she came out in her jeans and T-shirt again, brother and sister broke off their conversation and looked at her guiltily.

'Christina, I'll meet you tomorrow at two-thirty as usual. Goodbye, Carlo.'

She marched off down the drive, head held high. She felt exhausted, but grateful for small mercies. Carlo hadn't suggested driving her home. Half a kilometre from here she could get the 'bus back to Rome. She quickened her pace, and her spirits rose.

Happiness, just then, was being in her shabby rented room, with the chance to sit in the window, and look over the red tiled roofs of the city. She reached into her bag for the violets, which she had put there, and drew them out ruefully. They still smelt of spring, and of home. But they were wilted.

CHAPTER TWO

JULIA's apartment—though apartment was too grand a word for what was, in reality, one large studio room—was in a tall house with old louvred shutters and peeling ochre paint, that stood in a quiet courtyard off the Via Bocca di Leone. The road, so quaintly named, was in the centre of Rome, not far from the Spanish Steps, and was one of Julia's favourites. When she had first arrived here and was looking unsuccessfully for somewhere to live, she had spent a whole morning exploring it, and the narrow streets and secret courts that lay off it. How wonderful, she had thought, to live in a street called 'in the mouth of the lion'—particularly since, in Italian, that phrase had a particular meaning. It meant to be in a hot spot, in the lion's den, as it were.

But this part of Rome was now expensive; the side streets were lined with costly little shops selling the most exquisite shoes, bags of the softest Florentine leather, clothes that cost more than Julia earned in a year. She had been about to give up and move on somewhere much less romantic and more realistic when she'd met Hardiman Fletcher. Hardy, as he was always called, was English, and now nearly sixty. He was a painter—a good one, Julia thought—and he had lived in Italy for nearly forty years. Hardy was a bachelor, and something of an eccentric, occasionally vague, at other times alarmingly perceptive, and he had a passion for Rome to which Julia had instantly responded. They had started talking, and the upshot was that some hours later Hardy had persuaded Julia to rent the studio above his own apartment which he no longer used. He had told her that the small rent she paid would be helpful to him; indeed, with his customary charm, he had done his best to imply that Julia was doing him a favour by taking on the sub-let. Julia doubted that was the case, but she had liked Hardy from the first, and the moment she saw the room with its amazing view she had fallen in love with it.

Hardy had become a close friend. He had guided her around the city, introducing her to little cafés, to streets and houses and churches that were tucked away, undiscovered by tourists. And, though he did not know it, he had done much to ease the ache in Julia's heart since the death of her father—the unhappiness which had first decided her to come to Rome. Hardy had helped with her work too, introducing her to a number of writers and professors for whom she could do translations, and, when she felt exhausted or worried about Christina, it was to Hardy Julia turned. Hardy made her laugh; he gossiped and teased and cheered her up. Now if she thought of Rome, she could not imagine the city without his tall, angular, slightly shabby elegance.

Often—it was the only way she felt she could repay him for his generosity—Julia used to cook Hardy supper. So that evening, as she walked back from the bus stop, crossed the Tiber, and began to weave her way through the now-familiar streets, she decided to stop off at the little grocer's shop near her flat. She'd see if Hardy was free and wanted feeding . . .

It was well past six when she finally left the shop clutching her packages, and the light was beginning to fade. The streets were crowded with evening shoppers and children were playing on the doorsteps. Julia looked about her and smiled. How she loved this city! Loved its energy, its sprawling extravagant beauty. Sometimes she did think of England longingly, it was true. At an unexpected moment the past would suddenly come back to her, and catch her out.

She would think, then, of her childhood: of the old rambling house in a small Suffolk village; of her father reading to her, or carefully and patiently helping her with her homework. Sometimes, too, she would remember her mother, her smart, chic, bored mother who had always seemed unhappy and out of place there, and who had, in due course, inevitably removed herself. Julia didn't dislike her mother, she didn't hate her, though she knew she had made her father very unhappy. She just felt she did not know her, and was not related to her. It took an effort of will to believe that this woman had brought her into the world. And, since her mother was as uninterested in Julia as Julia was shy of her, their relationship had never developed. She recalled a few meetings, awkwardly taking tea together. One visit to Julia's school: an elegant stranger in a black couture suit, at her father's funeral. Her new husband had muttered a few kind words, she had climbed into the back of the Rolls, and then she was gone. That was nearly a year ago now, and Julia had had one letter from her, but she had not seen her since.

Julia rounded the corner, and stopped, suddenly unaccountably nervous. Was it that man again? She hadn't been thinking of him—indeed, she'd almost forgotten his existence. She had rounded a wall and out of the corner of her eye she had glimpsed—something. A man—wearing a pale linen suit. A tall man, with very dark hair, walking fast; he had turned off the street a few houses along.

There was an opening there that led into a small courtyard not unlike the one in which she herself lived. Julia paused, her throat suddenly dry. Then, telling herself not to be foolish, that she had probably been mistaken anyway, she walked back and stepped nervously into the shadowy court. There was nobody there. She hesitated, the back of her neck prickling with nerves, half expecting someone to leap out of the shadows and grab her. But of course no one did. If it had been the man, he must have gone into one of the houses, because there was no other way out. At the entrance to the courtyard, just as she turned back into the street, she stopped, her eyes falling to the uneven cobbles. There, still sending up a thin curl of smoke, clearly only just tossed away, was a half-smoked cheroot.

It was one of those long thin black things, neither cigarette nor cigar. And she knew when she had last seen someone smoking one. Yesterday—at the café in Trastevere. He had been three or four tables away at the time, and with his coffee, he had lit one of these things, and the smell of the smoke, aromatic, pungent, quite pleasant, had drifted across to the table where she and Christina had been sitting. She caught the same scent now.

She stared down at the cobbles for a moment, the memory

of the man's face suddenly vivid in her mind, then with a toss
of her head she turned away. She was being stupid. Many
Italian men smoked those things. It probably wasn't the same
man, and if it were, so what? He had to live somewhere, didn't
he? But still, she had better mention it to someone, she
thought guiltily, remembering she had intended to do just that
earlier in the day. She would tell Luigi tomorrow. After all,
Christina's safety was his ultimate responsibility, and Luigi
was thorough. He had objected, she knew, to these afternoon
expeditions with Christina. He had suggested to Giovanni
that he should accompany them—reluctant though he might
be to put up with Christina and her insolence. But Giovanni
had waved the idea away. He wanted Christina to have more
independence now. What kind of world was it, where a young
girl could go nowhere without a discreetly armed escort? It
was ridiculous, and besides, it was conspicuous. *Keep a low
profile*, Giovanni had said. *That way Christina and Julia will
look like any other girls—no one will look twice at them.*

Julia shut the old iron courtyard gate behind her with a
clang, and began to race up the wide flight of stone stairs that
led to Hardy's apartment and her own studio above. She
bumped into Hardy on the landing just as he was shutting his
door—which, to Julia's admiration, he never troubled to lock.

'Hallo.' He planted a firm kiss on her cheeks. 'You're in a
hurry. I was just coming to see you.'

'Hungry?' Julia waved the packages at him cheerfully, and
Hardy looked sheepish.

'Hungry? I suppose I might be . . .'

'Of course you are!' Julia linked her arm through his. 'You
know perfectly well that once you start painting you never
remember to eat, and I know you've been painting—I can
smell the turpentine. I bought some food—look. Pasta made
this afternoon, those lovely big tomatoes—Parmesan—fresh
oregano . . .'

'Mmmm,' Hardy sniffed appreciatively. 'I can't think of
anything nicer. Tell you what, you go on up. I'll just fetch a
bottle of wine. There's some rather good Chianti I found in a
little place round the corner yesterday. Just the thing with the

pasta—it's skulking at the bottom of the cupboard. I won't be a minute.'

Humming to herself, Julia took the remaining stairs two at a time, fumbled in her bag for her keys, undid the lock, and threw back the door. She stopped dead in her tracks with a moan of dismay. Then she dropped the packages, and just stared in front of her in disbelief. The studio had been burgled. More than that, it had been ransacked, and thoroughly. She had never seen anything like it.

The mattress had been pulled off the bed and lay with the linen in a heap on the floor. Everything had been scattered. Tables overturned, lamps, candles, boxes, cooking utensils, books, postcards—all her meagre possessions had been scattered over the floor. They lay now in random heaps, as if someone had done this in order to search them thoroughly and quickly.

The studio didn't contain a great deal of furniture, but everything there was had been investigated. Obviously whoever had done this had simply pulled out all the drawers and tipped their contents on to the floor. All her clothes were scattered about. The old bureau which belonged to Hardy had been opened too: a pile of papers, envelopes and old bills fluttered on the floor in the breeze from the open window.

Julia just stood looking at it, too dumbfounded to think. Then as her numbed mind started to work again she darted across the room, and began to rummage among the things that had been tipped from the chest of drawers. There was only one thing she cared about. She didn't *have* anything valuable anyway, damn it! Just a few worthless bracelets, a bead necklace, and the brooch. The brooch her father had given her for her twenty-first birthday, not long before he died. With a sob her fingers closed over it. It was there, and unbroken. A small cameo, old, set in gold. It wasn't worth a great deal, but it was absolutely the only thing she possessed that was worth anything. She knelt back on her heels, and stared around her in bewilderment. If whoever had done this left the only thing of any value, what was the motive for all of it? Was it robbery, or could it be something else?

'What the devil . . .?' Hardy's voice came from the doorway. He stood there clutching the bottle of wine, staring around the room in horror. 'Julia—are you all right?' He started across the room to her, and Julia saw the sudden anger in his eyes. He gestured around them. 'I don't believe it. I can't believe it. I've lived here in this house for over twenty years, and I've never . . . Nothing like this has ever happened! I can't believe it . . .' He broke off, and then bent and put his arm round Julia. She was shaking, and to her own annoyance knew that the shock had brought her close to tears. 'Don't touch anything, Julia, leave it just as it is. Look, sit down. I'll open the wine—have a drink. It will make you feel better, really. Then I'll call the police.'

It was later, much later, when they finally ate. The police had been, and had been efficient but—Julia could tell—resigned. It was regrettable, they explained, but this sort of thing happened more and more these days. It was probably some teenager, looking for cash, the officer explained gently. An impulse crime. A professional thief, he suggested tactfully, wouldn't bother with a place like this—the pickings were too small. Probably he had been prowling around the building, had been on the balcony below, and had seen how easy it was to get up from there to the open window . . .

Hardy had frowned. The balcony in question ran outside the windows of his own flat. He had been there all day, painting. He had seen no one.

The officer smiled patiently. He had been there *all* day—without any break? Hardy sighed. Of course, the officer was right. He got tired nowadays, he didn't have the energy he had as a young man. He almost always took a brief nap in the early afternoon, about three o'clock—just for half an hour or so.

The policeman raised his hands expressively. There it was—about three. And half an hour was plenty of time. This kind of job usually took no more than twenty minutes. He would send someone round in the morning, he said. They'd test for finger-prints and so on—there might be something on the balcony rail, or possibly on the window itself, but he doubted it. Nice shiny metal, that gave the best prints, he explained. Not peeling old wood that needed painting, that was hopeless. Meantime, the *signorina* could tidy up and put the things away, but certainly, and if she found anything missing, would she please make a list and keep it in readiness for him?

He bowed politely and left. For the next hour or so, Julia and Hardy carefully and painstakingly put everything back in its place. When they had finished at last, Julia, feeling calmer now, put the water on to boil, grated the parmesan, chopped and cooked the tomatoes. It soothed her, doing these simple familiar tasks, and it gave her the chance to think. Three o'clock. At two-thirty she had been at the foot of the Spanish Steps. She had bought the violets, she had seen that man. At three she had been in the café with Christina. At three she was never, ever, in this apartment. Anyone watching her movements over the past week or so could have been fairly certain of that ...

When they had finished the spaghetti, Hardy poured her another glass of wine, lit a cigarette, and leaned back in his chair thoughtfully.

'You're sure?' He looked at Julia closely. 'You're certain there's *nothing* missing?'

'Absolutely certain.' Julia shrugged. 'I didn't bring that much with me from England, and I'm sure that nothing has gone.' She lowered her gaze, keeping her voice deliberately casual. 'If it was just an amateur, someone wanting money, or something they could sell easily—well, then why leave everything behind? My passport, for instance. That was there, in the desk drawer, and you can sell passports, can't you? The brooch my father gave me—that's worth a little, and it would be easy enough to sell, I'd have thought. And there was even some money—not lire, English money, about twelve pounds— left over from the journey. I'd been keeping it—I thought I'd change it some day when I was really broke. It wasn't hidden, it was just loose, in the top drawer. It's still there.'

'Maybe something disturbed him. If he was in a hurry— maybe he just tipped everything out, and then heard something, and decided to beat it. It could happen. Except . . .' Hardy hesitated, 'except it didn't look like that, did it? It looked, well, as if they'd been searching for something.'

'That's what I thought.' Julia's voice was quiet, and Hardy leaned forward.

'Is there something you're not telling me, Julia? You look worried, what is it?'

'Well,' she hesitated, 'I know it sounds silly, but whoever it was : . .' She paused. 'They'd been through the desk especially thoroughly, didn't you think? There wasn't that much in it, but every single thing had been opened. All the envelopes, the old letters, they'd all been taken out—it looked as if they'd been reading them.'

Hardy smiled. 'I see. Incriminating correspondence, is that it? What *have* you been up to, Julia dear?'

Julia blushed, then smiled. 'Well, there were a lot of old letters from my father, written to me when I was away at school. They'd all been opened.'

She broke off. Hardy was watching her closely.

'And?' he prompted. 'Come on, out with it—you can tell me.'

'And there was a letter from Carlo Contadelli.' Julia stood up abruptly. 'It came yesterday. I hadn't answered it, and now I don't need to.'

'I see. A letter from Carlo.' Hardy's voice was bland, and Julia swung round.

'Oh, Hardy, it's not what you think—really. It was a love letter—I suppose you could call it that. There were reams and reams of it.'

'A declaration?' Hardy smiled. 'I still don't quite see what you're driving at. Who would want to steal Carlo's letter? Or even read it? Come on, Julia, it doesn't make sense.'

'No, listen.' Julia turned back, and sat down again. She leaned across the table. 'Supposing someone was interested in me—not because of me at all, but because of who I work for. The Contadellis. They might have thought Carlo's letter could be useful, don't you see? It had the Contadelli crest on the back of the envelope—they wouldn't have known what the letter contained.' She paused, and seeing the disbelief on

Hardy's features, she spread her hands. 'You see, Hardy, there's something I haven't told you. I think someone's been following me.'

'Following you?' Hardy's eyebrows shot up. Julia leaned forward. Quietly and carefully, knowing it sounded melodramatic, she told him about the events of the past week. Hardy listened in silence, occasionally interjecting a question, letting the smoke curl upwards from his cigarette, his perceptive blue eyes never leaving her face. When she had finished he sighed, and leaned back.

'I *see*. And you're certain of this—you couldn't be mistaken?'

'I'm absolutely certain.' Julia's voice was firm. 'I notice people anyway, and I remember faces. And this man . . .' She hesitated, the colour rising slightly in her cheeks. 'Well, he's remarkable to look at. Not a man you would confuse or forget.'

'An admirer, maybe?' Hardy smiled at her. 'Someone who finds you as striking and memorable as you do him? Someone who deliberately seeks you out?'

'I don't think so.' Julia shook her head. 'Someone who's interested in me because of Christina. And this——' she gestured around the room, 'could just be coincidence, but I don't think so. After all, if it was just a casual, random crime, why not try your apartment? It's larger than mine. You have such beautiful things, and you never lock your door.'

Hardy frowned. 'You may be wrong, you may be putting two and two together and making ten, but I don't like it.' He stood up. 'I think you'd better do two things. You'd better inform the Contadellis, first thing tomorrow—telegraph Giovanni, speak to that so-called bodyguard fellow, and tell the police. You should have told them this evening. And meanwhile, just in case, let's fix that window so it can't be opened. There's some nails and a hammer somewhere. I'll go and get them.'

Julia protested, but Hardy would have none of it. Half an hour later, the window firmly nailed in place, Hardy wished her good night. Julia thanked him, and kissed him.

'I feel like a prisoner now,' she said with a smile, as Hardy issued last instructions about barring the door. 'I've got you all worked up—and it's probably just stupidity.'

Hardy patted her arm.

'I hope you're right, Julia, my dear. But promise me you'll do as I say—first thing tomorrow, all right? I would be very upset if anything happened to you, you know.'

'Nothing's going to happen. Now stop worrying. And I'll do just what you say—promise.'

She forced herself to sound more cheerful than she felt, but, when Hardy had gone and she had bolted the door firmly, she knew it would be a long time before she could sleep.

She washed and undressed ready for bed, and then prowled back and forth, unable to settle, her mind working furiously. Finally, on impulse, she went to the bureau, and took out the envelope with Carlo's letter. Her hand shaking a little, she drew out the bundle of pages. The paper was thin, Carlo's writing was large and sprawling. There must have been nine or ten pages of it.

She cast her eye down over the sentences. There was a long, fairly formal, preamble all about their dinner together, and how Carlo hoped and pleaded that she would not have taken offence at his behaviour. How he was a man, with a man's instincts and he knew he had gone too far, but truly, he could hold back the truth no longer, he had to tell her . . .

She had come to the bottom of a page. She turned it over, started to scan the top of the next page, and then stopped. It made no sense. Carlo had not numbered the pages, but this was a later passage. The pages must have been muddled up. In her haste to put everything away, she had probably put it back in the wrong order. Eventually Julia laid the pages down on the table in front of her and stared at them. There was no mistake. Part of the letter was missing. How much she couldn't remember, but quite a lot, two or three pages certainly. The part where Carlo had most forcefully and at greatest length, described how he wanted her and how he loved her.

So she had been right after all. Whoever had ransacked the

apartment *had* wanted something; they had found it and taken it.

For some reason, they had wanted Carlo's letter. Why? Why? Desperately she tried to remember what the missing pages contained. Outpourings of devotion, certainly, but had there been anything else? Any reference to a meeting place or time? None that she could recall. And so why take *those* pages? It made no sense.

At last, stiff with tiredness, and cold with anxiety, she fell asleep.

'Luigi?' Christina looked at Julia in surprise, and downed the last of her coffee. 'What do you want to see Luigi for?'

'Oh, nothing very important,' Julia said evasively, hoping Christina would notice nothing odd in her tone. She had already decided not to tell Christina about the events of the previous night—not yet, anyway. She did not want needlessly to alarm her. 'I just wanted to have a quick word with him.'

'Well, you can't.' Christina drew on her cigarette, the fourth she had smoked during what had been an uneasy lunch. 'He's gone up to Tuscany, to the Ricionis' place—you know, Lucky's parents. He has to check out the security arrangements for that party I told you about. Daddy asked him to do it. They have their own people, of course, but Daddy doesn't think much of them. And he's getting some of the jewellery out of the bank for me to wear, he said, so . . .' She shrugged. 'Luigi will be back tonight. He flew up. You can talk to him then if you like.' Her eyes narrowed. 'Is it urgent?'

'No—no. It can wait.' Julia looked away. She glanced around the terrace of the restaurant where they were eating. There were several other diners, none of whom she recognised. She had not seen the man that day. She sighed, and gestured to the waiter for the bill.

She had seen the police officer as she had promised Hardy she would, and the whole interview had left her feeling more than a little foolish. The man's interest had been immediate when she mentioned the Contadellis and the time she spent

each day with Christina Contadelli. The missing pages from
Carlo's letter interested him not at all: he suggested, politely,
that she was mistaken. Who would want to steal a few pieces
of paper? She would probably find them, they had probably
been misplaced the previous night, and as for the tall dark
stranger ... Well, Julia had felt an idiot as soon as she
embarked on that side of the story, and the officer's reaction
had only increased her humiliation. He had heard her out, his
dark eyes twinkling. By the time she had finished an
increasingly stuttered and incoherent summary, his smile had
been broad. He stood up, held out his hand, and clasped hers
a little longer than was strictly necessary.

'*Signorina* . . .' He gave a little bow. 'Forgive me, but if you
will permit me to say so, you are in Rome now. In Rome, a
beautiful woman, such as yourself, gradually gets used to such
a phenomenon. In London, no doubt ...' He raised his
shoulders in an expressive shrug, in which the enterprise of
English manhood was at once dismissed. 'But in Rome—if a
man sees a lovely woman he will respond. He will seek her
out, yes, even follow her, I must admit this. For the lady
concerned it can be a little alarming at first. But no harm is
intended. What you describe—if you could think of it as a
compliment merely? There is no connection with the burglary
at your house. Of that I am sure.'

He paused and released her hand. 'As far as the Contadelli
family is concerned—there, of course, there is every reason to
be careful. If you will speak to the family as you say, then
when *Signor* Contadelli returns, I will contact him personally.
Next week, you have my word. *Signorina* Hamilton,' again a
half bow, '*arrive derci* . . .'

Julia sighed. She settled the bill and the two stood up, and
made their way through the tables. It was a beautiful day
again, and very warm, and now—out in the sunlight—her
fears of the night before did seem foolish. Julia gave herself a
little shake. No more looking over her shoulder.

'Now . . .' she turned to Christina, who seemed, if sullen, in
a slightly better mood that day, 'where would you like to go? I
had planned a rather different expedition . . .' She hesitated,

and Christina looked at her beadily. 'There's a district of the city, beyond the Piazza Navona, walking towards the river . . . It's rather run-down and dilapidated now, but it's where all the richest and most fashionable Romans had houses in the fifteenth and early sixteenth centuries. The Borgias kept a residence there, Lucrezia Borgia spent part of her childhood in the house. I thought you might enjoy that. The book says it's atmospheric—it gives you a very strong feeling of what it must have been like to live in Rome then.'

'The Borgias? Lucrezia Borgia? Yeah—well, I suppose she's quite interesting. I wouldn't mind seeing where she hung out. I feel like her sometimes. You know . . .' Christina gave Julia a wicked sideways glance. 'Like it'd be fun to have one of those poison rings, you know, and slip a little something in someone's glass when they were looking the other way . . .'

Julie laughed. 'Not mine, I hope!'

'No, not yours. You're not too bad really.' To Julia's surprise, Christina slipped her arm through hers. 'I know I can be a drag. It can't be much fun for you, all this.' She hesitated, then, as they began to walk down the street, her voice suddenly took on a confiding tone Julia had not heard before. 'The thing is . . . well, I may as well come out with it. The thing is, I thought you were after Carlo. I had it all weighed up. Not very nice of me, I suppose, but you get cynical being rich. I mean, sooner or later you find out all your so-called friends are after the same thing. And I thought you were just using me to get in with Carlo. I set up that meeting yesterday—I wanted to prove to myself I was right, I suppose. And then, when you'd marched off with your nose in the air, Carlo really let fly. He was wild. He really is crazy about you, you know . . .' She glanced at Julia, who said nothing. 'And he told me everything. How you'd turned him down flat, how you hadn't encouraged him or anything, how you'd talked to him about Lucky and so on . . . and then, well, then I felt mean. I'd misjudged you—yeah. I guess you could say that.' She stopped suddenly, and turned to Julia, and with an awkward gesture, held out her hand.

'So—pax, OK? From now on I'll behave. I'll try to behave.

I mean—I know you've really been trying, and no one's ever done that before. And. Well, some of the stuff you've told me has been quite interesting, really.'

Julia stared at Christina in astonishment, and then she began to laugh.

'Well,' she said happily, 'I'm bowled over! Nothing nicer than a compliment from an unexpected source. I thought you hated my guts.'

'I did.' Christina grinned. 'To begin with. Not so much now.'

Julia took her hand, and pressed it, and then, both laughing, they set off again.

'Let's enjoy ourselves then, shall we?' Julia turned to Christina impulsively. 'Let's look at the place I told you about—and then come back to the Piazza Navona, and have an ice-cream and some tea or something, and then let's go and choose that dress for your party. OK?'

'Terrific . . .'

It was as if some barrier that had always been between them had suddenly been swept away. For the first time in the last months, Julia felt relaxed with Christina, and Christina opened up. Consulting the map, they found their way from the Piazza through a maze of increasingly narrow and dark streets, until they finally found the district Julia had mentioned. She herself had never visited it before, and so it was a journey of exploration for both of them as, guidebook in hand, they wandered along the streets, peering at the tall and beautiful old houses. Some were little more than ruins, others appeared to be almost falling down; a few were being renovated. But their decay only made them more beautiful. Suddenly Christina gave a cry of triumph.

'This is it, look, Julia! The Borgia house. The fourth on the left after the turning—it must be this one. Yes, look, it's just the way the book describes it. Wow!'

Christina gave a little shudder.

'It's amazing—isn't it? To think of them all living there. Cesare and Lucrezia—which was her bedroom window, d'you reckon?'

Julia laughed.

'Probably at the other side of the house, I think. That way
the house would have looked out over the gardens to the
Tiber—but you can't get round there now.'

'Oh, I wish we could!' Christina looked up at the building
longingly. 'It makes it all real, don't you think, Julia? I mean,
seeing where they actually lived. Especially when it's like this,
all empty and silent and ghostly. Not some boring old place
with a guide, and billions of tourists . . .' She paused. 'It says
it's built round a courtyard on the inside—I wonder if you
can get in?'

'I don't think so. It's all boarded up.' Julia peered at the
crumbling doorway. 'We might be able to peer through here,
look . . .'

'You're right . . . Hey, this is great, Julia, look. It's all
overgrown.'

Christina had raced over to the doorway, and had her eyes
glued to the roughly-nailed wooden boards. More slowly Julia
followed her, and peered through the crack. It was shadowy
and dark beyond, but as her eyes got used to the light she
could just make out a courtyard. It was very overgrown, but it
had a well-head and arches, and she could see the outline of a
statue.

They both had their backs to the empty road, and they were
both intent on what they could see through the wooden
panels. Christina, by now in a state of great excitement, was
chattering away at the top of her voice.

'You're right, it's a well. And look, just beyond, in the
centre—do you see? There's a big flight of steps going up. I
just bet that led to the family apartments. Wow! Think of
Cesare and Lucrezia—they must have walked up there . . .
D'you think it's true they were lovers, Julia? I bet they were!
Brother and sister—think of that! Bet he wasn't anything like
Carlo—if he was I wouldn't have fancied him. No—I bet he
was terrific. I bet he kissed her right there, on the stairs. It
would have been night time, and all the servants would have
been asleep, and they would have crept out of their rooms for
a—what d'you call it, an assignation—and . . .'

She was talking so fast and so excitedly that neither of them noticed the car. They didn't hear it until it was right behind them. They reacted at the same moment, just as Julia felt her arms grabbed from behind. After that everything happened very fast. Julia heard herself give a cry. She swung round, and caught a glimpse of Christina's startled face—her skin white, her eyes wide. Christina's mouth opened, and a man's hand came over it roughly, then Julia was off balance, being half dragged, half carried towards the car. Behind her she heard a grunt of pain, as if Christina had succeeded in kicking or biting her captor. She was off her feet; the world spun before her eyes—a man's shoes, a cracked pavement, a large black car, its doors open.

She cried out, bunched her fist, swung wildly at the man who was holding her and caught him in the stomach. He gave a cry of pain and slackened his hold. Still off balance, she clawed upwards into air, towards his face; she heard her own voice yelling.

'Get hold of her . . . damn little she-cat . . .' A man's voice cut across her shouts. He spoke in Italian—a curt voice, an educated voice.

The arm grabbed her again, righted her. The world tilted, she looked up, and she saw him. He was standing by the car, looking at them both dispassionately, a slightly disdainful curl to his lip. The same man. The dark man.

'God damn you!' She kicked out again. 'Let me go . . .' The man holding her gave a grunt of anger. She must have connected with his shin—good! He released his hold on her for a second, no more. She just had time to see his hand go back, and then he hit her, slam across the side of her head and face with his open palm. Light flashed in front of her eyes; her ears sang. She felt her knees buckle. The man she recognised had stepped forward quickly, and she heard him swear.

Oh God, don't let me black out, she thought wildly. *Don't let me . . .*

She did black out, but not before she saw the dark man raise his arms to catch her.

CHAPTER THREE

SHE came round slowly. The side of her head was very sore, and her left arm ached where the man who had grabbed her had wrenched at it. She almost moaned; then, as her mind started to work again, had the wit to keep silent. She sat absolutely still, forcing herself not move. Wait, wait, she thought—wait and think.

Very carefully, under the cover of the darkness, she opened her eyes and peered out from under her lashes. They were travelling fast in a very large car—a Mercedes, she thought, though she couldn't be sure. It seemed to be the kind that was long enough to contain two back seats, one behind the other—at least she hoped that was the case, because if it were not, there was no sign of Christina. There was a smoked-glass panel between the rear section of the car and the front, where only one man sat, the driver, wearing a dark uniform of some kind and a chauffeur's cap. On the seat next to her, very close, was a man. Julia felt pretty certain she knew who it was.

It was the dark man, the one who had been following her. She could feel the warmth and strength of his body against hers. Her thigh was pressed against his; her head half rested against his shoulder. As her eyes got used to the lack of light she could just see his hands, resting against the plain dark material of his trousers. Perhaps he was asleep; certainly he did not move.

There had been four of them, she was certain of that. One man who had stayed behind the wheel of the car; the two men who had got out and grabbed Christina and herself, and this man. Julia bit her lip, fear and loathing and anger surging up in her so strongly that she almost spoke. The boss-man, that's who he was. The man who must have masterminded all this, the man—damn him—who had stood by the car as nonchalantly as he had stood at the foot of the Spanish Steps the previous day. Who had been so calm, so controlled—as if kidnapping were just another part of the day's work . . .

There was absolute silence in the car. No one spoke. The only sound was the muffled hiss of the tyres on the road; the only light came from the headlamps, which were full on. Desperately Julia forced herself to think. It must have been about five when it had happened. It began to grow dark just before seven, so the man must have hit her really hard—she had been out cold for at least two hours. And where were they? Somewhere remote, that was certain. She could see nothing beyond the windows of the car: no street lamps, no lighted windows, nothing. If they had been driving since five, and at this speed—she calculated they were doing about seventy or eighty miles an hour—then they could be a long way from Rome by now.

Her mind darted back and forth; panic made it difficult for her to concentrate. With a great effort of will, still not moving, she forced herself to think. They wanted Christina, that much was obvious. Such kidnappings and abductions were a regular occurrence in Italy now; she knew only too well that in spite of the increased security arrangements made by the very rich, like the Contadellis, the snatches and the blackmail still continued. Each year there were four or five cases. Those who delayed paying up—she remembered the Getty case from a few years back, and felt a shudder of fear run down her spine—suffered the consequences. Julia set her mouth, trying to fight the fear that surged up in her. In Italy kidnapping was no joke. It was organised, professional and vicious, and the police record of success was poor. She did not, at that moment, feel very optimistic about their chances.

Again she glanced under her lashes at the silent figure by her side. There were two obvious alternatives: these men were terrorists or Mafia. Either way she and Christina were in deep trouble. She tried to remember the accounts she had read of such cases; in all of them, it seemed to her, the behaviour of those kidnapped had played a key part in their survival. The ones who had come out of it alive weren't simply those whose families had paid up—that alone was no surety for safe release. No, the ones who had survived had been those who used their brains. She thought of an interview she had read a few months before, with a rich Italian businessman, released after being held for over four months.

What had he said? That it was important not to antagonise them, that was one thing. Because they could be nervy and trigger-happy, because the strain got to the kidnappers as well as to their victims. That it was important to notice everything and say nothing. To try and build a relationship with them, but never to fall for their tricks and their lies. 'You become dependent upon them,' the man had said. 'They feed you, they are with you day and night. You know nothing except what they choose to tell you, and that may be the truth or it may be lies—you never have to forget that . . .'

Julia swallowed. Just what advantages did she and Christina have? Not many, but there were perhaps a few. Christina's English was good, and virtually without an Italian accent. Might it be possible to bluff them, to pretend they had snatched the wrong people, that she and Christina were not who they thought?

She doubted it even as she thought it, though it might be worth a try. Apart from that, the only advantage she could think of was her fluency in Italian. If they had not investigated her too closely, they might not know that. If she pretended only to speak English, then perhaps they might say something among themselves, might become incautious. Yes, it wasn't much and it might not work, but it was something . . .

Who was this man? Very carefully and stealthily, she moved her head just a fraction, so that beneath her lashes she could look up at his face. He was staring straight ahead of him, so she could see his profile in the dim reflected light. Its perfection, its harshness, was etched against the dark glass. Long strands of her own hair, like burnished metal, clung to the plain black material of his suit. He did not look at all like a terrorist, or like a member of the Mafia. He looked as he had on every occasion on which she had seen him: like a powerful, successful and clever man. His voice was educated, the voice also of someone accustomed to command. His hands revealed no evidence of manual labour; the clothes he wore were those of a man with taste and money. The mouth looked severe, and cruel; she could feel the hard muscles, the power of arm and shoulder against which she rested her unwilling head. Instinctively she feared him. She knew, just knew with every nerve in her body, that this was a man capable of ruthlessness, a man it certainly would not be easy to fool.

The car was slowing, and Julia felt her body tense. Beside her, the man moved slightly. She saw his hands clench in his lap. Then very carefully he eased her body away from his, leaned forward and opened the panel between him and the driver.

'What is it?'

He spoke in Italian, crisply, without agitation. The driver turned his head slightly.

'There's some kind of road block ahead. Police . . .'

'Can you turn off?'

'No.'

'Then slow down. Approach them normally. It will be all right. It might be something to do with us, but it's unlikely this soon. It's probably an accident.'

He turned his head, as if looking behind them.

'Is she all right?'

'Fine,' a man's voice answered, then gave a low chuckle. 'Sleeping like a baby.'

'Good. Keep it that way.'

Julia felt a surge of relief. So she had been right! Christina was there, at least, and unharmed, thank God. She moved her head back against the soft leather of the seat, and peered ahead of them. She couldn't see much, but there were lights— torches or lamps of some kind—she could see them waving about on the road ahead of them. About three hundred yards away now, the car was slowing to a crawl . . .

Think, think, she told herself. You won't have another chance, so take this one. The door on her side was locked, she could see that, just, and the car almost certainly would have centralised locking, so trying to open it from where she sat wouldn't be possible. But if they were stopped—and yes, they were stopping—then she could do something. Lean forward. Scream. Start to struggle. They'd stop her, of course, but if she took them by surprise she ought to be able to convey the fact that something was wrong.

Her whole body felt as tense as a wire. In front of them now, in the headlights, she could see a wooden barrier, men in uniform, a torch waving at them ... Police, she thought, opening her eyes a little wider. Thank God. It was police!

The car was coming to a halt. She could see a man, carrying a flashlight, approaching the driver's window ... *Now!*

She moved, but the man beside her was too quick for her. As her mouth opened to cry out and her hand rose from her lap to attract the attention of the police, he slid across the six inches of space that now divided them. An arm like iron came round her shoulders, a hand gripped her and swung Julia round towards him. His grasp tightened, his fingers cutting in to the bare skin of her shoulders. He pressed her against him, close, suffocatingly close, so that her hair tumbled across his shoulders and her face was buried against his neck. She struggled, his grip tightened, and then his mouth came down on hers.

Julia's lips were imprisoned beneath the hard pressure of his. The hand that had encircled her shoulder now gripped her hair roughly, dragging her head back so her face was offered up to his. Her lips, parted to cry out, felt the demanding thrust of his tongue. He kissed her, kissed her with apparent passion, ravishing her mouth, pressing the softness of her body against the hardness of his.

It was impossible to escape his hold, impossible to cry out. The pressure of his lips, the thrust of his tongue silenced her as effectively as the tightest of gags. Dimly, through the blackness, she could hear voices: the chauffeur saying something she could not catch, the policeman answering him. She saw a flash of light—presumably the torch being directed into the back of the car. She felt it light her skin and her hair; she struggled more violently, and heard a low laugh.

The chauffeur said something else; beside her, the man

cupped her face up to his, his fingers shielding her face from
the torchlight. The light disappeared. His mouth did not relax
its pressure, but he let his hand slide down in a travesty of a
caress. Softly over the sensitive skin of her throat, then down,
tightening over the swell of her breast. And to her horror she
felt something in her body respond—felt a hot surge of
excitement swell up unbidden through her blood, relaxing,
just for an instant, her lips against his. He sighed; a deep sigh
as if of pleasure, and at once she was afraid again, and the
guilty, crazy sweep of physical response left her furiously
angry and ashamed.

Footsteps. The man in uniform was moving away from the
car. She struggled to free her hands, imprisoned against the
man's chest, tried to claw at him, but her fingers were trapped
and she could hardly move them. She tried, violently, to push
him away, then she felt something else, something cold and
hard, metal, jammed against her rib-cage, thrust beneath her
breast. The car was starting to move forward slowly. The man
raised his mouth from hers, just a fraction.

'I apologise for this.' He spoke in English, and to her
redoubled fury she could hear an insolent amusement in his
voice. 'But I advise you to keep still. If you try anything I
shall shoot you first, and your friend immediately afterwards.
Do you understand?'

'You bastard! Just what in hell do you think you're doing?'

She spat the words into his face, forgetting, in her anger, all
her resolutions about being careful, about not alienating him.
For a second her eyes flashed yellow fire; she stared into the
blackness of his. Then he smiled.

'I know just what I'm doing. And as a matter of fact, *cara*,
it's rather enjoyable. Forgive me, will you?'

Then he bent his head once more, and, as Julia felt the car
gather speed, saw the lights at the barrier go past, and recede
into the darkness, he gathered her into his arms again and,
holding her body in a grip of steel, kissed her lingeringly and
with insolent tenderness upon the lips.

He could have let her go almost at once. As he kissed her
they were already through the barrier, and into the darkness

beyond. But he did not; the kiss went on and on, his lips moving softly and persuasively against hers until finally, with a sigh, he drew back. He looked down into her face for an instant; she saw for a moment the harsh shadowed planes of his face. Then he smiled, released her, and—as if nothing had happened at all—slipped the gun back beneath his jacket and slid back across the seat.

Julia stared at him in passionate, silent hatred. She hated him for what he had done, and for the efficiency and casualness with which he had done it. More than that she hated *him*, with a fierceness that made her whole body tremble, for what he had made her feel.

After a brief silence, he turned to her with a cold polite smile.

'We still have quite a while to travel. Why don't you rest? Relax a while after your ordeal?'

The way he inflected that word made Julia grit her teeth with anger. She glared at him. 'Rest? Relax? Are you mad or something? That goon of yours pulled half my hair out, I can hardly move my arm, and then you . . . you . . .'

She broke off, and he gave a low laugh.

'Just where are you taking us? You realise you've made some kind of mistake, I suppose? We're perfectly ordinary people, just visitors, going round Rome with a guidebook, and then suddenly we get caught up in some kind of gangster epic. What are you playing at?'

He heard her out in silence, his face grave and still, and when she had finished, he gave a shrug.

'Well, I'm sorry you think of me as a gangster.' His voice was calm and unrepentant, his English accented but perfect. 'However, you're intelligent enough, I imagine, to know I'm not going to answer any of your questions, so it's a waste of breath asking them, don't you think?' He paused, and for a second she caught a flash as his dark eyes turned to her dismissively.

'Your name is Julia Hamilton,' he went on quietly. 'You've been in Rome five months. You live in the top floor studio, at sixteen Via Bocca di Leone. Your father died a year ago and your mother is married to Robert Carnegie Hunt, the American industrialist. I know more about you than you know yourself—so let's not play silly games, shall we?'

He turned away as if she bored him, with a quick impatient gesture, and there was silence. Julia looked at him, her mind working fast. What he said astonished her, and yet surely it opened up one tiny little avenue of hope? He hadn't mentioned Christina. Nothing about the Contadellis—not one word. Was it possible, could it be, that he didn't realise the identity of Christina?

She turned her head slightly. She could see Christina now, sandwiched between two swarthy men, her head resting tranquilly against one broad shoulder, her eyes closed. She slept as peacefully as a child in a nursery. Julia felt her heart contract and a wave of compassion surged through her. She turned her head again and looked at the tall dark figure beside her. So he thought they shouldn't play games, did he? Well, she intended to have a damn good try. And from now on, she wasn't going to be impetuous, and she wasn't going to make silly mistakes.

She sighed, then spoke softly.

'Well,' she said, 'I see you've done your homework. You know who I am. Supposing you tell me who you are?'

'But of course. Delighted.' He didn't even bother to turn and look at her. 'My name is Raphael Pierangeli.'

I'll bet, Julia thought bitterly. But he obviously intended to say nothing more, and so she, too, lapsed into silence. She turned to the window, and, mutinously, watched the night speed past, gazing out helplessly into the dark.

Wherever it was they had been taken, they arrived there very late. Julia looked at her watch: almost four in the morning. The last two hours of the journey had been very slow, bumping over twisting mountain roads, she judged, the road surface getting progressively worse. They must have driven south; they were now at least five or six hundred miles from Rome, but they were still on the mainland and that could only mean one thing. The mountains of southern Italy, that wild inhospitable region, where villages were few, and distant from each other, where you could hole up in some remote farm for months without risk of discovery.

She was being pulled out of the car. One of the men held her—not the one who called himself Raphael, one of the others. Julia stumbled; she felt rough stones cut the thin canvas shoes she wore on her feet. And it was dark and cold; she shivered. Then, suddenly, they were inside.

She looked around her, trying to memorise everything.

A large, simple room with a stone-flagged floor, some chairs, a wooden table, an oil lamp, an empty fireplace. It looked like a farm house. The walls were rough plaster, painted white. The shuttered windows were small. Raphael was sitting composedly at the table, incongruous in his impeccably cut black suit. The three other men, all of them young, looked rougher. One of them, holding a pale and trembling Christina, was very handsome in a flashy kind of way; he was wearing jeans and a black shirt and a fine necklace of gold hung around his neck. He looked as if he were enjoying himself.

The other two men were more difficult to classify. One looked surly and uneasy, constantly glancing towards the dark figure of Raphael. And the third man, too, looked uneasy. It was he who had been driving; he was still wearing the chauffeur's uniform. He looked so much like the faithful employee awaiting his master's instructions that Julia felt a wild desire to laugh. Raphael looked up.

'Get a fire lit. There's wood outside.'

One man—he looked like a farmer—moved instantly to the door. Julia cleared her throat. *Establish a relationship. Don't accept a subordinate rôle. Make it clear what you want and when you want it*: the phrases from the interview sprang into her mind, and she tilted her chin, and met those cold dark eyes.

'I assume you intend to keep us here?'

'You assume correctly.'

'Then we need something to eat. We need a bathroom, and then we need somewhere to sleep.'

'That had occurred to me.' He smiled coldly. He nodded at the young man with the gold chain, who at once moved to the far side of the room, and went into what looked like a kitchen. Raphael turned back to them. 'If you would both follow me?'

Julia put her arm around Christina and urged her forward. He led them into a corridor, a narrow one, more modern in appearance than the first room, and opened a heavy door.

Christina seemed hardly able to walk and Julia had to propel her forward. They followed him into a plain, square room. It contained two single beds, a table, a chair, a chest of drawers, and a simple rag rug. Julia looked around it swiftly. Obviously they were in some kind of modern extension, built on to the farmhouse. This room had electric light. It also had a window, one very small one. It was barred.

Raphael closed the shutters, then opened a door on the far side of the room.

'A bathroom. I would hate for you to be without modern conveniences.' He paused. 'You will find nightwear and a change of clothes in the chest. I hope they fit. We did our best . . . He gave a little smile. 'Food will be brought to you on a tray in about ten minutes. I would suggest you sleep then. Good night.'

With that he turned on his heel, and left them. The door shut, a key turned in the lock, and there was the sound of two heavy bolts being drawn across.

Christina gave a low moan, and sank down on the nearest bed.

'They gave me something to drink,' she said in a low, shaky voice. 'I was so frightened! My throat was so dry I could hardly swallow. I said I wanted some water, and one of them opened a flask thing and gave me something, I don't know what it was. It tasted foul. Then I went to sleep . . . oh, Julia!' Tears welled up in her eyes. 'They're kidnappers, aren't they? What's going to happen? What will they do to us?'

'Nothing. They won't do anything.' Julia crouched beside her and put her arm around her. 'They'll keep us here and try to get money for us. They won't hurt us—it isn't in their interests. We must just stay calm, and use our brains.

'Now listen,' she took Christina's hands and pressed them between her own, 'he knows who I am, he told me, but he said nothing about you. Do you understand? There's just a possibility that they haven't realised who you are—let's try and play it like that anyway, shall we? It can't do any harm, and it might do some good. Tonight we'll eat—we have to keep our strength up. And then sleep, and then in the morning we'll work out a plan. Okay? We can do it, I know we can— but we'll do it a whole lot better if we're not hungry and tired, all right?'

'All right.' Christina nodded woefully. She lay back on the bed, and Julia looked at her carefully, and felt for her pulse. It was regular and strong enough, but a little slow. Already Christina's eyes were closing again. Julia set her mouth grimly. Whatever they'd given Christina, it still hadn't worn off.

Exactly ten minutes later she heard the sound of the bolts being withdrawn. The young man with the gold chain came in, carrying a large tray; Raphael stood just behind him, barring the doorway. Neither spoke.

Carefully the young man laid the food on the table. Bread, two bowls of soup, cheese, some cold meat and salad. He picked up the empty tray, and left the room as silently as he had come. As he passed the bed where Christina lay, Julia saw him glance down at her. She didn't like the expression on his face, and Raphael didn't seem to like it either, because he suddenly spoke curtly, making her jump.

'Hurry up, get a move on. No need to take all night.'

The young man scuttled out fast. The door shut; the bolts were rammed into place.

In spite of herself Julia was hungry, and she managed to persuade Christina to eat a little. The food, if simple, was good. It gave Julia courage. As she helped Christina to wash and undress and then tucked her into bed, she kept talking. She said everything optimistic and everything encouraging that she could, though Christina seemed too drugged still to take much of it in.

Then, when Christina was at last asleep, Julia herself

washed and undressed. The nightdress so thoughtfully provided, she thought wryly, could have been worse. Plain white cotton, more or less the right size, and serviceable, anyway.

She crept between the coarse sheets of the narrow bed, and rested her head against the pillow with a sigh. In the darkness her mind swooped almost instantly toward oblivion. She slept—she didn't know how long. Some hours, perhaps, hours crowded with incoherent and oddly calm dreams. But at some point she woke. She didn't know what had woken her—the sound of the bolts being withdrawn, perhaps. But she came at once to full alertness and lay there, not moving, trying to keep her breathing regular, knowing that there was a third person in the room.

There was silence, then careful footsteps. Her heart pounded in her chest. She lay stock still.

The light of a small torch came on, moving in the darkness, trained well away from her face. Stealthily, as she had done in the car, she watched from under her lashes.

It was Raphael. She could see his dark figure, the flash of white cuffs. He was standing silently, not moving, at the end of her bed. For a long time he did not move, but simply stood there, a tall dark figure, half lit by the rays of the torch.

Then she heard him draw in his breath, sharply. Every nerve in her body sang. He reached out a hand and carefully, silently and slowly, drew back the blankets and the sheet that covered her. Still Julia did not move; she did not dare to. She was paralysed with fear, and also with a weird, intoxicated excitement. Her nightdress had ridden up in the bed to the tops of her thighs. Its loose neck had fallen open. She could feel cold night air against the soft skin of her thighs, over the curve of one breast. He stood absolutely still, looking down at her. She could feel the intensity of the gaze of those black eyes as strongly as if he touched her. The torchlight wavered. It fell on the red-gold of her hair, she knew, as it spilled out over the pillow. It avoided her face, travelled down the length of her body. Then, abruptly, it was flicked off.

In the darkness she felt him reach down. His hand brushed

against her thigh, reached for the edge of the sheet. Then, very quickly and deftly, he covered her up. The sheet, the blankets. Did he know she did not sleep?

There was a moment's silence. Then the sound of soft footsteps, the opening and closing of the door, the noise of the bolts being fastened.

CHAPTER FOUR

JULIA sat up sleepily, trying to think where on earth she was, then it came back to her. She looked at her watch—it was past ten; she could have slept for only five hours, but she felt refreshed, reinvigorated. Quickly she jumped out of bed, and stood listening. Christina's peaceful regular breathing was the only sound. Julia saw that the colour was now back in her cheeks. She would let her sleep, and meanwhile ... She hesitated, looking at the small window. Then, very carefully, trying to make no noise, she climbed first on to the chair, then on to the table, and quietly eased back one of the small shutters. Standing on tiptoe, she craned her head to peer out.

The view was beautiful, breathtakingly so, but in their present circumstances hardly encouraging. She seemed to be looking out to one side of the house. There was a loggia there, sheltered with a pergola and a flourishing vine; beyond that was rough ground, rocks, and mountains. They were quite high up, although she looked out over mountains much higher. Fold upon fold of grim rocky outcrops, still with a little grass, for it was early in the year, but on their higher slopes the ground was desolate, already burned brown.

Julia had good eyesight. She strained her eyes now, training them over the hillsides. She could see no sign of habitation, no sign of civilisation: no houses, no barns, no roads even— nothing. There were no trees, none of the beautiful straight dark cypresses that were such a feature of the softer country to the north, just a few scrubby bushes that could not have hidden a dog, let alone a house.

Very carefully, anxious not to disturb Christina, she eased the other shutter open, and then the small window itself. It creaked slightly; Julia felt the heat of the day on her face. At ten in the morning it was already hot, much hotter than she had ever known it in Rome. But there was a breeze. The air against her skin felt fresh and smelled clean and sweet.

Very carefully she reached up her hands, and clasped the iron bars. There were five of them, set about a hand's breadth apart. She gripped them, and pulled. Then she tried pushing: absolutely nothing happened. They did not budge an inch— but then Julia had hardly expected them to. One glance had told her they had recently been set in fresh concrete.

She touched the concrete with her finger. Perfectly set, no sign of crumbling. It looked as if all this had been carefully planned, she thought, as if this house had been made ready for this purpose. How long ago did he start planning it? she wondered angrily. Two months ago? Three? However long it was, the preparations had been thorough.

Carefully, she climbed down from the table and padded into the bathroom. She took a shower, and washed her hair, letting the cool water rush over her skin, freshening her. She noticed now, as the previous night she had not, that the towels were thick and expensive; that the soap was of the finest quality. A small cupboard set into the wall contained toothpaste, toothbrushes still in their wrappers, Roger et Gallet bath oil, and talcum powder.

She looked at these objects with wry suspicion. What was this set-up? The bathroom was equipped like that of a first-class hotel—she couldn't believe that kidnappers were usually so careful of their victims' requirements. What happened if you didn't co-operate with them? she thought with a bitter little smile. Did they threaten to take your soap away?

She padded back into the bedroom and opened the chest of drawers. One drawer contained things for Christina, all far too small for Julia, for Christina was only five foot three, and Julia stood five nine in bare feet. Her things must be in the other drawer; she had been too tired and too worried to look at them the night before. She opened the drawer curiously; might as well see what they had come up with—her own clothes were crumpled, the skirt torn, the thin shirt dirty.

She stared down in disbelief and then slowly, one by one, drew out the things that had been left for her. Underclothes:

silk panties, a lace and silk bra, two exquisite hand-embroidered petticoats of finest crêpe-de-Chine. Two shirts, one silk, one linen; a pair of cream linen trousers, a full skirt, a jumper of hand-knitted cotton. Julia stared at them in disbelief, rummaged for the labels. Her size exactly; even the details of the bra were precisely correct.

She felt colour flame into her cheeks. These were not ordinary clothes, they were beautiful, and very expensive. And the trousers she recognised. She had seen them about four weeks ago, in the window of Gianni Versace's boutique; Christina had been with her and they had both admired them. Then Christina had laughed. 'Come on,' she'd said, 'I couldn't wear them and you couldn't afford them. What's the point in looking?'

Julia ran her hand over the soft silk, then, setting her mouth, shut the drawer quietly and turned away. What the hell was going on? Some kind of softening-up process? Well, if so, she was having nothing to do with it. She'd damn' well put on her own clothes, whatever they looked like.

So, rebelliously, she pulled them on, and then stood before the glass brushing her hair thoughtfully. She looked at her own reflection. As it dried, her hair spread out in a full soft aureole around her face; its colour flamed in the light. She had inherited this hair from her father, though his had never looked as wild, nor been so untameable as hers was. She didn't look too bad, she thought, glancing at herself critically. There was colour across the wide cheekbones; the full mouth was firm; the yellowish topaz eyes looked back at her calmly and levelly from the glass. Just so long as she didn't look intimidated by them, that was all she cared about.

At about half-past ten there was a knock at the door, and then she heard the bolts being drawn back. She stood up quickly, feeling her heart quicken, certain that it would be Raphael, but it was not. It was the young man who had brought their supper the night before, and Julia felt an odd sense of let-down.

He nodded to her casually, and greeted her in Italian. Julia did not answer him, and she saw his eyes run over her, leeringly and unpleasantly. But he said nothing more, merely gathered up the supper dishes, replaced them with the breakfast he had brought, and then left the room silently, with just one passing glance at the bed where Christina was just waking.

Christina stretched and sat up. She looked around the room, looked at Julia, and then smiled.

'Still prisoners?'

'I'm afraid it looks like it.'

'Oh well.' She threw back the bedclothes and slipped out of bed. 'Just now I can't even think about all that. All I know is that I feel a helluva lot better, and I'm starving. What about you?'

Julia smiled. 'Then come and eat. It looks quite good actually.'

There was a pot of good strong coffee, warm milk, sugar, honey, bread and fresh fruit. They both ate hungrily. When they'd finished, Christina pushed back her chair and grinned at Julia.

'Well, it could be worse. At least they don't seem to want to starve us.'

'No, apparently not.' Julia paused. Already, she could see, Christina's natural resilience was reasserting itself. She looked refreshed, relaxed, and comparatively unworried. Julia hesitated. She wanted to keep her spirits up, but on the other hand it would be fatal to let Christina develop a false sense of security. She leaned across the table.

'Christina, listen, I've been thinking. You remember what I said last night? Well, it probably won't work, but it's worth a try. So, have you anything on you that would identify you? Anything you're wearing? Anything in your bag?'

Christina grinned. 'Oh, not much. Just a cheque book, a wallet with my initials on, a gold American Express card, and a Diner's Club in my name. This bracelet—it has my initials on the inside.'

'Christina, it's not a joke, it's serious! Now, take the bracelet off, and give me the other things. I'm going to hide them.'

Christina looked reluctant, but she eventually did as Julia said. Hopelessly Julia looked around the room. It was not exactly full of hiding-places, but if the men had no reason to suspect anything had been hidden they had no reason to search.

'Hey, wait a minute, I've got an idea.' She rummaged in her own large canvas bag and eventually, with triumph, drew out a plastic bag. Christina stared at her as if she had gone mad.

'I saw it in a film once. It's as good as anywhere. Watch this!'

Carefully Julia tipped Christina's belongings into the bag, tied it in a tight knot, went into the bathroom, and very carefully, having removed the lid, lowered it into the lavatory cistern. She replaced the lid and came back. Christina pulled a face.

'You're nuts—you know that, don't you? I mean, what good is it going to do? Obviously they know who I am—why else would all this have happened? I mean, they wouldn't want to kidnap you, would they? It's me they want.' She smiled at Julia smugly. 'As a matter of fact, I think it's going to be OK. I'll just write a message to Daddy, or send him a tape or something—that's what they do, isn't it? Then he'll pay up, and off we'll go. Quite an adventure really! Wait till they hear about this at Le Rosey . . .'

'Christina!' Julia cut her off in exasperation. 'It's not as simple as that. I . . .' She hesitated, seeing Christina's eyes grow round. 'I just think it's worth trying something else first. If we can persuade them they've got the wrong people, you never know, they might just let us go.'

'You think they're going to kill us!' Christina's voice rose suddenly. 'You're not saying it, but it's what you're thinking . . . oh, Julia! They wouldn't hurt us, surely they wouldn't? That man who brought the breakfast in—he looks quite nice. He's young, he's good-looking. I thought . . .'

'Christina, stop this. Forget about the man, and stay out of his way, for God's sake.' Julia softened her voice. 'And don't be melodramatic, OK? I don't think they're going to kill us, of course I don't. I'd just rather get the hell out of here as quickly as we can—and if lying is going to help, then I'll lie.

Now—go and have a shower, and get dressed. You'll feel a whole lot better then.'

She didn't convince herself, but what she said seemed to cheer Christina up a bit, for she didn't argue. She did as Julia said, docilely, which made Julia a little suspicious. Christina was not usually so amenable; she just hoped she didn't have some wild secret ruse of her own.

Unlike Julia, Christina was delighted by the clothes she found in her drawer and had no hesitation in wearing them. Julia watched her as she preened herself before the glass in a short tight skirt, and a fuschia-pink cotton sweater. Whoever had chosen these clothes, and she didn't doubt for a second it was Raphael, he was sharp and he had a sense of humour. He had matched their very different tastes only too exactly.

Christina was still admiring herself in front of the glass when the bolts on the door were drawn back, and the young man who had brought their breakfast stood in the doorway. He looked at Christina, then at Julia, his face impassive.

'Raphael wants to see you. Just you. On your own.' He spoke in Italian and Julia managed to keep her face blank.

'I'm sorry, I don't speak Italian. You'll have to speak in English.'

He looked her up and down scornfully, his mouth sneering. Then he shrugged.

'Okay, we play it your way. Raphael wants to see you, on your own. Now. *Pronto.*'

'Fine.' Julia stood up, calmly. 'I'd like to see him too, so that suits me perfectly.' She gave Christina a warning glance and the girl nodded silently. Then, head high, she walked out of the room.

She took her time, and waited to make sure the man came with her—she didn't trust him an inch, and she didn't like the thought of Christina being left to *his* ministrations. He shut, locked and bolted the door and then, with a rude jerk of his head, set off along the corridor.

Julia followed him. Her heart was in her throat and her legs felt like jelly, but she was damned if she was going to let him see that.

The house was roughly L-shaped, she realised. The room she and Christina were in was at the back, directly behind the sitting-room she had seen the previous night. The room she was being taken to was at angles to the rest of the house, set apart at the end of the corridor. There seemed to be no other doors, and she wondered for an instant where the other three men slept. Were there outbuildings? Stables?

They reached a plain wooden door, set in an archway. The young man straightened, like a soldier about to be inspected by an officer, and knocked. Then he opened the door, stepped back to let Julia through, and closed it behind her.

She stood on the threshold looking around her in astonishment. It was a large room, and quite different in kind from the rest of the house. It too had a stone-flagged floor, but there all resemblance ended. The room was both beautiful and luxurious. There were fine paintings and exquisite rugs. On either side of the old fireplace were two sofas, covered in heavy silk brocade. One wall was lined with books. At one end of the room there was a bed, a double one, covered in some kind of fur rug and half hidden behind a Chinese lacquer screen. She turned her eyes quickly away from that to the other end of the room. There, in front of wide windows, was a desk. Behind the desk, silhouetted against the light, was Raphael. On the desk in front of him were several folders, a lamp, and a dark green telephone.

Raphael was rising to his feet. He came round the desk, taking his time about it, and then stood looking down at her. He didn't look pleased, and Julia had to force herself not to lower her eyes before that hard dark gaze.

'You didn't like the clothes that were chosen for you? The sizes were incorrect, perhaps?' He frowned.

'Not at all,' Julia gave him a cool smile. 'I'm sure they would have fitted perfectly, but I prefer my own things.'

'I see.' He gave her a cold smile which did not reach his eyes. 'I wonder if you'll feel quite the same some weeks from now. We'll see. I've always thought, myself, that pride—especially futile pride—was rather a waste of time.'

'Then we disagree.' Julia's voice did not falter. 'I expect we disagree about many things, don't you?'

'Certainly not.' The smile widened and became a little warmer. 'By the time you and I have had a chance to talk, I expect us to see eye to eye. Now—let me see—eleven-thirty. Not too early to have a drink, I think. What would you like? Champagne? Campari? Wine? A glass of sherry?'

He was, as always, beautifully dressed, wearing his expensive clothes with a negligence that increased their elegance. Today he was more casually dressed—a silk shirt open at the neck, narrow trousers that emphasised his lean hips and long legs; Gucci loafers and a watch that could only have been Cartier. He looked like an Italian aristocrat on his home ground, and his manner was that of a host to a welcome guest. Obviously he expected her to refuse his offer: well then, she would accept it.

'That would be lovely,' she drawled, trying to sound as casual as he had done. 'A glass of champagne, I think.'

One dark eyebrow lifted slightly, but he said nothing, and turned away to the table. A Lalique glass ice-bucket; Bollinger champagne. Julia frowned. Curiouser and curiouser, as Alice once said. Whoever was running this show, whether Raphael or someone above him, they did not appear to be hard up. Had they made their fortune with a series of kidnappings, she wondered wryly, or were other types of money involved— Mafia money, for instance?

He returned, looked down at her, and then solemnly handed her a long fluted glass. He lifted his own.

'*Salute.*'

Julia caught the mockery in his eyes, and turned to sit on a sofa. She sipped the champagne, which was infuriatingly delicious, waited until he had seated himself opposite her and then leaned back and crossed her legs.

'Well, this is very pleasant. I have only one question.'

'And that is?' He inclined his head to her politely.

'When do we leave?'

She had hoped such direct antagonism would provoke him into some kind of direct response, but she was disappointed. He smiled.

'But you know what I'll say. That depends entirely upon you.'

'Fine, I'll leave now. Just tell your minions to unlock the door of our room and we'll be off at once.' She started to stand up, knowing the anger she suppressed burned in her eyes, but before she could rise he caught hold of her wrist and, with the slightest hint of pressure, he pushed her gently back into her seat. His mouth had tightened but he gave no other indication of anger. Julia, though, had no doubt that if she tried to move again he would prevent her.

The two of them looked at each other, like two fighters sizing one another up, Julia thought. His dark steady gaze, lit with a mockery that angered her almost more than anything else, met hers. He took a sip of champagne.

'Do you know,' he said casually, 'you have the most extraordinary eyes? Obviously you will have been told this before, but all the same they are—extraordinary. Eyes like a cat—a very beautiful cat—who also has claws.'

He lifted his hand as he spoke, and for the first time Julia noticed that it was scratched badly from wrist to knuckle, four long red scars against the even tan of his skin.

'Did I do that?'

'Yes, in the car last night.' He smiled composedly. 'It is of no consequence. It will heal. All the same—it was quite impressive, I thought.'

'Oh, good.' Julia gave him a charming smile. 'Try again what you tried in the car last night, and I'll be only too delighted to give you a few more.'

She no sooner spoke than she regretted it. What on earth was the matter with her? she thought angrily. Why was he affecting her like this—why should she worry about being rude to a man who was a bully and a criminal?

She hesitated, and then, setting down her glass, raised her eyes to his face.

'I want you to let us go,' she said quietly. 'We have done nothing to deserve this. My friend is only fifteen, and she's very frightened. You can gain absolutely nothing from keeping us, and I can only assume that ... that you have made some kind of mistake.'

'I told you yesterday, there is no mistake. I know precisely

who you are and what you have been up to in Rome.' He
paused and as he said that, with a kind of cold fastidious
distaste in his voice that puzzled her, she saw something like
anger darken those black eyes. 'So, let's stop pretending, shall
we?'

Julia's mouth tightened. 'I know you've been following me,'
she said quickly. 'I recognised you at once, if that's any
consolation—but then you didn't make much effort to be
inconspicuous, did you? I assume it was you who arranged
that charming break-in at my flat. None of that makes any
difference. You've still got the wrong woman.'

'Oh, I don't think so.' He gave a long, slow smile. 'I think I
have the right woman. Precisely the right woman.'

The way he inflected those words, as if they had a meaning
for him which Julia did not understand, alarmed her, but
before she could speak he stood up and moved to the desk.
He opened up one of the folders that lay on it and began to
read from one of the pages, his voice quite even and
businesslike, as if he were reading from a company report.

'Let me see, a few examples should suffice. Ah, here we are.
You arrived in Rome on Alitalia Flight 782, on November the
sixteenth of last year. You stayed first at the Pensione Sforza
and then, after picking up a Mr Hardiman Fletcher, English,
bachelor, long-time resident in Rome, at the Café Lucca, on
November the nineteenth, you moved the same day—rather
swift, that, I thought—into the studio conveniently above his
apartment . . .' He flicked through a few more pages. 'Thanks
to the complaisance of Mr Fletcher you were introduced to a
number of people—we'll take just one example, I think.
Professor Foscari.'

He looked up, his hard, dark gaze meeting Julia's across the
room, and Julia stared at him, her colour deepening.

'The *Professore* is married, with four children. A good-
looking man with something of a reputation as a libertine. On
November the thirtieth you had luncheon with him, alone, at
an expensive restaurant off the Via Veneto. On December the
second, you accompanied him to the Vatican Museum, where
you spent a great deal of time looking at the Raphael murals.'

He smiled. 'You have good taste in art, that at least can be admitted. On leaving the Vatican, you and the *Professore* were seen to embrace. I have a photograph here . . .'

He briefly held up the folder and Julia stared at the Polaroid in horror.

'What *is* this? Some kind of inquisition? I was *working* with Professor Foscari! We went out to lunch to discuss . . . to discuss work,' she added lamely, still not wanting to admit the question of translation. 'Yes, I went with him to the Vatican, and yes, he tried to kiss me when we came out. And if your photographer had taken his picture about two seconds later, he'd have caught me resisting him. I stopped working for the professor at that point.'

He nodded coolly. 'That is true, I gather, but then there were rather good reasons for that. Bigger fish to fry—isn't that the English expression?' He looked up, his eyes hard, and turned another page. 'On December the first you were picked up in a chauffeur-driven car and taken to the Palazzo Contadelli, five kilometres outside Rome. There you took tea with Giovanni Contadelli, who was once, I gather, a student friend of your father's. You had not met before. *Signor* Contadelli is a widower, of course. He is a handsome, well-preserved man of fifty-four, some thirty-two years older than you. Despite that, you got along together very well. Let me see: tea on the first. Dinner on the fifth. Present at a party at his estate on the ninth. Accompanied by him to the '81 Club on the night of the fifteenth—an occasion at which his son Carlo and his daughter, your "friend" Christina, were also present. They, however, left at eleven p.m., Carlo seeing his sister home, and you and Giovanni remained there until two a.m., after which he escorted you back to your studio and was not seen to leave.'

'That's a filthy lie!' Julie started to move across the room. 'He took me back to my studio and he left immediately. Your spies ought to know that . . .'

'That's not what it says here.' His voice was bland. 'After that, your meetings with Giovanni were more infrequent. However, both you and the ever co-operative Mr Fletcher spent part of Christmas at the Palazzo Contadelli. After that, Giovanni Contadelli left for an extended business trip. He ensured your continuing involvement with his family, however, by employing you to look after his semi-delinquent daughter. What do we have here? January the fifth: a visit to your old haunt, the Vatican Museum. You pick up, and then quickly discard, Charles Fisher, an American student . . .'

Julia began to laugh. 'Look,' she said, a little hysterically, 'this is getting a little ridiculous, don't you think? Whoever compiled that for you must have had a vivid imagination. That American—I don't even remember his name. We talked about paintings. We had a cup of coffee for about fifteen minutes after leaving the museum—I wasn't even alone with him, for goodness' sake, and then we . . . I left. I never set eyes on him again.'

'We'll skip on a little, I think.' Again he behaved as if she had not spoken. 'February the sixteenth. You have dinner, alone, with Carlo Contadelli . . . Really, your devotion to members of that family is quite touching, I find. First father, then son and heir. Still, I suppose it's quite understandable. So, February the sixteenth. An intimate and expensive *diner à deux*, at a restaurant off the Piazza Navona. During the course of dinner the unfortunate Carlo, who happens to be engaged, tells you of his need for you, his want for you, his love for you. You play hard to get. He holds your hand. He whispers in your ear. As you leave the restaurant he has his arm around you and fondles you. You return, on foot, to your apartment. Outside, he takes you in his arms . . .'

'Right, that's it. I'm leaving, now!' Julia's eyes blazed across the desk that separated them. 'Who on earth do you think you are—you and your lying, voyeuristic little spies? Just what right do you think you have to stand there and read me that stuff? None of it's true, not one word of it—all that's right are the dates and the places. Everything else is . . . is just foul invention and innuendo. But if it were true, if all of it were true, I still don't have to account for my behaviour to a . . . a man like you.' She tossed her head, and turned. 'You can go to hell. I'm not listening to a word of this!'

'On the contrary.' He was round the desk with the speed of a panther, catching her wrist in an iron grip and pulling her round to face him. 'You have no choice in the matter. You'll listen to anything I choose to say. It's about time you faced up to what you are, to what you've been doing.' His eyes blazed dark, his face had paled, and instinctively Julia shrank from him. He was angry, that was clear; furiously angry. He looked as if he might strike her at any moment.

'You're the liar . . .' he went on, his voice rougher now, all composure gone. 'You've been lying to me, playing the little innocent English girl, turning on the charm when you think it might get you somewhere and turning into a little alley-cat when you think it isn't working.' He paused, and then, very deliberately, pulled her round so she was forced to look into his face, holding her in a grip so tight his long fingers cut into the flesh of her wrists. He lowered his voice, and began to speak to her in Italian. Julia hardly heard him, she was so angry, and now so frightened.

'Oh, go on, go on,' she said furiously. 'Talk to me in Italian, do. Then I can't understand a word you're saying— and that's preferable.'

'Is it? Is it?' His eyes narrowed, and he wrenched her closer to him. 'You little liar—is that what you told Professor Foscari when you worked on translations for him—among other things—that you couldn't speak Italian?'

Again, he lowered his voice, speaking in Italian once more, speaking each word with a cruel deliberation, straight into her face.

Julia stared at him, white-faced, unable to speak for shock. Insult after insult: a woman interested in only two things, men and money. A woman who had deliberately set her sights, first on Giovanni, and then on his son—who didn't care how much heartache and pain she caused to others, to women who were not so easily available, women who would not stoop to her kind of behaviour . . .

'Women? What women?' Before she could stop herself, the words sped from her lips, and he smiled grimly.

'Oh—so you do understand all of a sudden. Remarkable!'

'I said—what women?' Julia took a step towards him, her eyes blazing. 'What women have been hurt by my behaviour? Have you some trumped-up answer to that charge as well, or does your research fall down at that point? Not that it matters—I don't care. You're mad—or sick—one or the other. Every single thing you've said is a lie, and if you want to believe it go right ahead ... it doesn't alter the truth.'

There was a little silence; Julia could feel his gaze, but she did not flinch. When eventually he spoke again, he did so in English once more, and his tone had altered. The anger, the impassioned indignation she had heard in it before, had gone. It was flat, and there was just a second's hesitation.

'You mean you deny *all* this? Everything? Just like that? It is all a tissue of lies——' He paused. 'The Professor? Carlo?'

Julia swung round. 'Deny it?' She gave him the most withering glance she could muster. 'I've already denied it! I don't have to repeat myself. I told you—I don't feel that I have to account for the morality of my actions to a man like you. I can see you might enjoy it if I did, but I'm not going to give you that pleasure. I've no intention of defending myself— who are *you* to call me to account?'

'Who indeed?' He gave a small, cold smile, his eyes never leaving her face. Then, with a quick impatient gesture he threw the papers to one side, and took a step towards her. 'It interests me, though, how emotional you become, how hotly you deny the charges. How neatly everything can be explained by—coincidence, by accident. By a photograph taken a second too early ... It's very convenient, don't you think?'

'So what?' Julia's temper snapped. 'What is it to do with you anyway? Believe I had affairs with half the men in Italy and one-night stands with the rest! Believe anything you damn well like ... and don't look at me with that damn contemptuous look on your face!'

'If I look at you with contempt it is because you provoke it,' he said, his mouth tightening. 'We are not in England now. In Italy a man expects that a woman should ...'

'Should behave like a nun—don't tell me! Be modest and

chaste and sweet and good—except the woman he wants to get into bed, of course, and then it's a very different story!'

Julia shouted her answer at him, and she saw his face darken.

'Is it? *Is* it?' He took another step forward, and suddenly his hand snaked out and grabbed hers in an iron grip. 'You seem to know a lot about it suddenly. You have first-hand experience after all?'

'No—I don't—I didn't say that! You're twisting my words—and you're twisting my wrist as well.' Julia struggled angrily to free herself. 'You—you *animal . . .*'

That insult registered. He was still for a moment, and she saw dark colour wash over the high cheekbones. His face was close to hers, very close, and she thought for a moment that she saw in his a blackness, a desperation, as if he hated not her but himself. It was there and then gone in an instant; his mouth lifted in a cold smile, his eyes glittered dangerously. When he spoke his voice was silky with threat.

'An animal—yes? That is what you think? Then we make a good pair, don't you agree, you—and I?'

Julia tensed. She knew what was coming next, she could read it in the sudden focusing of his eyes, in the new and sudden purpose with which he moved closer. Instinctively she tensed, backing away from him as far as she could. She felt the desk behind her, and like a cornered animal she shrank back against it. Desperately she fumbled on its surface with her one free hand. There must be something—a paperweight, a paper-knife, something she could use to defend herself.

She expected him to grab her, to pull her against him roughly, to force her head back for his kiss—but he did none of those things. Instead, slowly and deliberately, he lifted his hand and pinning her against the desk, began to stroke her breast through her thin blouse.

His touch was very light, almost teasing, circling the full curve with his fingers, then cupping the weight of her breast in his hand. Julia bit her lip and turned her head away with a low groan. Instantly he touched her, fire shot through her blood; even then, even when he had her trapped, when she was desperately afraid.

He smiled, keeping his eyes on her face, his manner quite calm, although his breath was coming quickly, and as he touched her, she felt his body harden against her in quick response.

He moved his thumb then, slowly and gently across the tip of her breast, tracing the wide circle of the aureole. Julia shuddered; to her horror, she felt her own body begin to betray her. Her nipple stiffened and hardened under that gentle parody of a caress, and in spite of herself she felt her neck arch back in a second of response, quickly checked. She wrenched her head back hard, forcing herself to look at him, to confront him, hoping she might shame him into stopping this now, but to look at him was a mistake. Their eyes met, and held. She knew the desire she saw in his was mirrored in her own wide, startled gaze; she parted her lips to cry out—to deny it—and he bent his mouth to hers.

He kissed her as he had kissed her in the car the night before, with a quickness of passion that took her breath away and made her body shudder involuntarily against his. Her mind spun away in horror: this could not be happening to her—it could not. It was insane that frightened though she was, angry though she was, her body responded to him. She gave a little cry, half fear, half pleasure, and his kiss deepened. Then, slowly, pinning her against the desk with his weight, he moved his mouth down the long curve of her throat and his hands to the fastening of her blouse. His mouth moved against hers, softly, persuasively: she thought he said her name. Then his hands were roughly parting the blouse, lifting her breast to his seeking lips. They closed over the tip of her nipple, teasing it with the warmth of his tongue, sucking its hardness into his mouth. She cried out despairingly, feeling her body go limp, her hands relaxing for an instant, then fumbling once more on the wooden surface behind her.

He raised his mouth to her lips and kissed her again, seeking her mouth gently as she tried to turn her head away: it was a long, slow exploring kiss that broke down her resistance inch by inch as force could never have done. She heard her breath catch in her throat; then quite calmly, quite suddenly, he drew back from her. As he did so her scrabbling fingers closed, at last, over cold metal. Scissors.

He stood for a moment looking down into her face, his breath coming quickly, his eyes dark and questioning, as if what had just happened had surprised him in some way, as if he were—momentarily—uncertain. Julia stared at him for a second, transfixed; neither spoke. Then he moved his hand, just a fraction but enough to unleash the stored fear and anger she felt, and sweep all uncertainty away. Quite slowly, knowing she was shaking all over, Julia lifted the scissors from the desk behind her and brought them round, their sharp points toward him.

'So help me God . . .' Her voice would hardly function, it was little more than a whisper. 'So help me . . . if you touch me again, I'll kill you.'

He did not move and his eyes never left her face. Then, very quietly, he simply reached up and twisted the scissors out of her grasp with one quick, easy movement, and tossed them away across the room.

'A child of five could take those away from you,' he said quietly. 'You're shaking so badly you have to lean against the desk. Do you imagine you could do anything—anything at all—to prevent me right now from doing whatever I wanted?'

Julia raised her eyes to his face. In spite of his words there was no triumph in his expression, and no mockery. He looked grave, and also immeasurably sad. She swallowed, then looked away.

'No,' she said slowly, 'I don't suppose I could. However . . .' She looked back at him and her eyes flashed. 'I'd have a damn good try.'

He laughed then, a little bitterly.

'Well—you have spirit. I like that.'

'Do you? You surprise me.' Julia tried to make her voice sound cool, but the words almost choked her. 'I thought sadists liked their victims to be afraid. I thought that was the whole point—spirit was the last thing I'd imagine a man like you would want.'

'Do you believe that? Truly? That I am a sadist—an

animal?' He looked at her searchingly, and Julia turned her face away. He paused. 'We shouldn't argue. You seem to have a most inflammatory effect on my—temper. And surprisng as that may seem to you, it is not what I wish. So, now . . .' He opened a cupboard that, Julia saw, contained shelves and neat stacks of clothes. He reached up, pulled out a shirt and tossed it to her.

'One of mine—it will be too large, but put it on, will you? Your own is a little torn.'

Julia hesitated. She looked down at her own torn blouse, at the shirt in her hand. It was of fine cotton, faintly striped; the initials *R.C.G.P.* were hand-embroidered on the pocket. She touched them lightly, thoughtfully—was it possible Raphael Pierangeli *was* his real name?—then she pulled it on over her own blouse.

He sat quietly on the sofa, watching her. His legs were crossed; he had lit one of those long black cigarettes, and his eyes were narrowed, thoughtful.

'Now,' he said, 'won't you sit down? We got a little sidetracked, I'm afraid. And we have business to discuss—don't you think?'

CHAPTER FIVE

'I WOULD like you to write a letter to your mother and your stepfather.' He paused, tipped the ash from the thin cigar into an ashtray, and then looked up at her.

'You will explain, if you would, that you have been unwillingly detained by some exceedingly violent, unprincipled Italian gangsters——' he smiled as he said that word, 'and that you will be safely released, unharmed, in due course, provided they concur with my wishes.'

'With *your* wishes?' Julia looked up. 'Really? I assumed you must be the side-kick, working for someone else. You mean you're the boss of this little enterprise?'

'But absolutely.' He smiled.

'Well, you seem to do very well out of it.' Julia gestured around the room. 'How many people's misery paid for all this?'

'My own,' he cut in sharply. 'But we're not here to discuss that. You will write the letter, and . . .'

Julia began to laugh. 'Oh sure,' she said at last. 'And if I do, what do you imagine is going to happen? It seems to me that your precious research has let you down again. I won't write, and if I did you wouldn't get much of an answer . . .'

'Really? You think not? Your stepfather is a very rich man and he has no children of his own. I think he would be only too swift to come to your rescue.'

'Then you're wrong.' Julia hesitated. 'I . . . I hardly know my mother,' she went on at last, 'let alone my stepfather. When my parents separated, I stayed with my father.'

'I know all this.'

'Then you should also know that I've seen my mother— what? Maybe four or five times in the last five years? And my stepfather precisely three times—the last occasion at my father's funeral.' To her horror, she felt tears sting at the back of her eyes, and she turned her face away. 'I'm afraid my mother is perfectly indifferent to my fate, and my stepfather would express polite concern, ring up someone in the Embassy, and then do precisely nothing.'

He heard her out, his manner abstracted, as if there was something he couldn't quite work out, something that puzzled him.

'You don't ask about your friend,' he said sharply, 'fifteen-year-old Christina Contadelli along the passage . . . and that surprises me. There's an obvious question, isn't there?'

'Is there?' Julia raised her innocent face to his. 'I don't know what you're talking about.'

'Please don't waste my time. We're not children.' He turned away impatiently. 'If you're trying to help her—which you seem to be, and no doubt you have a devious reason for it—you won't do so by being ridiculous. Co-operate with me, and maybe you will.'

'Oh, I see.' Julia sighed. 'It's classic, isn't it, the two techniques? First you rough me up, then you try the soft touch. All right . . .' She leaned back against the cushions behind her, watching him closely. 'If you think that girl is Christina, then indeed, why not appeal to her father? You might do very well out of it. You could buy a few more paintings, a few more antiques. According to the scenario you'd certainly be better off than you would trying to blackmail my stepfather. That's going to get you precisely nowhere.'

He gave her a quick, cold smile, and Julia was pleased to see that her words had stung him.

'So—all right. I'll explain. Giovanni Contadelli is a powerful man—a very powerful man, with very powerful friends. Contact him, and half the police force in Italy will be galvanised into action. The rewards would be high, and so would the risks. Whereas your stepfather is an American, rich it's true, but he has no particular pull in Italy. I don't think the abduction of his daughter would stir the police to quite such energetic efforts, that's all. The rewards will be less, but the risks negligible. I prefer to play safe, you see?'

'No, I don't.' Julia smiled at him, her eyes watchful. 'It makes no sense at all. Perhaps you don't know, but I went to the police yesterday morning. I told them you'd been following me, I told them I was worried and I gave them a full description of you. It will have been flashed to every police unit in the country by now.'

She had hoped to surprise and alarm him, but she did neither. There was a little silence.

'You knew that already?' Julia said at last.

'But of course.'

'Then surely you can see . . .'

'No, I can't. I know this country better than you, and I know just what the gaps are in its policing system . . .' He paused. 'And besides, I just might be prepared to let your friend go in certain circumstances. Not immediately, but we won't discuss that yet.'

Julia rose to her feet eagerly. 'You mean you'll let her go if I write to my stepfather? Then I'll write now, I promise. Just give me some paper and a pen. I'll write it as . . . as persuasively as I can. Maybe I was wrong just now. Maybe my stepfather will do something . . .'

He smiled. 'You're very quick to co-operate all of a sudden. What's happened? Were you so busy pretending the girl wasn't Christina that you hadn't realised you might be able to bargain on her behalf? That was rather slow of you, don't you think?'

Julia coloured. He was right, he was at least three jumps ahead of her. What a fool she had been! Why, if she had played along with him, she might have persuaded him to let Christina go almost immediately. His arguments about the police seemed a little weak, but why should she argue with his reasoning if it could secure Christina's release? She turned to him, pleadingly, her beautiful eyes wide with distress.

'Please don't play cat and mouse with me. You don't need to. If you'll let Christina go then I'll do anything you want, I'll . . .'

'Ah, so she *is* Christina, suddenly?' He turned to her with a smile of triumph at having trapped the admission, and impotent anger at her own gullibility made Julia's eyes flash.

'All right,' she cried angrily. 'All right! You're very clever. And very cruel. Christina is fifteen years old. She's a young, frightened, innocent girl who's done nothing to harm anyone. And you've already admitted she's no use to you. So—if you mean what you say, let her go. Please. I'll do anything you say if you release her.'

'Anything?' His eyebrows lifted a fraction, and Julia looked quickly away.

'I'll write the letter,' she muttered, 'once I'm sure Christina is safe.'

'Oh no.' He smiled. 'I'm afraid you weren't listening. I said I might be prepared to let her go—*might*, mark you—at a later date. If your present docility and co-operativeness continue. But not now. And believe me, you will write that letter.'

'I shall?' Julia's chin lifted. 'Well, you can forge it if you like, but I'm not writing it.'

'Such heroics.' He smiled coldly, and she saw the dark eyes flash. 'I shan't need to make you. If you don't write the letter, then I shall send your stepfather something else instead.'

'Something else? What could you possibly send him? You can't write—he might not believe you. You can't fake my voice on a tape. Oh no—you need me every bit as much as I need you. Mutual co-operation. Without that, your demands will never stand up.'

'How imaginative you are—you seem very up on the subject.' He looked at her sarcastically. 'But not imaginative enough. It's really quite simple. If you refuse to write to your stepfather, then I shall start sending him some photographs.'

'Photographs?' Julia stared at him blankly. 'I don't understand.'

'It's obvious enough. A series of photographs, I think. At carefully calculated intervals. To begin with, they could be innocuous enough, dramatic, of course, but not over-stated. A photograph of you, simply standing against a wall, for instance. Just as you look now, except perhaps your hands might be bound. And then, something a little stronger. Sitting tied to a chair. Gagged, maybe—I think that would start to work, don't you? And then . . .' He paused. 'Well, if they didn't work, then I think really one would have to start to make them a little more lurid. I can leave the rest to your imagination, I hope. I've no wish to submit you to unnecessary indignities.'

Julia rounded on him furiously, tears of anger starting to her eyes. 'You'd relish it—every moment of it.'

'Would I?' He turned to her with an icy smile. 'Well, in some senses you may be right, though not, I think, in the respect you mean. And no . . .' he reached for her hand as Julia raised it to his face, 'no more violence today, I think. This meeting has gone on long enough. I think you should go back to your room and think about what I've said, don't you? Time to reflect. As much as you like, I'm in no hurry. We can discuss it again, this evening if you like.'

'There's nothing to discuss. I'm not frightened of you, and I'm not going to do what you want because of your cheap threats either. You can go to hell . . .'

'I'm sure you'll think differently in time.' He looked at his watch imperturbably, and then pressed a bell on his desk. 'Pietro will take you back to your room and he'll bring you lunch at one. If there is anything you need, just ask him for it, will you?'

When she was back in their room and the door was securely fastened, Julia went straight into the bathroom and retrieved the plastic bag with Christina's belongings, and handed them to her.

'You may as well have them back,' she said quietly. 'I'm afraid it was hopeless. He knows exactly who you are, who I am—he knows everything about us. They've obviously been watching us for much longer than I realised—months.'

This information did not seem to worry Christina greatly. Quite calmly she put the cards and cheque-book and wallet back in her bag, and refastened the gold bracelet, turning her wrist back and forth so the bracelet glowed against the light.

Julia turned away. She was deeply shaken by what had happened, and she wanted just then to give in, to sit down, to cry, to pour out to Christina everything that had happened.

But she knew she must not. Christina was too young: it was better she shouldn't realise how violent Raphael was. The longer Julia could protect her from that knowledge, the better it would be.

Quietly, Julia went into the bathroom. She stripped off Raphael's shirt with loathing and flung it on the floor. She peeled off her own torn clothes, ran some cool water in the basin, and washed. She felt as if she wanted to go on washing for ever, rinsing the touch of his hands from her skin.

'Well, aren't you going to tell me what happened?' Christina called through the open door. 'Come on, Julia— what did he say?'

'Nothing.' Julia retraced her steps, stuffed the old clothes at the back of her drawer and pulled out some of the things left for her. She stared at them angrily and then began to pull them on, conscious of Christina's puzzled gaze. 'I want to change these clothes. Those things of mine are showing the wear and tear a bit . . .'

'Oh.' Christina was not really interested. She hadn't even noticed Raphael's shirt, and for once Julia gave silent thanks for her innate self-centredness. She leaned back on the narrow bed, and propped her hands behind her head.

'So—come on, what happened? Hey, you look really good in those trousers, you know that? And the shirt. You've got a terrific figure, you know, Julia—it's not fair! I wish I was tall and slim like you . . .'

'Okay.' Patiently, Julia sat down on the bed. 'I'll explain as well as I can. It's crazy, and I don't understand any of it.'

'Are you all right, Julia?' Christina suddenly sat up, and looked at her searchingly. 'You're terribly pale, and your hands are shaking. What did he say, for goodness' sake?'

Carefully, Julia told her. She chose her words and she left out Raphael's threats, but Christina's eyes widened. By the time Julia had finished, her mouth had taken on a sulky pout.

'You mean it's not me they're after, it's you? Are you sure you got it right, Julia? It doesn't make any sense. Who is this stepfather of yours, anyway? He's not that rich, is he? Why did you never mention him before?'

'I never mentioned him because I hardly know him,' Julia answered patiently. 'I've seen him about three times—and, yes, he is rich. Not by your standards, maybe, but by most people's—yes.'

Christina drew her brows together in a frown. Clearly she was deeply affronted that she was not the centre of attention and the object of the plot.

'Did you tell him all that—this Raphael man?'

'Of course.' Julia sighed. 'It didn't make any difference—I told you, Christina. He thinks your father would make too much trouble for him. My stepfather wouldn't have the same pull, so it's less risky.' She shrugged. 'I don't know.'

Christina looked slightly mollified by this. She paused thoughtfully.

'But my father's going to come down like a ton of bricks anyway,' she said at last. 'I mean, the minute I didn't return yesterday the alarm would have gone out . . .'

'I know. But think, Christina—I realised something after I left him. You see how cleverly they chose the moment to kidnap us? Your father's in South America, Luigi was up in Tuscany, but he wasn't due back until this morning, right? So that means they took us on the perfect day—the day when there was no one person who could really organise things. Once Giovanni gets back, obviously all hell will break loose—but until then, there'll be confusion, muddle. It's given them a couple of days' grace, I think.'

'You may be right, it makes sense. Carlo couldn't organise his way out of a paper-bag. All he'll have done is panic and prevaricate.' Christina paused. 'So, what's the next move?'

'I rather think it's mine.' Julia looked away. 'He wants me to write to my stepfather. I said I wouldn't unless he let you go.'

'And he wouldn't play ball?'

Julia smiled wryly. 'In a word, no, so it's deadlock at the moment. But I think there *is* hope, Christina—he said, he hinted, that he might let you go if I were co-operative. At a slightly later date, he said. But obviously just writing the letter isn't enough. He wants something more . . .'

'Oh yes?' Christina's eyes narrowed, and flicked over Julia's slender figure with more than a trace of jealousy in their gaze. 'And what would that be, need one ask?'

'Not what you think. You've been reading too many trashy books.' Julia's voice took on an edge as she stood up and moved away. Christina's coarseness stung her, and also alarmed her. Naively, stupidly, that possibility had not occurred to her. Could Christina be right? For a brief second she remembered the touch of his mouth on her, the touch of his hands as he cupped her breast. And then she remembered the contempt in his eyes, and her heart burned.

'Well, if you don't mind my saying so, I think you're playing this all wrong.' Christina levered herself up and leaned back reflectively, her arms hugging her knees. 'What have you done? You've antagonised him straight off. Said you *won't* do this and *won't* do that. Tried to make conditions. It's stupid. We're in no position to make any demands—surely you can see that? What you ought to have done is played it cool, spun him along—vamp him a bit—why not? You were in there long enough. It's worth a try, isn't it?'

'No, it isn't!' Julia rounded on her angrily. 'For God's sake, Christina, be sensible. I can't think of anything more potentially dangerous—and anyway, I simply couldn't do it. I despise him. I loathe him.'

'All right, all right. Keep your hair on.' Christina waved a hand at her placatingly. 'I know you and men! The original snow princess. But I don't see what you're being so vehement about. He's very handsome. I thought he was madly attractive. Criminal or not, I wouldn't mind co-operating with him a bit.'

Julia turned away. 'You don't mean that, Christina, so why say it? You've got to grow out of trying to shock people, you know.'

'Oh yes?' Christina's voice was scornful. 'Well, there's no need to be so high and mighty about it—and you're wrong. While you were in there being aggressive and demanding and getting nowhere, I've made progress. So there!'

Julia turned round slowly. The younger girl's face was

slightly flushed, and wore an expression Julia had come to know and dread—one of excitement and defiance. She had seen that look before, and she knew what it signified: a man. She felt a quickening of alarm. Christina's teenaged obsession with boys was one thing in Rome, on their sight-seeing expeditions when it never progressed further than attempted sexy walks and backward glances. It was something quite different now. She crossed back to the bed and sat down.

'All right,' she said quietly, 'obviously something's happened. What is it?'

Christina drew in a long breath. She raised her eyes to Julia's worried face, and gave a little smile. 'You were away ages, you know. And after a bit, I got bored. So, after about an hour I got fed up, and I started pounding on the door. And he came in—that good-looking one, Pietro.'

'And?'

'And I said I was fed up, and I wanted to go outside and get some fresh air, and he said no, I couldn't do that, we weren't allowed out unless he had permission from Raphael or something. So I said well, could I borrow a wireless—I wanted to listen to some pop music, and he said no, radios weren't allowed.' She pulled a face. 'That dished me a bit—I thought I might pick up the news, find out what was happening about the kidnapping. Not a chance. Well, I wheedled a bit, and chatted him up, and eventually he said he'd try and find me some magazines. He went away, and when he came back—he said he'd stay and talk to me for a bit. I could see he fancied me. So. Just like I say, I played him along—and no, Julia, don't look like that! I'm nearly sixteen, you know, I'm not a child. I was very careful. I didn't come on too strong—just enough to get him talking. And I found out a few useful things . . .'

Julia swallowed her anxieties. She knew from experience that reprimands and warnings only made Christina more stubborn.

'You did? What?'

'More than you have anyway. Just odd things . . .' Christina paused tantalisingly. 'First of all—the men. There were four of them last night, yes? Well, now there's only three. The chauffeur one has left—he let that slip. So there's just Raphael and Pietro, and the peasant-looking one. He's called Lorenzo.'

'That's very good.' Julia frowned. 'Anything else?'

'Just bits and pieces . . . obviously I couldn't ask too many questions, he'd have got suspicious. So I just rabbited on about nothing in particular, and threw in the odd one. So—he's younger than the others, and he's the outsider in some way. He didn't say much, but it was obvious that the chauffeur one and Lorenzo know Raphael well—have done for years. Whereas Pietro, well, he's obviously been roped in from somewhere else. He's frightened of Raphael, I think, but he doesn't like him. Not that he said anything direct—I could just tell.'

Christina grinned. 'He fancies himself quite a lot, does Pietro, especially as far as the ladies are concerned—that sticks out a mile. And obviously he thinks Raphael outranks him in that respect. Also, they're a different class—did you notice their accents? Raphael's educated, very grand; Pietro's working class, and not from Rome either—further north, I'd say. Florence, or Siena maybe. And not a country accent, a town one. Very chippy, resents Raphael like mad. And I thought that might be useful—you know, if we could get him on our side—divide and rule, you know what I mean?'

Julia nodded. After what had happened that morning she knew it was totally illogical, but she still felt with every instinct in her body that she would rather trust Raphael than the leering Pietro. However, she said nothing, but encouraged Christina to go on.

'Well, I didn't find out much else. Obviously what I really wanted to know was where we are, and why they did it—but I couldn't draw him at all on that. He clammed up straight away. But there were a couple of little things.' She paused. 'First, they obviously *have* been watching us for ages, and Pietro did some of the watching, because he made a few nasty remarks about you and your behaviour. He said something like . . . "Oh, I've seen her. I've seen her put-downs. Maybe

she'll be a bit different with Raphael"—something like that.
Then he grinned and looked at his watch, and said what a
long time you were being. It was obvious what he thought,
and I pretended to be frightened, though I wasn't really, I
know you can take care of yourself in that department, and so
I said, "Raphael wouldn't do anything to Julia, would he?"
And he laughed and said, "He was doing plenty in the car last
night, and she loved every minute of it ..."' Christina
paused, and looked at Julia closely. 'Did he do something last
night? Is *that* what he's after?'

Julia looked away. 'He kissed me, that's all. To shut me up.
We were going through some kind of road block, and there
were police.'

'And did you love every minute of it?'

'No, I did *not*,' Julia said quickly, her voice fierce.

'Okay, okay . . .' Christina frowned. 'Now let me think, was
there anything else?'

'Did you get any hint that there were other people
involved—higher up? Raphael said there weren't, but he
might have been lying.'

'I don't think so.' Christina shook her head. 'Raphael was
obviously *numero uno* as far as Pietro was concerned. I think
he's the boss and Pietro wishes he wasn't. And that's odd. I
mean, he's not exactly your typical kidnapper, would you
say?'

'No, he's not. But then we don't know very much about
him.'

'Yes, we do.' Christina gave a sly little smile. 'I know two
things. He's not married, for one thing. And Pietro has been,
because he said something—it was meant to be disparaging, I
think. Maybe he thought I was too interested in Raphael,
asking too many questions, and not paying *him* enough
attention, I don't know. But anyway, he said, "What does he
know about women? He's never even been married. Now me,
I know about them. I know how to treat them. My wife
treated me like a god . . ." Something like that. And I said—
very innocently, you know—"Oh, doesn't Raphael like
women, then?" And he laughed, and said, "Oh, he likes them

all right. For a while. *She'll* find out." He meant you. Then he changed the subject. I think he was getting edgy. Anyway, he left not long after that.'

Julia digested this information in silence. It tallied with what she had seen of the man, and it was not encouraging.

'Two things,' she prompted gently, 'you said there were two things. What was the other?'

'Oh, that's the best. I was keeping it for last.' Christina gave a little smile. 'Raphael's going away this afternoon, Pietro said so.'

'Going away?' Julia stared at her blankly. A little mad insistent pulse began to beat somewhere in her temple, and she passed her hand across her brow tiredly. 'How can he be?'

'Oh, not for long. About three or four hours, Pietro said. I got the feeling it was something to do with the kidnapping. That he needs to see someone or talk to someone—something like that. Anyway, he won't be back until this evening. And ...' She looked up at Julia mischievously. 'And Pietro promised we can go out for a bit while he's away. I wheedled and wheedled, and eventually he said yes. I think he wanted to be macho, you know, to show off. To show he wasn't that afraid of Raphael, that he could do something off his own bat ... So this afternoon, there'll be two of them and two of us, and we're going to be able to go outside.' She leaned back against the pillows with a smug smile. '*Now* do you see what I meant? Admit I did better than you, Julia.'

'You did better than me.' Julia's mouth widened in a slow smile, and their eyes met in a glance of mutual conspiracy.

Christina grinned. 'I'd say it was a perfect chance, wouldn't you? We're not likely to get a better one. So—how do we escape, Julia? Let's plot! Come on—how shall we do it?'

Raphael must have left, Julia calculated later, at some point while they were having that conversation, because shortly afterwards Pietro reappeared, and it was obvious from his manner that he now considered himself in charge. Christina handled it very well, Julia had to admit. Her years of practice in getting her own way now proved extremely useful. By a combination of appeals and sulky pouts, of coy flirtatious glances and flattery, she eventually persuaded Pietro that it would be all right for them to take lunch out of doors.

'Oh, go on, please,' she said, fixing him with a winning glance, while Julia stayed quiet in the background. 'It's so hot in here, and it would be lovely outside. No one need ever know—we won't say a word, will we, Julia? And anyway, it's your decision now, isn't it, Pietro? You're in charge. Go on—what harm can it do?'

Reluctantly at first, then with growing confidence, Pietro agreed. He led them out to the small shaded loggia at the back of the house, and, after some argument, persuaded the man called Lorenzo to bring the two girls their food there.

He stayed to keep guard over them, whistling, leaning against the wall in what he clearly imagined was a decorative manner. Julia and Christina sat down, and Christina kept up a flow of coy chatter. When the food arrived, it looked excellent: grilled escalopes of veal, with sauté potatoes and a delicious salad. Fresh bread, fruit. Julia regarded the bread with interest. Its freshness was revealing. Clearly it had been baked that day, but when Pietro had led them out past the kitchen there had been no smell of baking. Did that mean, could it mean, that there was a village fairly nearby after all—out of sight perhaps, in some valley?

Julia ate it thoughtfully, suppressing her optimism. Probably it was simply frozen and re-heated, but possibly not. There was a chance—Lorenzo could have gone off that morning on a shopping expedition. Was there a car here, she wondered? Or more than one car? If Raphael had left by car—and he must have done—then was there another?

Perhaps, she thought, if they could persuade Pietro to let them take a little stroll after lunch she could get a better idea of the layout. From here they couldn't even see the track they must have driven up the previous night, and on this side of the house there were no outbuildings—no barns, stables, nothing that might have served as a garage.

With the lunch they were brought a small carafe of some rough white wine, and a carafe of San Pellegrino mineral

water. Carefully Julia took only the San Pellegrino, and
Christina, catching her eyes, poured only a very little wine
into her glass.

'Won't you have a little wine, Pietro?' she said engagingly.
She smiled up at him, then poured a substantial amount into
Julia's unused glass and held it out to him.

'After all—this is all so mad and topsy-turvy, isn't it? You
don't seem like a kidnapper at all. I mean, I know you are . . .'
she smiled up at him, 'but somehow I can't think of it like
that. Do have just a glass, won't you? Julia never touches
wine.'

Pietro shot Julia a glance then, and Julia had the firm
impression he had seen her drink wine on some occasion and
knew Christina was lying. He shook his head surlily.

'I do drink it sometimes,' Julia said quickly, 'but not today.
I've got a headache. Do have some, Pietro.'

He demurred a while longer, but eventually Julia's docility
and Christina's bright chatter seemed to disarm him. He took
the glass and half drained it. The second he looked away,
Julia refilled it. There wasn't enough of it to have much effect,
but it might loosen him up a bit, she thought.

It seemed she was right. As the lunch wore on Pietro grew
more expansive. He didn't join them at the table, but he
continued to talk—about generalities, in a boastful kind of
way. Julia, seeing the effectiveness of Christina's approach,
gritted her teeth and made an effort to flatter him.

He was wearing tight black trousers, a white shirt open to
the waist to display the hair on his chest, and a shoulder
holster. Occasionally, his eyes on the two girls, he would
finger the butt of the gun in it with a silly lascivious smile on
his features. Eventually, Julia raised her eyes wide to his, and
faced him with their topaz fire. 'Oh Pietro,' she said, with a
simper that made her mind writhe with self-disgust, 'I'm so
frightened of guns—I wish you wouldn't touch that one. It
might go off.'

He leered back at her suggestively. 'No way. The catch is
on.'

'I bet you're a really good shot . . .' Julia smiled at him. She spoke in Italian, having decided to give up the pretence, and having seen quickly that Pietro's English was poor, and unless they spoke in Italian they would get nowhere.

The flattery obviously did not strike him as excessive. He grinned once more.

'Oh, sure. Watch . . .' He pointed to a boulder on the far side of the rising ground before them. 'You see that little stone there, on top of the big one?' He drew out the revolver from his holster.

'Goodness! You couldn't hit that, surely? I can hardly see it!'

Christina stifled a giggle in her napkin, but Pietro took the challenge seriously. He swaggered forward a few paces and took up a two-handed stance, squinting along the barrel. Julia wanted to laugh—what did he think he was doing? Starring in a Hollywood movie?

There was a click, and a whine. The pebble on top of the boulder exploded in a shower of dust.

Julia paled, and she and Christina exchanged glances. He might be a clown, but Pietro could shoot.

He swaggered back to them, replacing the gun in the holster, and Julia did not need to pretend to look a little frightened.

'Heavens!' she said. 'However did you learn to shoot like that?'

'Never you mind, eh?' Pietro's face took on a cunning look. 'Just don't attempt to run away, pretty little girls, or . . . peow——' He made the noise of a gun going off. 'Just like that, eh?'

Julia privately thought that was unlikely. Dead hostages wouldn't be that much use to them, but on the other hand you couldn't be certain even of that. There had been cases where money had been extracted on behalf of someone who was already a corpse . . .

She felt glad of the way she and Christina had organised their plan. Christina would distract him; Julia herself would try and slip away. They had argued back and forth on this question, and Julia was unhappy with either alternative. But in the end she had to agree. Obviously they couldn't both make a break for it, and it seemed, on balance, more dangerous to try and escape than to try and distract Pietro.

She looked out with a sense of despair at the beautiful but savage country beyond. Could she find her way to a road? To a village? How long would it be before she could get help? She might wander around for hours, getting more and more lost—and what would happen to Christina the while?

She almost gave up the idea then, but she told herself not to waver. Christina was right, they might never get a better chance. Pietro was easy to dupe—it would not be easy to dupe Raphael. And, once they realised she had disappeared, Pietro would put Christina back in their room and come after her. He wouldn't pursue the flirtation they intended to distract him with. She just hoped Christina had the sense not to let it go too far . . .

At the end of their meal Christina and she exchanged glances, and, on cue, Julia stood up.

'Oh, that was delicious, Pietro. Thank you.' She looked out across the hillside. 'It's such a lovely day—so warm. Would you mind if we went out into the sun, just for a little while?'

Instantly he looked suspicious. Christina promptly stretched. She lifted her arms decoratively, and stuck out her chest. 'Oh, please Pietro,' she said, with a little cat-like yawn. 'The wine's made me feel sleepy. I need a bit of fresh air . . .'

Pietro hesitated, and then shrugged. 'Okay, but not too far. Just ahead up there. That's okay . . .'

He gestured at the dry scrubby ground ahead of them. Slowly, side by side, Julia and Christina set off. They walked a hundred yards, maybe a hundred and fifty, and then stopped. Julia looked around her innocently, as if she were admiring the view, and Pietro, just behind them, watched them closely.

They were now a little way from the house, and Julia could see it more clearly. That must be the room where they were kept, and there was the passageway, and there was the large room belonging to Raphael. She turned slowly, lifting her face to the sun. On the other side, just to the right of the main door, there were other buildings; what looked like a barn,

with windows above it. Maybe the men slept there. There was
no sign of a car, and no sign of a track. That must be further
away, behind the outbuildings. She turned and looked in the
other direction, away from the house, across the land before
them. And she caught her breath.

They were high up, much higher than she had realised. The
house was built close to the edge of an escarpment. Below
them the land dropped sharply away into a series of rocky
ravines dotted with small thorny shrubs. The ravines seemed
to lead down to a valley, but from here the valley floor was
invisible, hidden by outcrops of rock and by the lie of the
land. But in a valley there might be a road, and in the shallow
ravines there were hiding places. She touched Christina's arm
lightly; it was their signal.

'Isn't it beautiful, Christina?' she said. 'So wild—I've never
seen anything like it.'

'Me neither,' said Christina, in a suggestive tone, and
glanced at Pietro as she said it.

They spoke in English. Julia laughed; Pietro laughed with
them, and demanded to know what they were saying. Smiling
up at him, Christina translated. He got the message. Julia saw
his wiry body relax a little as he, too, laughed.

Christina sat down on a wide boulder, facing the house. She
pretended to be sunning herself. Julia moved away from her,
just a few yards, as if she were still intent on the view.

Eventually, after about five minutes or so, Pietro moved.
He stood next to Christina, who had stretched out long bare
legs to the sun, then he sat down next to her on the rock.
Carefully Julia watched him, not moving. Time passed.
Christina had started talking again, and occasionally Pietro
answered her. She was saying something about palm-reading,
and a few minutes later, when Julia cautiously looked back,
she saw that Christina was holding Pietro's hand in hers, and
solemnly scanning his palm.

Very cautiously, uttering up a silent prayer that Christina
would be all right, Julia began, slowly, to inch forward. Pietro
did not turn his head. She looked down. Just below her was a
shallow rocky ravine, on the far side of which the land rose

again sharply. Once over that rise she could be out of sight from above. It might be quite a while before they realised which direction she had taken, and then Pietro couldn't follow her at once. He'd have to get Lorenzo first, and leave Christina with him . . .

She stood on the edge, poised. Behind her, Christina giggled.

'Honestly, Pietro, it's all there! I'm very good at this. The palm cannot lie . . . Well, yes, it means you have a *very* sensual nature. You're the kind of man who just looks at a woman, and then . . .'

God, Julia thought. Where did Christina learn all this stuff? It was quite disgusting, and obviously extremely effective. Pietro was rapt. Now, she thought, and moved.

She was wearing her own flat, rubber-soled shoes, and, naturally athletic, she could move fast. She had to be wary of dislodging sharp stones, she knew that, but luckily there was still a little dry scrubby grass underfoot. In a minute she was slipping quietly down into the ravine. There was no shout, no cry from above, but she hesitated, knowing she was very vulnerable here. She could be seen—she could be picked off, come to that. Go on, she told herself, don't hesitate, go on . . .

The rocks were sharp. They cut into her hands and feet as she scaled the rise on the far side. She winced in pain, her breath catching in her throat as she pulled herself up the steep incline. For a second she glanced back. Pietro and Christina still had their backs to her: now.

A moment later she was over the crest and crouching down out of sight on a narrow rocky ledge. Her heart nearly missed a beat.

Below her the ground fell away sharply in a dangerous and terrifying fall of scree, but what she could see exceeded her wildest hopes. It was a valley, very deep and sharply cleft, so that even from this vantage point she could not see right into it. But she could see something else. A narrow dry track, running round the side of the mountain—the track they must have taken the previous night. If she could only reach that, and follow it down! Not walking along it, obviously, but keeping out of sight just below it perhaps—it must lead somewhere, surely?

Very carefully, her heart in her mouth, she began to traverse the steep gritty slope before her, leaning in against the hillside, making her way always to the cover of rocks or bushes. She was making some progress, but the heat was intense and her hands were already raw from scrabbling over the rock, when suddenly, above her, she heard the shout.

She had been expecting it, but still it terrified her. In an instant, her foot slipped and she was falling. Even then she managed not to cry out, but she was out of control, skidding and bumping down over the scree. Desperately she tried to grab at tufts of grass as she tumbled past, but they only came away in her hand, and scarcely slowed her progress. There were more shouts from the top of the ravine—two men's voices now. And before her, as she skidded down on her back, she could see an outcrop of rocks. Oh, God, she was going to crash straight into them and kill herself, she thought, in a moment of slow dreamlike clarity. She grabbed at a thorny bush as she hurtled past it, and for a second, before it broke, the branch held her.

It did not stop her fall, but it slowed it considerably. She just had time to swivel round and brace her legs, and then she crashed into the rocks, feet first. She tumbled over, scratched and battered, and found herself, gasping, in a hollow of rock.

She lay there half-stunned for an instant, all breath knocked out of her body. Then, hearing another shout, she quickly scrambled over the protruding rock, summoning up her last energy, and crouched down low on the far side of it. Very cautiously, Julia raised her head a fraction, and then quickly ducked down again.

Standing at the top of the escarpment was Pietro, gun in hand, shouting furious instructions to Lorenzo, who was out of sight but obviously somewhere behind him. She saw him lift his arm in the air; a gun shot rang out. She crouched, trembling, pressed against the rock, praying she was invisible from where he stood. There was silence then, but she did not dare to move. Her hands and arms were bleeding. Her face was covered in dirt and sweat and blood, the thin linen shirt was ripped, her breath came in painful, gasping pants: for what seemed like an age she crouched there. The road, the track, was only a few yards behind her, but she didn't dare to turn around. There was a little grass, peppered with dry sheep or goat droppings, at her feet. Just then the dry red texture of the rock was so close to her face it was like a whole world, a planet viewed from space.

At length, very cautiously and slowly, she raised her head a fraction, and looked up. The skyline now was empty: Pietro had gone. She could hear nothing, just the sound of the wind which whistled up the escarpment and over the scree, and lifted the gravelly soil with a dry whisper.

She relaxed. It was all right. For the moment it was all right. He had gone elsewhere to look for her. Now, if she could just make it to the track, and drop down on the far side of it . . .

'Don't move. Stay absolutely still. I have you covered.'

The clipped voice cut into her thoughts, and Julia, recognising it with despair and hearing the menace in its tones, froze against the rock. She pressed herself against it, not daring to turn around, gripping its broken surface as painfully hard as she could in an effort to stop herself from shaking.

There was a light footstep behind her. She waited resignedly for the jab, the thrust of hard metal in the ribs, but it never came. Instead she felt the pressure of two hands—Raphael's hands, she knew that. They encircled her waist tightly, and she heard her breath escape from her throat in a long ragged moan.

His hands tightened just for a second beneath the soft flesh of her breasts, then he released her.

'Now. Turn around to face me,' he said. 'Turn around. Slowly.'

CHAPTER SIX

SHE had expected to see anger, and threat; instead his expression took her by surprise. He was pale, yes, and his breath was still coming quickly, but—had she not known it to be absurd—Julia would have thought his face expressed consternation. He was looking at her searchingly, his dark level brows drawn together, his mouth tight. He was not holding a gun.

Julia let out her breath in a long shaky sigh, and Raphael, whose hands were tightly clenched, seemed to relax a little.

'I saw you fall.' He spoke flatly, then paused. 'I thought you would be killed.'

There was a little silence. For a moment Julia thought he sounded relieved, glad she had not been hurt. Then she looked away—naturally he was. He was hoping to get money out of her, wasn't he?

Very slowly he stepped forward and lifted his hand. Instinctively Julia flinched, thinking he was about to strike her, and she saw anger in his eyes then.

'You think I would hit you now? You think I am that kind of man? Stay still . . .'

Expertly, with a gentle firmness, he ran his hands down her body. She felt his hard fingers press against her rib-cage, her upper arms. They moved gently over her hips and down her legs, and then he slowly straightened up. Their eyes met.

'You can lift your arms? You can walk?'

Julia bit her lip. The gentleness of his tone took her by surprise and, after the shock of the fall, brought her closer to tears than anger or violence would have done.

'There are no bones broken, if that's what you're worried about,' she said flatly. 'Just a few bruises, that's all.'

'You're cut to pieces . . . look, your hands—your arm. Your face is cut . . .' He reached up, as if to touch her, his

86

dark eyes intent, and Julia turned her face away. He let his hand fall.

'The car is just over there. Can you walk to it?'

'Of course I can. I told you, I'm perfectly all right. I . . .'

Julia took about five steps, and then felt her knees give. Raphael said nothing. With a quick easy movement he bent and swung her into his arms, and strode off in the direction of the car, moving effortlessly, as if she were weightless. Julia did not even struggle. She felt only resignation. What was the point?

She could feel the hard muscles of his chest and arms as he carried her; she felt the beating of his heart through the thin material of his shirt. Although she tried to hold it upright, her head swayed against his neck. For a second her cheek brushed against the softness of his dark hair, against the warm skin of his throat. She smelled the slight scent of his cologne and of his skin, familiar from that morning and from the previous day, and the remembered scent had an extraordinary effect upon her. She felt something arc through her body; something fired in her, pulsing through the nerve-endings of her skin, so for a second she felt her body relax against his, as if it ached for, yearned for, his touch. He looked down, then, into her face, and Julia gazed up into the blackness of his eyes. What she saw there reflected what she had felt: she knew then that he wanted her as she had wanted him. Every rational part of her mind was horrified at the thought. How was it possible? The man was a criminal, a vicious heartless exploiter who made a business of other people's suffering, who had shown her only violence and contempt . . . and yet when she looked into his eyes she forgot all that. She saw only a man; she thought she glimpsed a kind of angry and exasperated tenderness.

She looked quickly away. She was deluded, of course. She was a captive; he was her captor. If she let herself forget that for an instant, she knew it would be the beginning of the end.

The car was pulled off the side of the road just on the bend. Its engine was still running, the driver's door only half shut, as if he had stopped and leapt out of the car very quickly. He opened the passenger door and gently lowered her on to the seat. Then he went round to the other side, climbed in, and threw a switch which locked all the doors. He looked at her then, his hand on the gear lever, his face now grim.

'You realise how stupid that was, I imagine? Just where do you think you were going?'

'To find help. A village. Something like that.' Julia looked at him, and he smiled derisively.

'You obviously don't realise how far we are from another house, let alone a village. It would have got dark. You might have fallen, and you might have been less lucky than you were.' He slammed the car into gear, and accelerated away fast. 'It's lucky for you I returned early. I won't tell you not to try such a thing again—I don't need to, you won't have another opportunity.'

There was a pause, then he turned to her again.

'How did you get out? Which of those damn fools let it happen?'

'Find out for yourself. You're the inquisitor.' Julia set her lips.

'I don't need to ask anyway, I can guess. That bloody fool Pietro . . .'

As he said that they swung round the last turn in the steep road, and the house came into view. Now, in daylight, its geography was clear. The road came up behind the outbuildings, as Julia had expected. It ended in a small cobbled courtyard which lay between house and stables. There, outside the main door, were three people. Lorenzo was standing in the doorway, saying something. In front of him, cowering on her knees, was Christina. And standing over her, fist raised ready to strike her, was Pietro.

Even at this distance Julia could see that his face was contorted with rage. So angry was he, so loud were his shouts, that he did not hear the car until it screeched to a halt behind him. He reached forward and wrenched Christina violently upright. Lorenzo stepped forward and Julia heard him shout out, but Raphael was quicker than he was. In a second he was out of the car, across the space that separated them. He caught hold of Pietro by the collar, and half-lifted him off his feet. He slammed him back against the wall of the house and held him there. Julia too was out of the car; forgetting her own pain, she ran across the cobbles to Christina and knelt and put her arms around her. Christina's face was streaked with dust and tears, and there was a purplish weal on her wrist as if Pietro had twisted her arm, but otherwise she appeared to be unhurt.

They both crouched there, shaking, clinging to each other, staring up at the two figures of Pietro and Raphael. Julia thought, for a moment, that Raphael was going to hit him. He held the smaller man with contemptuous ease, in a grip from which Pietro clearly could not free himself. Raphael's other fist was bunched, a stream of low-pitched Italian issued from his lips. Eventually, with a contemptuous gesture, he released Pietro, who reeled back from his grasp, his handsome face flushed. Like all bullies he was a coward, Julia thought. His first instinct was self-preservation and he rounded now on Julia, pointing at her with a quivering finger, the abuse tumbling forth in an incoherent torrent.

'I warned you about her—it's her fault. She planned it, not the other one. I wouldn't have hurt the girl, I was just threatening her, I wanted to know which direction *she'd* taken—how else was I to find her in this godforsaken wilderness, I ask you? She might have been anywhere . . .'

He paused to draw breath, and Julia saw his eyes shift from her to Raphael, who stood motionless, his face dark with anger, hearing him out. His voice took on a high-pitched, needling whine.

'I told you she was a bitch—I told you what she was like. She even took me in . . . The moment you'd gone, it started. She called me into their room, It was obvious what she wanted, she couldn't keep her hands off me, even in front of the girl. She said they wanted to eat outside, and, in the end, I agreed—what was the harm? I was only being kind. I never let them out of my sight . . . and all the time she kept touching me, looking at me.' He hesitated, and wiped his hand across the back of his mouth. 'Then, suddenly, she made a run for it—well, what could I do? I just fired into the air. I couldn't leave the other one and go after her. That stupid bastard Lorenzo was asleep—much help he was. I had to get him, and then I was going after her. I was frightened, worried—God knows why. I don't know. I wish she'd broken her neck . . .'

'Shut your foul mouth!' Raphael spoke suddenly, his face black with rage. His fist clenched, then fell. He turned away with a gesture of contempt. 'Get back to your quarters. I'll talk to you later. You're an incompetent, stupid, conceited fool.'

Pietro hesitated, and gave Julia a glance of such venomous hatred that she looked away instinctively. Then, with a toss of his head, keeping well out of Raphael's reach, he swaggered away in the direction of the stables. There was a little silence, broken only by the sound of Christina's sobs. Julia turned to her, and held her tightly.

'Are you all right? Oh, Christina,' she said softly, 'we should never have done it—we might have known it wouldn't work. I blame myself. If that creep did anything to you . . .'

'He didn't.' Christina made a choking noise. 'I'm OK, it's just that he frightened me. He didn't have time to do anything—it was all just as we planned, but when he realised you'd gone he went spare. I think he's crazy. He was acting like a madman. If you hadn't come back then . . .'

She broke off, and looked from Julia to Raphael. It was obvious enough what had happened: Julia knew there was no need to explain. She was still shaken by her fall, but she was more shaken by the scene which had just taken place and by her own rashness and stupidity. If they hadn't returned when they did, what would have happened to Christina? She held the girl's trembling body close, and a terrible futile anger swelled up in her that these men, that Raphael above all, should do this to them.

Slowly she rose to her feet and turned to confront him, her face pale, her voice shaking with emotion.

'You see,' she said. 'You see what you've done? This is your responsibility. How can you do this? She's still a *child*. You saw what could have happened—he's crazy, that man, and you left us alone with him—I hate you. I *hate* you. If

I were a man, I'd . . .'

She broke off, unable to control her voice, and to her fury felt tears of anger and impotence spring to her eyes. Raphael stood in silence, his face dark and unreadable. Beside him, Lorenzo's kind features crumpled. He laid a hand, as if in plea, on Raphael's arm, and Raphael shook it off impatiently. Julia sprang forward, lifting her hands to him.

'Please,' she cried, looking up into his eyes, 'please—can't you see what you're doing? Don't you feel *anything*—have you no heart? What have we ever done to you? What do you want from us?' When he didn't answer, she brushed the tears angrily from her eyes. 'Do you want to humiliate us, is that it? Haven't you humiliated us enough? What do you need before you let us go? You want us to grovel? All right!' With a furious gesture she tossed back the full aureole of flaming hair. 'I'll grovel. I'll crawl! I don't care what I do if you promise to let her go . . . please, Raphael. Please . . .'

As her voice broke she sank to her knees at his feet and bowed her head. A sob broke in her throat, her whole body shook. She stared down at the reddish dust, at the polished toe of Raphael's shoes. There was a long silence. Then, above her, she heard Raphael expel his breath in a shaky sigh. He bent; she felt his hand come under her arm and strongly lift her to her feet. For a second hope flooded through her.

She looked up into his face, and saw it to be as dark and as implacable as it always was, and with a little cry of hatred and contempt she turned her face away from him.

'Go back to your room.' His voice shook just a fraction. 'Both of you. You should wash your cuts, and both of you should rest. Lorenzo will bring you everything you need. Now go. I have other matters to attend to.'

He turned away abruptly before Julia could say anything more. Slowly she turned; Christina was getting to her feet, and Julia held out her hand to her. Christina took it, and together they followed Lorenzo. Raphael watched them from across the courtyard. He stood still, feet spread, arms folded, silhouetted against the light. As they went into the shadow of the doorway he called out, using her name for the first time.

'Julia.' She stopped, and turned her face wearily. 'We shall talk. Tonight I shall send for you. Now—rest.'

He turned away in the direction of the stables without a backward glance, and Julia, feeling only a dull and leaden hopelessness, slowly followed Lorenzo and Christina back to their room.

During the long heat of the afternoon both girls slept. Julia's sleep was uneasy, shot through with dreams and dangers, and she awoke feeling still on edge. At about seven there was a knock at the door, then the bolts were withdrawn and Lorenzo entered bearing a tray. He looked shamefaced and uneasy; unhappiness clouded his open farmer's face. Julia saw it was difficult for him to meet her eyes.

She was sitting at the table staring into space, trying desperately to think and knowing her thoughts went round and round, hopelessly, like rats in a cage. Christina lay on the bed. She was not asleep now, but she was quiet and shaken— Julia could see that. She had said very little since they returned to their room, and her uncharacteristic silence and despondency worried Julia almost more than anything else. The reality of their situation had been borne in on her now; all her energy and spirit seemed to have left her.

Lorenzo carefully placed the tray on the table in front of Julia, and she looked up at him. 'Only food for one—why is that?'

'Raphael says you're to have dinner with him. He wants to talk to you.'

Julia looked up at him coldly, determined not to let his obvious concern touch her.

'I have nothing to say to him,' she said proudly, lifting her chin, 'and I'm not hungry anyway. Tell him I shan't go.'

'No . . . no!' Lorenzo's kind features took on an expression of alarm. 'It is better that you go—truly. Raphael will not harm you. Believe me . . .' He hesitated, and looked down at the floor. 'He is a good man. I know him . . .'

He half-muttered the words, which took Julia by surprise. A caustic reply rose at once to her lips, but she bit it back. She looked at Lorenzo and then, slowly and expressively, she raised her hands and indicated the room.

'This is good?' she said quietly. 'To do this to two women is good? How can you think that?'

'There are reasons . . .'

'You mean money?'

'No!' He raised his face with a kind of weird shocked pride, as if Julia had suggested something unforgivable. 'You do not understand,' he muttered. 'I must not explain. And you are English—it is difficult for you, perhaps, to understand, but . . .' He broke off. 'You should talk to Raphael.'

Julia gave a little shrug.

'Well, I suppose if I don't go he can always make me. So, all right, tell him I'll go.'

Lorenzo shambled back to the door. There he turned and looked back at her. 'It was not an order,' he said simply, 'I thought you understood. It was a request.' Then he turned and left the room.

Gently, Julia helped Christina to eat, wash and undress, and tucked her into bed. Without her usual make-up, with her short hair ruffled and spiky against the pillow, Christina suddenly looked much younger and very vulnerable—more like a little waif than the tough, brassy, jet-set schoolgirl she tried to pretend to be in Rome. Julia sat with her quietly, and watched Christina's dark eyes fill with silent tears. She pressed her hand.

'Tell me, Christina. Tell me what you're thinking of.'

'Of home.' Christina's mouth trembled. 'Of Daddy. And Carlo. And my mother, I don't know why—I've kept thinking about her, ever since we came here. She died a long time ago, but . . . oh, Julia! I want to go home!' She cried then, awful convulsive sobs that shook her whole body, and Julia held her tightly and stroked her hair, her own eyes full of tears.

'Now, listen,' she said gently, when the sobs eventually died down, 'what we did today was silly, I see that now. But it's going to be all right, Christina. I'm going to do what you said—I'm going to co-operate. I'm not going to be angry and hostile any more. I daren't risk it after what happened today.

So I'll just agree to everything he wants. I won't even argue, I promise you. And then . . .' She hesitated. 'Then he'll let *you* go at least, I'm sure of it. And that's all we need to worry about for the moment.'

'But what about you?' Christina's voice rose in pitch again.

'I'll be fine, you'll see,' she said with a calmness she did not feel. 'Either my stepfather will pay up and they'll let me go, or . . . or he won't, in which case they'll probably release me anyway. Eventually, when they realise I'm no use to them. Don't worry about it. I'll talk to Raphael, and you sleep. You'll feel better in the morning . . . That's it. Turn over . . . now sleep, Christina.'

You'll feel better in the morning—Julia sighed. That was what they had said to her when her mother had left home. Last year, when her father had died. It wasn't true, of course, and everyone knew it, yet there she was, telling the same comforting lie. Was that when you finally grew up, she thought sadly, when you told others the same gentle untruths that you yourself had been told?

Wearily she stood up and looked at herself in the glass. There was a long scratch down the side of her face where she had fallen. Since she had no choice in the matter, she was wearing one of the simple cotton shifts she had found in the drawer. It was almost the exact colour of her eyes, smoky, like topaz, and as she looked at herself in the unfamiliar glass she felt herself insubstantial, a ghost. She did not know this woman in the glass any more, this woman who could fight and plead. She was a stranger to herself; and it was Raphael who had done this to her.

Quietly she turned away from the glass, lit a small lamp and sat down at the table. In her bag she had writing paper and envelopes; she had often whiled away the time in cafés in Rome, writing letters to friends in England. How long ago all that seemed now!

Carefully she opened the pad, and began to write. When, just after eight, Lorenzo came to fetch her, she tore out the sheet of paper, folded it and took it with her.

She hesitated outside the door, glancing back at the

sleeping Christina, and Lorenzo seemed to read her thoughts, for he touched her arm shyly. 'It's all right,' he whispered, 'Pietro's gone. Raphael chucked him out.' He gave a low laugh. 'He won't be back, that's for sure. And don't worry— I'll see that she's safe.'

'Thank you,' Julia said, and then followed him along the corridor. She sighed. It didn't take long, she thought. Everything she had ever read on the subject was right. Once you were a prisoner you learned quickly enough to be grateful to your captors, to appreciate even the most minimal of reassurances or kindness.

Lorenzo left her at the door of Raphael's room, opening it for Julia to step inside, then shutting it quietly behind him.

The room was softly lit; a log fire burned in the grate. In the light of the flames the gold of the Chinese screen, the gilt frames of the many paintings, flickered into richness and warmth and then faded back into the shadows. Near the fire a small table was laid for two; next to it Raphael was sitting, staring into the fire. As she entered, he rose to his feet.

He was wearing evening clothes, a velvet jacket of a soft, very dark green, a silk shirt open at the throat. His physical beauty then was such that Julia was silenced. The darkness of his hair, the watchfulness of his eyes, the harsh and forbidding perfection of his strong features, all this held her eye, and cut off the bitter remark which might have sprung to her lips. In any case, had she not resolved to be quiescent?

Quietly she advanced across the room to him, conscious that his dark eyes never left her. He looked at the soft folds of the dress, then up into her eyes, and he half smiled.

'I was right . . .' His voice was very low. 'Almost the exact colour. Not quite, of course, for your eyes change constantly, and no material could do that.' He gestured to the chair by the fire. 'Will you sit down?'

Julia sat. She looked up at him and then, silently, she held out to him the piece of paper she carried.

He frowned, and then as she nodded took and read it. There was silence for a while, and Julia looked into the fire. At last he looked up, and she raised her face to his.

'Is that right? Will it do? It wasn't very easy to write—but if it's wrong, I'll do another. You see I've left a space blank for the amount of money. You didn't say—I didn't know ...' Her mouth twisted a little. 'I didn't know what value you set on me.'

'Did you not?' His voice was soft. 'No—well, I suppose you wouldn't.' He paused, and looked down at the slip of paper once more. ' "Dear Mr Carnegie Hunt",' he read aloud. He looked up once more to meet her eyes. 'Is that normally how you would address your stepfather?'

'I don't know. I've never written to him before,' Julia said simply. 'I thought of writing "Dear Robert", but it seemed wrong. I did tell you. I hardly know him.'

'I see.' He paused, and if she had not known better, she would have thought there was something like pity in his eyes. 'Perhaps it would be better if you wrote in the first instance to your mother ...'

'I thought of that too.' Julia's voice was bleak, and she hesitated. 'But, you see, we don't get on very well ... no, that's not true. We don't dislike one another, or quarrel or anything, it's just that I hardly ever see her either. She left when I was about six, I've rarely seen her since. And ... and I think on the whole my stepfather would be better. He's practical and capable, he'll try to help.'

'Very well.' He folded up the piece of paper without further comment, and put it in his pocket. Julia looked up at him wide-eyed.

'Is that all? Is it all right then?'

'It's very eloquent.' His voice was flat. He turned away to the table and without asking her, poured her a glass of white wine. He handed it to her, took one for himself, and then sat down opposite her.

'Lorenzo has made us some cold food—it's quite good, I think. That will be all right? I thought it would be easier, and we would not be disturbed.'

'That's fine ...' she said faintly. 'I'm not very hungry. I ... Are you sure the letter's all right? There's nothing you want me to add to it?'

NOW THAT THE DOOR IS OPEN...
Peel off the bouquet and send it on the postpaid order card to receive:

Harlequin Presents®

4 FREE BOOKS!
An attractive burgundy umbrella—FREE!
And a mystery gift as an EXTRA BONUS!
PLUS

MONEY-SAVING HOME DELIVERY!
Once you receive your 4 FREE books and gifts, you'll be able to open your door to more great romance reading month after month. Enjoy the convenience of previewing eight brand-new books every month delivered right to your home months before they appear in stores. Each book is yours for only $1.95—30¢ less than the retail price.

SPECIAL EXTRAS—FREE!
You'll get our free monthly newsletter, *Heart to Heart*—the indispensable insider's look at our most popular writers and their upcoming novels. You'll also get additional free gifts from time to time as a token of our appreciation for being a home subscriber.

NO-RISK GUARANTEE
- There's no obligation to buy—and the free books and gifts are yours to keep forever.
- You pay the lowest price possible and receive books months before they appear in stores.
- You may end your subscription anytime—just write and let us know.

RETURN THE POSTPAID ORDER CARD TODAY AND OPEN YOUR DOOR TO THESE 4 EXCITING, LOVE-FILLED NOVELS. THEY ARE YOURS ABSOLUTELY FREE, ALONG WITH YOUR FOLDING UMBRELLA AND MYSTERY GIFT.

HARLEQUIN READER SERVICE
P.O. Box 609,
Fort Erie, Ontario,
L2A 9Z9.

PLACE THE BOUQUET ON THIS CARD. FILL IT OUT AND MAIL TODAY!

*Place the
Bouquet
here* →

Yes! I have attached the bouquet above. Please send me my four Harlequin Presents® novels, free, along with my free folding umbrella and mystery gift. Then send me eight new Harlequin Presents® novels every month as they come off the presses, and bill me just $1.95 per book (30¢ less than retail), with no extra charges for shipping and handling. If I am not completely satisfied, I may return a shipment and cancel at any time. The free books and gifts remain mine to keep.

308 CIP U1BC

Name _____

Address _____ Apt. _____

City _____ Province/State _____

Postal Code/Zip _____

Offer limited to one per household and not valid for present subscribers. Prices subject to change.

PRINTED IN U.S.A.

Take this beautiful
FOLDING UMBRELLA
with your 4 FREE BOOKS
PLUS A MYSTERY GIFT

If order card is missing, write to Harlequin Reader Service,
P.O. Box 609, Fort Erie, Ontario, L2A 9Z9.

'Nothing.' He gave a brief smile. 'I will insert the—value.' He paused. 'You could write an envelope before you leave tonight, then the thing is done.'

'Very well.' Julia bent her head. Raphael said nothing, and the speech she had prepared for this moment spun incoherently in Julia's mind. She grappled with the words, and at last, still uncertain of what she would say, raised her head.

'I wanted to ask you now . . .' She hesitated, and then went on in a rush, the words tumbling over one another. 'You said yourself that keeping Christina was dangerous to you. By now her father will have returned—he'll move heaven and earth to get her back. She's a danger to you, and she's desperately frightened. That man this afternoon—he's unbalanced. Please—now that I've done as you asked, won't you let Christina go?'

'Her father will move heaven and earth?' He gave a slightly bitter smile. 'Rather different from your case, is it not? Is there anyone, do you think, who would move heaven or earth for you?'

Julia stared at him blankly, for his tone puzzled her, and she could only assume that he wanted to cause her pain, though the words were said with an angry bitterness, not cruelly.

'No,' she answered quietly, 'I don't suppose there is. I do have friends, though . . .' She raised her face proudly to his. 'Friends in England—people I was at school with. And in Rome. Hardy . . .' She broke off, and he gave an impatient gesture.

'Friends? *Friends?* I'm not talking about friendship—milk and water stuff. You know what I'm talking about. You have fire in your heart . . .' His voice had risen, and he struck his hand against his chest. 'You know very well what I mean.'

Julia hesitated, not understanding him. 'My father,' she began, in a shaky voice. 'If he were alive . . .'

'I know that,' his face softened, 'but I don't mean a father, not in this case. Is there no one else who would,' he smiled sardonically, 'in your eloquent phrase, move heaven and earth on your behalf?'

Understanding him at last, Julia met the question in his dark eyes. He meant a man, lover or a husband, she saw that now, and, she realised, on a sudden stab of instinct, that she had only met one man in her life who had such passion, or who was capable of it. She looked away, pushing that thought from her.

'No,' she said flatly, 'there's no one.'

'Then there should be.'

He spoke grimly. A little silence fell. Then, abruptly, he stood up, and began to pace up and down the room. Eventually, as if he could stand the silence no longer, he banged his glass down on a table so that Julia jumped, and wheeled round to her.

'I want you to understand why I say this . . .' His voice, and his gesture as he spoke revealed a kind of pent-up agitation. 'I say this because I was affected by what happened today. Byn everything that has happened since . . . since we left Rome.' He paused, and made an angry gesture of his hands, as if he knew he was not expressing what he thought. 'When you knelt before me today, in the dust, with your hair so . . . do you think that did not affect me? That I rejoiced to see you brought so low? Well, I did not! It was I who was humiliated when you did that—not you. I . . . and that moment, that scene has been in my mind ever since . . .'

He paused and then, as if trying to force himself to be calm, returned, and sat down opposite her. He leaned forward, his eyes burning dark in his face, holding her gaze absolutely.

'I want you to understand,' he said more slowly. 'I was wrong about certain things—I think I was wrong—about you. I feel . . .' He hesitated, and spread his hands palm upward. 'I feel nothing but respect for you. Admiration, even. Whatever you have been, or are—you have courage. I respect that in a man, I have rarely encountered it in a woman.'

'Perhaps you refused to see it,' Julia cut in sharply. 'Lots of women have courage, it just tends to take a quieter form than men's.'

'You may be right.' He inclined his head, as if to acknowledge a debating point, then he lifted his hand and gently touched the scratch that still scarred it. 'However, your courage is not always quiet. It can take quite dramatic forms too.'

In spite of herself Julia smiled, and his face immediately became more grave.

'I say this,' he went on, 'for a reason. Because I am going to refuse what you ask, and when I do so, I want you to understand my motives. Or part of them at least.'

'You're going to refuse me?' Julia stared at him. 'You mean you're not going to let Christina go?'

'I'm afraid not, not yet. It is not . . .' He broke off. 'Let's just say it is not yet possible.'

'But I don't understand!' Impulsively Julia sprang to her feet. 'I've written the letter! You don't need her—if you keep her you will certainly be caught yourself. You will gain nothing. Why?'

'Let's just say that I began doing it for one reason, and that now . . .' he paused, 'that now circumstances have changed. I cannot say more than that.'

She stared at him, knowing her whole body was trembling. She wanted to cry out in anger, to strike him, to burst into tears, to plead with him all at once. But she remembered her earlier resolution; the image of Christina's tear-stained face sprang into her mind.

Slowly she sank to her knees in front of him. 'If kneeling to you affects you, and you say that it does, I kneel to you now. Let her go.' She swallowed, and then hesitantly raised her hands, and placed them gently on his knees, lifting her face in entreaty to his. 'Please,' she went on. 'I saw Christina tonight. She hardly ate and she cried. She wants to be at home with her family. Let her go. I'll do anything if you do that. Anything you ask, I don't care what it is—I'm beyond caring. I want only one thing, and you are the only one who can give it to me . . . Please.'

As she said that she saw the corners of his mouth lift in a bitter smile. His eyes darkened. He leaned forward slightly and looked down into her upturned face, into her eyes, down to the parted fullness of her lips, to the curve of her upturned throat, the thrust of her breasts, and then back to her eyes.

'I think you mean it,' he said slowly, his voice low. 'Dear God, I think you mean it.'

He lifted his hand, and very slowly brought it up to her throat, so his fingers encircled it like the stem of a flower. 'Do you know what you look like?' he said, his voice thick. 'Do you *know* just how beautiful you look at this moment? Your hair . . . loose like that, the colour of fire, of sunset. Your eyes, your lovely cat's eyes, which can look as clear as the daylight—except when you look at me? And your skin, your English skin, so soft and cool to the touch . . .' He raised his index finger, and drew it gently down her cheek, so that Julia quivered. 'Oh yes—I think you must know,' he went on softly. 'And if you don't know that, you must know what you make me feel. What you do to a man, when you kneel like that, your lips parted, your mouth offered up. Your breasts . . . I want to hold them—you know that, don't you? I want to feel their softness and their weight, now, in my palms—against my heart. I can't look at you without thinking of those breasts, of touching them, of seeing you naked, taking you naked in my arms. When you knelt to me today, out there in the courtyard, in front of the others—you know what I felt? I felt shame and then, just as I do now, I felt desire. I wanted nothing more than to lift you in my arms again, and carry you to my bed, and take you, under that fur rug. Take you once. Take you twice. Take you again and again . . .'

Julia stared up at him, hypnotised by his low voice, by the quiet of the room, by the touch of his hand. She felt as if she were in a dream, as if she were going mad; a pulse lit and pulsed in her blood; warmth stole up through her body and coloured her cheeks. He saw her blush, and he smiled.

'You know, don't you? You know I tell the truth? You blush like an innocent girl, but you know I want you. I can read it in those eyes of yours, yes, even when you lower them. Look at me, Julia. Look at me, and tell me—don't you feel it too?'

Slowly, unwillingly, Julia raised her eyes to his. She ran her tongue over her dry lips; her throat felt as if it were on fire.

'I don't know . . .' she said desperately, her voice little more than a whisper. 'I don't know anything any more. I don't understand anything. I just know ... that I want you to let Christina go, and ...'

'Oh, I don't think so.' He smiled a little grimly. 'I don't think it's just that. You may prefer to tell yourself that it is, but it's a lie. Doesn't your body tell you it's a lie? What are you saying—that you'll go to bed with me if I let Christina go, is that it?'

'I told you. Yes—all right!' Julia turned her face away desperately. 'What does it matter, after all? It's a little thing, compared to her freedom.'

'A little thing? Oh, I don't think that's the case. Not with you and me ...' He moved suddenly, as if her words angered him and he was determined to make her acknowledge the truth of what he said. He slipped his hand down, down her throat, and then under the opening of her dress. Julia shuddered as his hand felt for the curve of the breast, for the hard jut of the nipple against the palm of his hand.

'You see?' He looked down into her upturned face. 'You want to make love—your body is ready for a man to make love to you. Just as mine is ready for you—just as mine hardens and grows strong every time I look at you, every time I undress you with my eyes. Touch me, Julia. Touch me—you can see that it is true ...'

She drew back then, but he caught her hand and held it tightly between his own. Then, slowly, he drew it along the hard muscles of his thighs, up to the flatness of his stomach. Julia's breath caught in her throat, and with a low moan she tore her hand away.

'Stop this. Stop it ...' she said in a low voice. 'I don't understand why you are doing this to me. You're just playing games. If you want me, you want me, it's as simple as that. You don't have to ... to dress it up with fine words and romantic phrases. That's just lies. You're just setting a price— the price for Christina's freedom—and, and it excites you, that's all, knowing I'm your prisoner, that I'm in your power, that I have to do what you want. If we weren't here, if I just met you—somewhere else, perfectly normally, you wouldn't feel that.'

'That's not true.' He cut across her with a smile. 'I *have* met you, under just the normal circumstances you describe.'

'What?' Julia swung round and stared at him.

'Well, not met you, but seen you. Long before all this began, before you were being watched. I saw you . . .' He hesitated. 'I saw you across a room in Rome, at a party, and you had the same effect upon me then that you have now. You had the same effect on every healthy male in the room between the age of fourteen and seventy, and I can't believe you were altogether unaware of it. So, no, Julia, you are wrong. It is not our circumstances. And it is not that you "are in my power", as you quaintly put it. You're not free to leave yet, that is the extent of my power. It begins and ends there. And . . .' His hand tightened over the warm swell of her breast. 'Much as I want to, angry though you may make me, going to bed with me is not the price of Christina's freedom. It is not the price of anything. That will happen—and it will happen, I know it—because you want it. Because you ask me for it . . . that's when, Julia, *carissima.* That's when.'

He lowered his face to hers then, and bent his lips to her mouth. Julia did not draw back, just then she could not have done. She let him draw her lips into a kiss, let him part them with his tongue, let him open them to the warmth of his touch and exploration. He kissed her deeply, slowly, with a great and powerful gentleness, and her mind sang at the suck and caress of his lips. Her breasts, the nipples engorged with the blood of desire for him, hardened to a point of pleasure under the stroking of his hand, and slowly, shyly at first, she kissed him back, reaching up her hand to touch his cheek, drawing his mouth down to hers.

At last, slowly, he drew back, and they looked at each other. Julia was trembling, but she managed to keep her voice even.

'I shall never ask you,' she said steadily. 'You know that, don't you? You can force me, you can blackmail me into it, but I shall never ask you of my own free will.'

'Then why did you kiss me?'

'Because I wanted to—then. That at least is true. I can't explain it, and I won't excuse it. There it is—and it's over.'

She stood up, and he gave a low laugh.

'That's honest, at least. We'll leave it there, shall we?'

He stood up, and straightened the collar of his shirt which was in some disarray. She saw the glint of laughter in his eyes.

'I think we should eat. There are other things I want you to tell me. We can continue this particular discussion—some other time.' He gestured with ironic gallantry in the direction of the table. 'Food. Wine. Candles. Firelight. The perfect setting—apart from the locked door, of course. Won't you join me?'

CHAPTER SEVEN

STRANGE though her circumstances were, crazy though it seemed to be sitting there with this man, Julia found that she was, after all, hungry. Raphael plied her with food and drink with a courteous solicitude, as if this were a normal dinner, she his guest and he the host.

He plied her, too, with questions: about her home and childhood, her school, her time in Rome, her work there. At first, suspecting him of seeking information that might assist him, she resisted his enquiries and answered in monosyllables. But gradually, perhaps because of the pale gold wine, with its heady spring taste, perhaps because of the way he listened and responded to the few things she said, she grew more open and more relaxed.

At the end of the meal he left the table, made coffee, and brought her a small glass of Armagnac. He sat down again, and lit one of the long black cigarettes he smoked occasionally, and that—reminding her of the day of the burglary in her flat—gave her the cue she needed. She looked at him levelly across the table, meeting his gaze.

'You've asked me so many questions ...' She paused. 'I suppose I'm not allowed to ask any about you?'

'You may ask.' He shrugged. 'I can tell you the main things if you want to identify me further. You already know my name. What else can I tell you? I'm not poor, I'm not married. I'm not—in spite of what you said—a degenerate or a bully.' He paused. 'I have a temper ...'

'Do you live in Rome?'

'Occasionally.'

'Near where I live?'

'I visit that area sometimes.'

'Where did you learn your English?'

'From my mother, initially. She speaks it perfectly.'

Julia stared at him. 'How strange,' she said softly. 'You have a mother . . .'

He gave a bark of laughter. 'But of course. Most men do. And a father too, but he is dead.'

Julia smiled. 'I know it sounds ridiculous—but I hadn't thought of you like that, you see. As a man, with a family. With a life outside—outside of all this. I can't think of you, except in this context.'

'I assure you I have another existence.' His voice was dry. 'I visit my mother. I visit my brothers and sisters. I sometimes remember to go to church. I read. I look at paintings. I eat. I drink. I listen to my mother's advice and then pay no heed to it . . .' He smiled. 'Very ordinary. Very dull.'

'And this?' Julia leaned forward suddenly. She gestured around the room. 'Your illegal activities. Do you discuss *them* with your mother?'

She spoke quietly enough, but her words were barbed, and she saw his eyes darken at once. He stubbed out the cigarette.

'No.'

'You lead a double life then?'

That idea seemed to amuse him; the corners of his mouth lifted.

'That hadn't occurred to me, but yes, I suppose—now—you are right.'

Julia was disconcerted by that smile, by the ease with which he deflected her challenge. She looked away quickly, trying to think: had this man a conscience? Sometimes she felt as if he had, and it might be appealed to, at other times he seemed brazenly conscience-less. There was a silence, and at length Raphael smiled.

'Well, you haven't asked very much. Is there nothing else you want to know? Most women, even in circumstances very different from yours, are a great deal more curious.'

'I *am* curious.' Julia turned back to him impulsively, 'but not in the way you seem to expect. After all, what kind of abduction is it where the kidnapper lets you see his face, where he tells you his name? I know you're lying. I could ask you to tell me your real name, where you come from, who you are—but you would only lie again, and anyway I feel . . . I feel as if those things hardly matter.'

'I see.' He frowned. 'We have moved beyond that, maybe. Then what does make you curious?'

'You do.' Carefully Julia took a sip of the Armagnac to give herself courage. 'You see,' she went on, 'I should like to understand you. It's after all a matter of self-preservation that I should, and I don't understand you at all. Yesterday in the car . . .' She hesitated. 'This morning, you frightened me then. You were very angry, very violent, when you were reading those things in the file. I couldn't understand why. After all— if all those lies were true, why should it matter to you, why should it affect you?'

She broke off then, seeing his hand clench and unclench on the polished surface of the table. But he said nothing, so she went on.

'And then this afternoon you said you had a gun, and I think you hadn't. You showed me something very like kindness and concern. Tonight you take a different tack altogether.' The colour rose a little in her cheeks. 'Your behaviour changes all the time—and I don't understand why.'

'I see. So, you have me marked down as some kind of madman—a psychopath with a reasonably civilised veneer, is that it?' He smiled drily, a little bitterly.

Julia shook her head. 'No, I don't. That's just the point. This morning, perhaps I thought that then, but not now. I feel . . .' She paused then, meeting his eyes, and feeling suddenly a great lurch of uncertainty, a surge of contradictory emotions. Raphael leaned forward, his voice low, his eyes intent.

'Tell me. What do you feel?'

'I feel as if I could trust you.' The words suddenly burst out, impetuously, and the moment they were spoken she knew they were the truth. 'I feel as if you could be brave. And kind. Even good, someone I could admire and like. And yet you are none of those things. You aren't trustworthy. If you were, I wouldn't be here, and we wouldn't have met.'

A lump rose in her throat, and her voice faltered to a halt.

To her horror she felt tears prick behind her eyelids, and she turned her face quickly away.

'I can't explain it. I first saw you a little while ago. You mystify me. And yet in some ways I feel closer to you than I've felt to anyone in a long time. And that makes me afraid— because I know it's foolish, and I know it's wrong.'

'But I feel that too.' He spoke quietly, with a sadness and bitter regret in his voice that made Julia swing round to him once more. This time it was he who shrugged and looked away. 'Maybe, as you said earlier, it is just the drama of the circumstances.'

'*Why* are you doing this?' She leaned forward again, the question that had been in her mind all this while at last rising to her lips. She spread her hands in a wide helpless gesture, and in the candlelight her topaz eyes blazed.

'I can't believe you don't know how wrong it is. I can't believe you would do this for personal gain—and yet you must be. Why are you doing something I think you know is hurtful—painful? You of all men?'

For a moment she thought he was not going to answer her, and that her appeal had angered him, for his brows drew together in a frown and his mouth tightened. Then, to her surprise, he smiled.

'Maybe my reasons for doing this now are quite simple.' He leaned back in his chair. 'I want you with me.'

'Oh, don't joke. How can you joke now?' Julia cried. 'That's not true, and if you were the man I think you are, you would know that it is useless to keep a person against their will. That's not possession, that's prison. If you wanted me here, truly, you would make me free to go.'

'You are free to go.' He lifted his hand from the table, and watched her. 'The door is unlocked. Leave.'

Julia stared at him; she half rose to her feet, and saw his body instantly become rigid with tension. She sat down again with a sigh.

'You don't mean that,' she said dully. 'You don't mean it and you're just mocking me. You're not even attempting to answer what I asked you . . .'

'All right.' His voice was suddenly decisive. Slowly he brought his hands together, and rested them palm against palm. He looked at her thoughtfully, speculatively—weighing every word, Julia thought, and noting her every reaction.

'I did what I did not on my own behalf, but on behalf of—a friend. For that friend's sake, I have to continue with it for as long as it takes. More than that I cannot say.'

Julia stared at him, disbelief rising stubbornly in her heart.

'For a *friend*?' she echoed. 'You did this for a friend? But why? You mean they need the money?'

'Not exactly, no.'

He stood up abruptly and moved away from the table.

'Look, you don't believe me, and there's no reason you should. I will say nothing more—there's no point in discussing this. I knew it would be futile . . . It's getting cold. Come and sit by the fire . . .'

Slowly Julia rose and crossed the room, his words ringing in her head. She sat down on the couch, and—after putting another log on the fire—he hesitated, and then sat beside her. His whole manner betrayed some inner agitation, and, for the first time since she had met him, Julia looked at him, and sensed that she was at last gaining the upper hand. *I must go on*, she thought, *I must; I must not relent*. But it was not easy. To her own distress her heart was softening towards him, however fiercely her mind told her that was insane—more than insane, dangerous. She must press home the temporary advantage she had won, she thought; talking to him in this way, calmly, directly, telling him the truth—all this was getting her further than anger and abuse had done. Maybe he was lying, maybe he was acting—but somehow she did believe he had a better nature, she must try to appeal to it. She drew in her breath and turned to him.

'You said you have sisters.'

'Yes.'

'Then think, imagine how you would feel if your sister were in my place. And your sister—think how frightened she would be—how terrified.' She leaned across to him pleadingly. 'If you can imagine that, surely you can see how wrong this is?'

'You have no brother.' He cut her off sharply. 'Your father is dead, you scarcely see your mother. No one is suffering as a result of what has happened to you, you told me so yourself. And you ...' He paused, and the corners of his mouth twisted. 'I would have said many things about you, but I would not have said you were afraid.'

'But Christina ...'

'*Are* you afraid?' He swung round to her suddenly, cutting off her words. Julia stared at him, held by something in his eyes. He reached forward and grasped her wrist.

'Answer me. Are you afraid? Of me?'

For an instant Julia's mind spun. She knew what the truth was, but she did not mean to say it. She did not fear him, she thought, but he made her fear herself, he made her fear the wild and unpredictable, irrational emotions she felt now, and which she knew she ought not to feel. She lowered her eyes.

'No, but I think I ought to be.'

He expelled his breath in a long sigh. The grasp on her wrist did not slacken.

'Why?' he said softly. 'Tell me why you think that.'

'Oh, for God's sake ...' Julia felt some control snap in her mind, and she tried desperately to free her wrist. 'How can you ask me that after all you've done? You've had me followed, you've had my flat broken into. You've stolen my personal letters. You've abused me—stuck a gun in my ribs. You've ...' She broke off angrily, the memory of his kisses suddenly palpable between them. 'Who knows what you might do next?'

'I think you're lying.' His voice was suddenly sharp, and she raised her eyes nervously to his, fearing his acuity, the quickness of his instincts. 'You may have resented all those things, but I don't think they made you afraid. If you fear at all, I think you fear—this.'

He leaned forward as he spoke, and very deliberately lowered his mouth to hers. He took her by surprise; before she had time to think or react, she felt the warmth of his mouth on hers, and at once, instantly, the fire shot through her blood. She gasped, and he drew her close against him, pressing her breasts against the soft material of his jacket and the hard flesh beneath, kissing her mouth, her face, her eyelids as they fluttered shut. Her mind held, then swooped into some black place. She heard him sigh, felt him seek her lips again with a kind of desperation. Then slowly he drew back, holding her so he could look down into her eyes.

'That is what you fear,' he said deliberately, 'what happens when I kiss you. When you forget you are a prisoner, and remember you are a woman. That is what you fear—and if it is any consolation to you, I fear it too.'

'*You* fear it?' Julia's eyes widened. His mouth twisted a little, and he drew back from her arms.

'But of course, I am not a fool.' His voice was suddenly dry, at odds with his words. 'To want something so much—it is always dangerous. I *know* that is what you feel; I feel it too— do you imagine a man is immune to such feelings? They cut across everything—don't you think? All barriers? Across age, across nationality, across sex. They cut across all divides— between man and woman, even ...' He gave a little smile. 'Even between prisoner and guard. They do not recognise taboos, or creeds, or codes. And so they are dangerous, for me as for you.'

'*Not* for you!' Julia cried passionately, and his grip on her wrist tightened.

'Yes, for me.' Slowly he lifted his hand and turned her face so she had to look at him. His eyes blazed down into hers, so she could not doubt the passionate sincerity with which he spoke. 'For me, because they make me forget everything. Who we are, why we are here. What I have to do ...' He released her hand and turned abruptly away. 'And I cannot afford to do that,' he finished, 'unfortunately.'

'You mean ...'

'I mean that you make it harder for me.' His voice grew cold. 'Do you think it is easy to cause pain to a woman you have kissed like that? To harm her in any way?' He turned back to her for a second and lifted one long strand of hair in his hand, then let it fall. 'It is not. Which is perhaps why you allow me to kiss you ...'

'*Allow* you . . .?' Julia's voice rose. He stood up.

'But of course.' He gave a sudden angry gesture. 'You know how to use your power over men. I cannot trust you any more than you trust me. I have to remember who you are, what you are, what you have been—how experienced you are when you kiss me so innocently . . .'

'Kiss you? *Allow* you to kiss me?' Julia sprang to her feet, furiously. 'I never did any such thing. You . . . you forced yourself on me, you made me kiss you. You're just the same as all the others—the Professor, Carlo . . . you hypocrite!'

'The same as Carlo?' He swung round to her, his face darkening. 'You compare me to that . . . that lying, stupid, irresponsible boy . . .'

'And why not?' Julia's eyes flashed. 'You want the same thing Carlo wanted, and you lie about it just the way he did.'

'Did he?' He took a step toward her, and Julia held her ground, her eyes blazing at him, her face pale.

'Yes! He did! You don't know what you're talking about. You don't know me, you don't know Carlo . . .'

'On the contrary, I do,' he cut her off sharply. 'I know Carlo, I know his family, I know you, and I know the kind of filthy drivel he wrote you when he was betrothed to another woman . . .'

'Oh, of course!' Julia's voice rose scornfully. 'His letter. You read his letter. I'd forgotten how low you stooped. I hate myself for listening to you, for being taken in by you even for an instant. And I hate you for touching me and then lying about it—pretending.

'I wasn't lying. Not then.'

'Then let me go now.' Her lip curled. 'If it's true you find it so hard to harm a woman you've kissed . . .'

The taunt went home; she saw him pale with anger as she threw his own words back at him, and her heart rejoiced. Then, with a sudden angry gesture, he turned back to his desk. She moved to the door as he took something from a folder, then he strode back across the room to her and thrust a sheaf of papers into her hand.

'There! Obviously you wanted it very much. There is your letter. I certainly have no wish to keep it.'

Carlo's writing sprawled, page upon page of it. Julia gave an angry cry and without thinking, tore them across and across and then tossed the fragments into the air.

'You think I want that letter now, when you've read it? When your minions have pawed over it? Well, I don't! I told you—you know nothing—nothing.'

There was silence. Raphael looked at the little white pieces of paper that were scattered at his feet, his mouth set in a hard line. Without a word he opened the door, grasped her arm and propelled her back down the corridor.

At the door of her room he turned the key, drew back the bolts.

'Good night.' His voice was now quite even, almost formal. 'Sleep well. It's the last time you'll be sleeping in that bed.'

'What?' She swung round, her gaze wide and startled. He gave a low laugh.

'You misunderstand me, I think. I meant something much duller, far less pleasurable. From tomorrow you will have a different room and a different bed—we're moving on. Didn't I mention that?'

'You know very well you didn't,' Julia snapped. She tilted her chin, and set her mouth. Damn him! Why was he always at least three jumps ahead of her—why hadn't she thought of that? She pushed open the door.

'It doesn't make any difference anyway,' she said over her shoulder, 'what room, what bed. They're all the same when there are locks on the door.'

They left the farmhouse just after dawn. It was a different car, and Lorenzo drove, at speed, while Raphael sat silent in the back with the two women. They drove down the track Julia had seen from the hillside the previous day, and on through the mountains for mile upon mile.

Julia sat there in silence, her face wan from lack of sleep, her nerves taut with exhaustion. The previous night she had hardly slept and now, as then, she was trying desperately to make sense of it all, to piece together a jigsaw of clues which would not fit.

She could imagine the man by her side to be motivated by many things—passion, revenge, anger, hatred—but not financial greed. More and more, she felt convinced the story about her stepfather was a lie, a blind, concocted to hide the true reason for this kidnapping.

No, he was duping her, lying to her, she thought. There was another reason for this kidnap, and it must concern the Contadellis, not herself. She frowned, trying desperately to concentrate. He claimed to know the Contadellis; certainly when he spoke of Carlo there was no disguising his loathing and contempt. So was that the connection? Was there some feud between his family and Giovanni's, or some business rivalry? Was his aim to cause the Contadellis anguish rather than extract money from them?

That was certainly possible: she did not know a great deal about Giovanni's business activities, but she knew his reputation for ruthlessness. And then Carlo—could it be his fault? He harped on him enough, on his engagement, on his faithlessness. What if Carlo, stupid, amoral, shiftless Carlo, had behaved to one of Raphael's sisters as he had behaved to her? What if it had gone further—if the girl had been hurt in some way, jilted, perhaps made pregnant?

That made sense—yes. Julia drew in her breath, and glanced cautiously at the dark closed face of the man beside her. Her instinct that she might have hit upon the truth grew stronger. Of course: then the kidnapping became a straightforward act of revenge, and she could well imagine this man might enjoy revenge. He had snatched not just Carlo's sister, but the woman Carlo now professed to love—the woman Raphael persisted in believing was Carlo's mistress. And he did it, what was more, just before Carlo's marriage, less than two months away.

Did he think Carlo would break off his marriage now, as he had threatened to do in his letter—Carlo who would revel in the drama of the whole situation, who could now claim an impossible barrier to his marriage to Lucretia—for how could he marry when the woman he loved was in danger?

She leant back against the seat, where she could look at

Raphael's harsh profile without being observed, and for the first time in two days she felt a new fear.

If he did this because of passionate love for a member of his family, what then? He was ruthless; she did not doubt that. Was he ruthless enough to harm them on behalf of someone he loved? Would he believe then that the ends justified the means?

He might, she thought, with a dart of alarm. He might. He was dangerous enough, unpredictable enough, to make it a possibility—one she shouldn't rule out, for Christina's sake above all. She shut her eyes, as she felt her thoughts and fears suddenly eddy out of control. She must be careful, careful, she thought desperately. Let him believe she accepted his story about her stepfather—let him believe that! It was safer to appear gullible, she decided. Much safer . . . Instinctively she reached across the seat and pressed Christina's hand.

Just after eight, when they had been driving hard for about three hours and Julia's head ached with her efforts to make some kind of plan, they crested a hill, and she caught her breath. Below them was the sea.

Raphael moved in his seat, leaned forward and said something in Italian to Lorenzo which Julia could not catch. She felt his closeness as he moved, the brush of his thigh against hers. Then he leaned back and moved cautiously away from her, turning to Christina.

'You are tired? We are almost there.'

Christina looked up at him wanly, but said nothing. The car slowed, turned off on to a track and eventually came to a halt. They were in a narrow bay, quite deserted. There was a crescent of pale sand, rocks—and out in the bay, at anchor, was one of the most beautiful motor yachts Julia had ever seen. She gazed at it, as it rose and fell on the waves, white against the blue, like a bird on the water.

Raphael motioned for them to get out of the car, and as Julia climbed out into the sunshine, glad to stretch her aching legs, she saw that a small tender was bobbing across the waves towards them. On the cool breeze she caught the purr of its engines. She was very tired, having hardly slept the night before, and it was a moment before she realised that all this was arranged; the beach, the meeting place, the yacht. The tender was coming to collect them.

She turned to Christina, seeing she had realised the same thing in the same instant, and their eyes met. Christina sighed. 'I don't care,' she said wearily. 'Honestly, I don't care any more, Julia. I don't care where he takes us . . .'

'But it means we won't be on the mainland—he could be taking us anywhere.' Julia heard her own voice rise. 'That yacht's huge—it's got radar, look! It's an ocean-going yacht—that means it could even take us out of the Mediterranean.'

'I don't think so.' Christina sat down on a low rock. 'I think he'll take us to Sicily. It's what I've thought all along. He's Mafia, he has to be.'

'If you will come with me.' Raphael had walked down to the water, but as the tender drew near the beach, he returned to them. 'He can't get in any closer, there's a strong swell. We'll have to wade out a few yards . . .'

Lorenzo, it seemed, was to remain behind, though Julia heard Raphael say something to him which indicated he might join them later—wherever it was they were going. But he helped Raphael get the two girls out to the boat, and when it drew away at last, Julia saw his stocky figure fade into the distance with something like regret.

Once aboard the yacht, Raphael at once took command. There seemed to be a large crew—six or seven swarthy-skinned men, southern Italians or Sicilians, Julia guessed. They looked at her and at Christina impassively, and then hastened to obey Raphael's quick commands. He turned back to them, switching back to English as he always did in Julia's presence, his manner blandly polite.

'I regret, but you will have to go below for a little while. Adjoining staterooms have been made ready for you. A steward will bring you breakfast, and will let you know when you may come back on deck.'

The staterooms were very luxurious, and to Julia's delight Christina seemed to revive at last when the steward had gone and she set about exploring them. She darted about, opening cupboards, experimenting with tables that lifted up and folded away. She fingered the beautiful mahogany fittings, the shiny brass of the window frames, the beautiful silks and velvets that covered the chairs and the beds.

'Classy,' she pronounced at last, with the air of an expert—which she was, of course, Julia remembered. Giovanni also possessed an ocean-going yacht. Its one-and-a-half million dollar refit the previous year had been an endless source of gossip in the Italian papers. 'Probably capable of sixty knots. She's quite a ship. Even Daddy might be a bit green if he saw this. Look at this, Julia——' She opened a beautifully fitted cupboard. 'Baccarat crystal glasses, no less! I hope it doesn't get rough. And linen sheets. That rug's silk—it's a Shiraz, I think.' She frowned, looking around the huge rooms. 'You know it's funny, but there's something familiar about all this. Something nagging away at the back of my memory, and I can't quite place it. It's odd. I feel as if I'd been on this yacht before . . .'

'Familiar?' Julia looked up quickly.

'Yes, and it's not just the yacht, either. It's Raphael himself . . .' She paused thoughtfully, and then sat down on the silk-covered bed. 'Normally when I've heard him speak, he's been speaking in English, hasn't he?'

'He spoke to Pietro in Italian yesterday . . .'

'Yes, I know. But I was very upset then, and I wasn't paying him that much attention. It wasn't until we got on the yacht just now, and he started to give orders to the crew. I mean, I'd noticed his voice before—it's very distinctive, isn't it? And I'd clocked his accent . . . but then it was different. Bells started ringing somewhere, just for a moment . . . I thought I'd met him before.'

Julia stared at her. 'Are you sure, Christina? You're not imagining it?'

Christina still looked puzzled. 'I don't think so, I just can't place it. I meet so many people, you know, in the summer vacations especially—and that's what I'm associating him with somehow. The summer. The sea. A yacht—either this one or one very like it.' She paused. 'He said his surname was Pierangeli, right?'

'That's what he said.' Julia shrugged. 'I don't believe that any more than that his first name is Raphael.'

'Pierangeli. Pierangeli . . .' Christina frowned. 'It's not that unusual a name. I can think of several, straight off. I think my mother had some Pierangeli cousins, but then she had thousands of cousins—she was related to half Italy, I sometimes think. Oh, and of course, there's the Marchesa di Montesole—her family name is Pierangeli. She's great mates with Lucky's family, in fact I think she's one of Lucky's godparents. Very much the *grande dame*, I believe. I've only met her once . . .'

'He has a mother—his father's dead, but he mentioned a mother; and brothers and sisters . . .' Julia leaned forward. 'Oh, and he said he'd seen me once, before all this happened. At a party in Rome.'

'A party, eh?' Christina looked sceptical. 'He didn't say where?'

'No, he didn't, but I haven't been to that many parties. There was that reception at your father's house, and the party he gave at Christmas, for Lucky and Carlo—and I went to a reception at the British Embassy as Hardy's guest in the New Year.' Julia frowned in an effort to remember. 'And there was a first night party at the Opera—I went to that with Hardy too. But nothing much else. A few dinner parties, writers and academics I was working with, and it couldn't be those—they were small. I'd remember him.'

Christina pulled a face. 'What a limited social life you lead. Still, I suppose it's useful in this case, it narrows the field. You don't remember seeing him ever?'

'Absolutely not.' Julia shook her head. 'I know I'd remember. I never saw him until the first day I realised he was following us.'

'Oh well, he was probably lying anyway. And he probably picked on that name because it sounded plausible, that's all. It's not that common—I mean it's not like being called "Smith" or "Jones" in English, but it's not that unusual either. Still, I wish I could remember if I had been on this yacht before, or met him. It's going to drive me mad. It's *there*, I know it is—just at the back of my mind somewhere.'

Christina pursued this line of thought for some while, until breakfast arrived and then she decided to abandon it.

Both she and Julia ate hungrily. Not long afterwards, the steward reappeared, and announced that they might like now to go on deck. There, Raphael joined them briefly, and it became clear why permission had been granted. They were well out to sea. On all sides all that could be seen was water; there was no glimpse of land, no possibility that they could identify their whereabouts in any way. Julia checked her watch, and the position of the sun again; it seemed to her that they were still travelling slightly eastwards—south-east perhaps, and that encouraged her slightly. Surely, if they were making for Sicily, they would be travelling due south?

She imparted this information to Christina once Raphael had left them, but Christina now had an irritable and preoccupied air, and she dismissed Julia's theories crossly.

'Oh honestly, Julia—who do you think you are? Sherlock Holmes? Why don't you go and read a book or something? You're getting on my nerves . . .'

Christina was leaning over the rails, but she had positioned herself, Julia noted, so that she could watch Raphael. Mostly he stayed on the bridge—but whenever he came down on deck, Christina's eyes never left him.

Julia stretched out on one of the deck loungers, let the sun wash over her face and limbs and tried to relax. She dozed a little, fitfully, but again her sleep was broken by dreams. Raphael's face kept haunting her sleeping mind, as well as her waking. His voice came to her over the sound of the yacht's engines, over the wash of the sea. *When you choose, Julia, and that moment will come . . .*

She dreamed his hands and his lips touched her. She dreamed of slow, gentle, fierce intimacies, from which her waking mind would have shied away. And, when she woke, feeling her body bathed in pleasurable warmth, it was to find Raphael standing by her side, looking down at her. His face was intent; his eyes dark and thoughtful, so that for one terrible moment Julia feared she might have spoken in her sleep and betrayed the nature of her dreams.

As if he could not restrain himself, Raphael reached across, touched her hair gently, and smoothed it back from her face. The moment he saw her eyes open fully, he quickly withdrew his hand.

'I woke you, forgive me. But we are nearing our destination. I should like you to go below.'

Julia looked up at him, her topaz eyes wide. For an instant he was still the man of her dream, her lover: infinitely gentle, infinitely arousing. Then consciousness came back, and she sat up. She must stop all this, she thought angrily. She couldn't understand what was the matter with her. Why were the edges of her judgement being blurred in this way, simply because a man happened to know the tricks of physical arousal, and didn't hesitate to employ them?

She stood up, looking away from him, and saw that Christina, still leaning against the rails, was watching Raphael closely.

'If you would listen a moment.' He detained her with a light touch on the arm as she turned to the companionway, and the touch shot through her body like fire. 'We will be landing at a small town, in about an hour's time. You will both wear these dark glasses . . .' He held out two pairs to her. 'And you, Julia, will wear this headscarf, please. I would like your hair completely covered.'

'Too recognisable for you?' Julia tried to force her features into an expression of cold contempt.

'Something like that, yes.' He smiled drily.

'Then you must be worried. The search must be well under way. You realise you aren't going to get away with this?'

He cut across her crisply. 'You will wear the glasses and the scarf. You will get out of the tender. I will have my arm around you; one of the stewards will be with Christina. You will walk a few yards across the quay, and you will get into the car that will be waiting. You will not shout, or otherwise try to attract the attention of anyone who may be there. You will behave perfectly normally. I wouldn't advise you to try to run away.'

'Oh really?' Julia's lip curled. 'What are you going to do—shoot me in the back with your Walther in front of a whole crowd of people?'

Again he smiled grimly. 'You will give me your word that you will do as I say. If you will not do that, regrettably I shall have to ensure that you are not conscious when you leave the yacht. I should prefer not to have to resort to that, however. So. Do I have your word?'

'My word?' Julia looked at him scornfully. 'Why should I keep my word to you, of all people?'

'I have no idea why,' he said quietly, 'but I believe you will. Now, do I have that promise?'

Julia looked hesitantly from Christina back to Raphael. Finally she nodded. 'Very well. I give you my word.'

'Thank you.' He inclined his head mockingly. 'Now. If you would go below until we anchor . . .'

CHAPTER EIGHT

Just under an hour later, Julia and Christina, sitting in the stateroom, felt the yacht cut back its engines and slow. They both hurried to the window, and, in the distance, they could make out a shape, land—shimmering in the heat haze on the horizon. But then the yacht altered course slightly, and it was not until it finally went about that they could see anything more.

'Do you recognise anything, Christina?'

'Not a thing.' Christina turned away from the beauty of the view with an irritable little shrug. 'Obviously we're still in the Med . . . More than that I couldn't say. Come on, Julia—let's get ready.'

Julia sighed and turned away. Slowly she wound the headscarf Raphael had given her around her head. It was of plain black cotton. She tucked the rich strands of her hair beneath it, and put on the large dark glasses. She was wearing the white Versace trousers which Raphael had left in their old room, and a simple white shirt. Christina looked at her and giggled.

'God—he is clever, you have to admit that! He chooses clothes brilliantly. He's transformed you, for a start. You look fantastic. Like a movie star being obviously incognito.'

'Oh, shut up, Christina!' Julia turned away. 'I think he does it deliberately. I feel a fool. Let's just do as he says and get it over with . . .'

But, when they went up on deck and the tender came alongside, Julia began quickly to revise that opinion. From Raphael's remarks she had expected a very small place—a tiny quay, very few people; but this place was quite large. A number of other large white yachts were anchored a little way out from the quay, and the quay itself was crowded with people. It opened off what looked like a small market square.

121

She could see stalls, hear the cries of the vendors, see people milling back and forth carrying baskets. Some of them looked like tourists, or visitors. Others—the inhabitants, she presumed—were almost all wearing black, but that told her nothing. That was so on most Mediterranean islands, and she didn't even know if this were an island. They could be in Yugoslavia, she thought quickly, or on one of the southern Italian islands, or even in Greece . . .

Raphael positioned himself close at Julia's side. As they drew closer to the shore, he moved his body deliberately, so he was pressed against her. She felt the hard muscles of his chest, and—as he had no doubt intended she should—she also felt the hard shape of a shoulder holster. She glanced sideways at him. He was wearing a loose linen jacket; just at the neck she could see the holster's leather strap. He read her thoughts and gave her a charming smile.

'They suit you—the glasses. The scarf. You look ravishing, *carissima*.'

She could see what she guessed would be their car, and it was hardly discreet. Large, black, gleaming—another Mercedes. Standing leaning against it, wearing uniform, was the chauffeur who had driven them from Rome. It was the only car near the quay, and it was already attracting the attention of a crowd of bare-footed little boys. Even as Julia looked she saw the chauffeur shooing them away.

They were landing. Christina appeared to be almost enjoying herself. She stepped out quite calmly, leaning on the steward's arm, walked the few paces to the car—preening herself the while—and climbed inside it without incident. Raphael gave a low sigh.

He stood, pulling Julia up with him, his arm tight around her waist. 'Don't forget. You gave me your word . . .'

His voice was low. Julia lowered her eyes demurely. Like hell, she thought. If he thought she was such a fool as to miss a chance like this simply because she had given her word to a liar and a cheat, then he was damn well wrong. Raphael stepped out of the tender first, turned and held out his hand to her.

Julia delayed; then, like an answer to a prayer to the gods, she saw him. A short, fat man, sweating in the heat, wearing a grey uniform. His shirt had some kind of badge on it; he wore a greasy peaked cap with somewhat frayed gilt braid on it, and he was clearly an official of some kind. Police, possibly; if not police, then maybe the harbourmaster, or Customs ... She hesitated. He had been looking out at their yacht, frowning, squinting his eyes against the hot glare of the sun. Now, as the tender drew up, he had begun to push his way importantly through the press of people. Julia's heart missed a beat. Oh, don't let him stop, she silently prayed.

'*Kalimera sas* ...' She heard just that phrase, and her heart leapt. Greek—he was speaking Greek. So she had been right. They had left from the east coast, and they had been travelling east, and this was either one of the Cyclades, or possibly the eastern seacoast of Greece. And, what was more, the fat man was now waddling towards them with a self-important air. Raphael had seen him too. She saw his mouth tighten.

The fat man was almost upon them. He was advancing rapidly now, a wide smile plastered across his features, his hand held forth as if to stay them. Raphael took a step forward; Julia did not move. Let him damn well try and drag me, she thought, let him—then they'll know something is wrong.

The fat man was saying something, trying to attract Raphael's attention. He had taken off his cap, it sounded like a greeting. Julia opened her mouth to speak, but Raphael was too quick for her. Before she could say anything he turned, and—as if he had noticed the fat man for the first time—he gave a gesture of welcome. The fat man's smile widened; he threw up his hands as if in delight and he clasped Raphael by the arm.

Julia stared, rooted to the spot, uncertain what to do next. The hat, she realised now, had been doffed for the benefit of Raphael, who was speaking rapidly in Greek. He was smiling broadly; what he said appeared first to astonish the fat man and then delight him. Raphael said her name, then, before she knew what was happening, his fingers tightened like a vice on her arm.

'Darling,' he said distinctly, in English, 'I'm so sorry—let me translate. This is an old friend of mine—Georgiadis Ioanni; he's Chief of Police on the island—what am I saying? he *is* the police, pure and simple—or have you acquired some new recruits since I was last here, Georgiadis?' He translated this for the fat man's benefit. He laughed, launched into a flood of Greek, then, as if recollecting himself, drew himself up importantly and turned to Julia with a low bow. Raphael turned to her with the sweetest of smiles.

'And this is my fiancée. Julia darling, this is Georgiadis ... He wants to congratulate you. I'm afraid his English is a bit rusty ...'

Georgiadis was holding out his hand. Stunned, unable to think, Julia took it. He pumped it up and down exuberantly, a torrent of Greek, then fractured English spilling from his lips.

'Excellent. Top-hole. I am entirely delighted. Good news, yes?' From the recesses of his memory Georgiadis drummed up these phrases, then he lapsed back into Greek. He looked at Julia; he looked at Raphael. He gave him a very broad wink indeed, and followed it up with a nudge in the ribs. Raphael appeared to take this in good part. He smiled, and laughed, and all the while his arm around her waist never relaxed its grip.

'Darling, he's paying you a compliment,' he said smoothly. Julia looked up into his face with furious resentment, and saw that his eyes danced with laughter. 'He says that you are a very beautiful woman, and that I am a very lucky man—but then I know that already. And he says it's about time a good woman made me respectable, and he's sure you will do it. Moreover, he hopes ...' here Raphael smiled widely and Julia seethed, 'he hopes—well, I think the English phrase is, that all our problems will be little ones.'

A thousand phrases tumbled into her mind, obscured by rage and indignation at Raphael's quick thinking and insolent aplomb. Georgiadis probably wouldn't understand any of them anyway—Raphael would pass it off as a joke.

She swung round to him furiously, her eyes flashing behind the dark glasses. 'You . . . you creep. You unspeakable liar, you . . .'

'Darling. I love you too. To distraction . . .' Raphael drew her to him and kissed her gently on the lips, then turned back to Georgiadis with such a smug smile of satisfaction on his face that Julia's fingers itched to hit him. Already Georgiadis was making his farewells. He bowed to her again. Raphael said something . . .

'It's all right, darling. He quite understands that I'm in a hurry to get you home. We can go now.'

The hand tightened around her waist painfully, he pulled her round in the direction of the car.

'Walk!' he said in a low voice into her ear, smiling the while as if he spoke an endearment. 'Get in that car, now, or you'll regret it . . .'

Julia made one last tardy effort, to free her hand, to reach for the door-handle as she was thrust into the car—something, and Raphael's grip on her tightened. His face was close to her own, his eyes dark with amusement, but also a touch of anger.

'You gave me your word . . . I know what you were trying. You promised me——'

'So? And just what in hell do you think you're going to do about it, *fiancé* of mine?' Julia spat the words angrily into his face. She was conscious, somewhere in her mind, of a reaction from Christina, who was watching all this with avid interest from the front seat of the car. Julia wrenched off the dark glasses and threw them on the floor of the car. Raphael clicked his tongue reprovingly, like an adult with a small child who was having a temper tantrum.

'What are you going to do? Thirty lashes? Bread and water for a week?' Her golden eyes flashed at him. 'Don't you see, there's nothing you can do? I might have failed then, but I won't next time, you'll see. And your threats and your punishments won't make a shred of difference!'

Raphael smiled. A long, slow, lazy smile. He released her and settled himself back comfortably against the leather seat.

'We'll see,' he said imperturbably. 'But I think you may be wrong, darling . . .'

They drove for about an hour, along a narrow winding road that edged the coast, and meandered through olive groves. Below them rocks fell to a sea the blue of lapis lazuli; the tall dark pillars of cypress were outlined clear in the radiant light. It was spectacularly beautiful—one of the most beautiful places she had ever seen, but its beauty did not console Julia. She had been outwitted yet again. She had had two opportunities to do something now, and both times she had failed. That angered her, but that alone did not account for the tumult and complexity of her feelings. They had their origins in Raphael, she knew that now, and acknowledged it to herself with a sense of bafflement and fear.

Why, why, when she had every reason to hate him, when she knew he was just using her, did he affect her as he did? When he had called her 'darling', when he had announced he loved her, she had felt for a second as if her heart had stopped beating. Half a second later, when she knew he lied and mocked her, she had felt a most violent and painful misery. And when he touched her—even in threat—she could not argue away what she felt. It was there, clear in her nerves and her blood, a response of excitement and joy. She hated herself for it. It was as if her body were set on defying her mind.

They reached the house not long after noon. It was very hot; the sun was almost directly above them. It was more than a house, Julia thought, tiredly trying to force her mind to concentrate on her surroundings once more. First there had been a high wall by the roadside, which they had followed for several miles, then a lodge with high iron gates, then a very long driveway.

The house itself was not one house but several long, low, white buildings with shuttered windows, built against the hillside, surrounded by terrace and gardens. As she climbed from the car, her eyes dazzled by the light, she saw the perfection of its position. It looked out over a wild and rocky hillside to the sea; it was a view that spoke of beauty, and of freedom. And, as far as she and Christina were concerned, it was just another prison.

She leaned against the car, tired to the bone. They were not even in Italy now. He had succeeded in spiriting them away. As the enormity of that bore into her, her spirits sank. It was a moment before she realised that Christina was sidling up to her, her features lit with excitement. She glanced warily at Raphael. For a moment he was speaking to their driver, issuing instructions: he was only a couple of paces away but he had his back to them.

'I've got it!' Christina's voice was a low excited whisper. 'It suddenly came to me when I was in the car, when you and he were standing on the quay. Julia, listen—I know who he is. And what's more—I know where we are. He's . . .'

Raphael swung round. He had caught something, perhaps half heard what Christina had said, for he moved quickly. He caught Julia by the arm and pulled her away.

'Take her inside.' He thrust Julia towards the chauffeur. 'I'll deal with this one.'

'Through here . . .' The driver's grip was firm but not painful, and Julia allowed him to lead her into the house. It was all right, she thought. She would see Christina again shortly; Christina would tell her then . . .

The man opened a door and closed it behind her; Julia heard the sound of bolts being pushed into place. She stared around her in confusion and disbelief for a moment. Then, seeing a door on the far side of the room, she ran across to it, turned the handle and flung it back. She gave a cry of alarm at what she saw, hesitated, and then sprang across to the only other door that led out of that room. She turned the handle: nothing happened. She pulled. She hammered against the heavy wooden panels. She shouted. Nothing happened.

Eventually, her face pale, she turned round, and slumped back against the door.

There were just the two rooms, opening out from each other and into a corridor. Both corridor entrances were securely locked. The first room—clearly intended for her—contained one narrow single bed. The second room, larger

and more opulent, contained a double bed. And she was in no
doubt who it belonged to: Raphael. On the wide bed a man's
linen suit was laid out—cream linen, the kind of informal suit
he often wore. She stared around the room hopelessly, like an
animal at bay.

He was separating them. Clearly Christina was being put in
a room somewhere else. Oh why, why had she not thought of
that possibility? It made sense—absolute sense from his point
of view. How much easier to control them, to manipulate
them, when they could not turn to each other for support,
when their only contact with each other might be messages via
Raphael, who might lie or tell the truth! If he wanted to break
her, what easier way of doing it?

She turned from the door and ran to the windows, first in this
room, then in the other. They were wide open: a breeze blew in
from the sea. Like the previous room she and Christina had
shared, they were both securely barred, the bars set in clean new
concrete. Desperately she began to open doors to what she knew
would be closets. Those in her room were full of clothes: she
didn't need to take them down to know they would be her exact
size. Those in Raphael's room contained his clothes. Rows of
beautifully laundered shirts, trousers, jackets. Day clothes.
Evening clothes ... She opened door after door and banged
them shut. The last door of all opened into a marble-floored
bathroom. It had a bath, also marble, sunk into the floor. A
huge basin; a long marble shelf surmounted by a large
looking-glass. On it were men's shaving things and women's
cosmetics. The brand she used, when she wore make-up, which
was rarely. The bottles all new, still in their wrappings. There
was a window there too, also barred.

Julia sank down on the floor, bent her head, and cried. It
was something she rarely did, but now she gave way to her
tears of tiredness, anger and frustration. When she had
finished, she felt a little better. She washed her face and dried
it. Damn him. Damn him. Damn him, she thought. There was
only one bathroom, and its door was right next to his bed.
She couldn't go and clean her teeth without his knowing
about it, and she knew, just knew, that that was deliberate.

At about half-past one, the door of her room opened and the chauffeur came in, wearing a different uniform this time, carrying a tray. He set it down on a table, and turned to the door without a word.

'Wait.' Julia raised her voice as haughtily as she could. 'I want to see Raphael, I want to see him now. Where is Christina? I demand to know. Tell him to come here . . .'

'I am sorry.' The man gave a polite half bow. 'He is busy.'

He went out and shut the door. The bolts were rammed back into place. There was silence.

For a while Julia paced back and forth in the room. Maybe if she didn't eat the food, she thought, maybe if she refused to eat at all until he reunited her with Christina . . . That was one possibility, but, growing calmer, she rejected it. If she didn't eat she knew she would only get weaker and more emotional—be even less of a match for him than she was now.

She ate a little of the lunch, which was delicious, but she did not have much appetite. Then she wandered back and forth between the two rooms. Eventually, frustrated and tired, she lay down on her narrow bed, covered herself with the plain white cotton bedspread, and slept.

When she woke, it was early evening. The sun was low on the horizon. Outside in the garden water-sprinklers had been turned on, and the shadows lengthened across the flowers and grass. As she looked out of the window and out across the azure sea, she saw a ship in the distance. A white yacht, steaming out to sea. It came into view for a while and then disappeared. Julia watched it sadly. It was like the yacht they had travelled on this morning; maybe it was the same yacht and—mission completed—it was travelling elsewhere.

She had no way of knowing. She had no way of knowing *anything*, she thought resentfully, unless Raphael chose to tell her. No telephone, no radio, no television. No newspapers or magazines. She might as well be on a desert island. Presumably Giovanni and the police would be searching for them, but she had no idea if they had any leads, any notion who was responsible, or where she and Christina were. Even the letter she had written—she had no idea what he had done with that. Maybe he had it still. After hours alone her sense of reality was already slipping. All her confidence was gone. Her theories of the morning which had seemed so clever—even those seemed hollow now.

She prowled around the two rooms once more, noting their contents more carefully. They had been prepared, thoroughly prepared, she felt sure of that. Her room was a pretty but anonymous guest room—usually it would serve as Raphael's dressing-room, she guessed. His room, though stamped with evidence of what she had come to recognise as his taste, was carefully devoid of all personal clues. There were no books, no papers, no photographs, nothing that might have betrayed some information about him. All the room suggested was that its owner was a man of taste—and of means. One of the paintings, she realised with astonishment, was a Monet. Another was a Pisarro. On his dressing chest the brushes were silver, tortoishell and ivory. If they were his brushes, of course. Or his paintings . . .

As time wore on she began to get more and more uneasy. This silence, this solitude—it had not happened before, and it was increasing her nervousness, as it was probably calculated to do. Well, she would not let it affect her like that, she thought determinedly. *Damn him.* The place looked like an hotel—well, her room did anyway. She'd treat it like one! She'd have a bath, in that exceedingly tempting bathtub—and then she'd change into one of the dresses in the cupboard, and if he returned, *when* he returned, she told herself firmly, there she would be. Calm, collected, bathed, changed, and damn' well ready for any new trick he might be going to throw at her.

She opened the closet doors, and, wonderingly, fingered the clothes that hung there. It was all like a mad dream: silk, velvet, lace, the most delicate chiffon. Long dresses. Short dresses. Day clothes. Evening clothes. How long did he intend to keep her here, for God's sake? She drew them out one by one, seduced by their beauty in spite of herself. Gently she ran her hands over their soft folds. What a strange man he was . . .

Eventually she chose one of the dresses. It had been hand-made in Rome. Black silk velvet—she had never worn such a dress. It was cut on the bias, so she knew that—once on—it would cling gently to the figure, skim her narrow hips. It fell, she judged, holding it against her, and looking into the long glass on the back of the closet door, to mid-calf. It had a belt designed to hang loose around the waist, an exquisite construction of gold and silver metal. It was quite plain except for the neck, which plunged low at the back—too low to wear a bra with it, she thought sardonically—and which was circled at the front with a collar of pale silk organdie, fastened with a white silk camellia. Chanel: from their Rome showrooms. Julia laid it reverently on the bed. She might hate him, she thought, she did hate him, but it was the most beautiful dress she had ever seen—and there were shoes that were clearly meant to go with it, for they were on the rack just beneath it, still boxed. High-heeled black suede shoes, very soft, very delicate, designed by Frizon. They had little diamond chains carefully stitched across the front of them . . .

She put them beside the bed, switched on the lamps, for the light was now fading fast, and went into the bathroom and turned on the taps. In for a penny, in for a pound, she thought. This was certainly therapeutic. She felt much less nervous now, and much more confident. She would be so controlled, so careful, he'd give in—he'd let her see Christina, she felt sure of it, before the evening was out. She stripped off her clothes, hesitated, shut the door, which would not lock, and wedged it with her shoe. The water was scented, opaline, cool and inviting. All this luxury might have its drawbacks, but it also had its advantages, she thought wryly, and slowly, luxuriating in the refreshing coolness of the water, she lowered herself into it.

Gradually, Julia felt herself relax. She soaped herself with soap that smelled of garden roses. She lifted the huge natural sponge, drenched it with water, and then held it over her face and let the cool water fall on to her skin. It felt marvellous—as if she were bathing in some magical spring; she felt like a mermaid, no, a nereid . . . Carefully she lowered herself beneath the water, and let it wash up through the weight of her hair. She saw her hair darken, cling to her skin. She lay there like that for a while, feeling quite unreal, like Ophelia, she thought wryly, in that Pre-Raphaelite painting, or the Maid of Astolat.

Humming gently to herself, she stood up. There was a porcelain and silver shower attachment; she bent over, lowered her head so her hair fell forward in a thick chestnut curtain, and began to rinse it. It was not until, with a gasp, she turned the temperature gauge too far and cold water rushed over her hair and shoulders, that she straightened up. She turned off the shower, lifted the thick curtain of her hair, and gave a cry.

Raphael was standing there, leaning against the bathroom door indolently, a slight smile upon his face. It looked as if he had been there some while; it also looked as if he had no intention whatsoever of leaving. He folded his arms, and the insolent smile widened. Julia let go of her hair, and felt it fall loose around her shoulders. She moved her hands in front of her, and looked wildly round for a towel.

'Is this what you're looking for?' He moved, and she saw that he was holding a huge white towel, the one she had laid down near the bath in readiness. All the others were on the far side of the room.

'Yes, it is.' Julia felt the colour mount in her cheeks. She could not meet his eyes, but she had seen already the way they had raked her hungrily from head to foot. 'May I have it, please?'

'But of course.' He paused, and she heard the mocking drawl and cursed him. 'Come and get it, won't you?'

Julia glared at him furiously. She hesitated, and then she let her hands fall defiantly to her sides.

'All right, if that's what you want. Look at me. You . . . you voyeur . . .'

'Oh, I wouldn't advise you to insult me,' he said smoothly. 'I already feel less than calm, shall we say, and if you provoke me and I lose my temper again—who can say what would happen?' He gave an expressive shrug. 'I think, on the whole, that you'd be better advised to come and fetch the towel quietly.' He glanced down at it. 'It's a very *large* towel,' he added infuriatingly. 'You'll feel much better when you're safely wrapped in it, I'm sure.'

Julia stared at him. She was getting extremely cold, and the intensity of his gaze, the frank admiration she saw in his eyes—all this confused and alarmed her. She had never stood naked before a man.

'Very well.' She set her lips. 'Since you leave me no choice.'

Carefully she stepped out of the water and approached him. Until she was no more than a foot away he did not move, but simply watched her. She hesitated, and took another step.

'Please,' she said, lifting her hand, 'give me the towel.'

Without a word, he handed it to her.

Julia breathed a low sigh of relief. She started to shake out the folds to wrap it around her, and then he moved.

'Damn you . . .' He gave a low groan and reached for her naked body. 'Damn you—do you think I am made of ice, that you can simply stand there, naked like that, and expect me to do *nothing*? To hand you a towel and turn my back, leave the room, behave like an English gentleman?' Julia cried out as she felt his hands lace around her waist, and he caught her against his hard thighs, against the demanding thrust of his flesh. 'Damn you,' he said again, his voice low and husky. He caught her by the hair, and lifted her face to his, speaking very deliberately, his lips close to hers, his eyes burning dark into hers.

'I *want* you—you know that. I dreamed of you naked—for *weeks*—do you know that? And now I see you and . . . and you are more beautiful, more desirable than you were even in my dreams. Do you think now, now that I see you like this, I am going to let you go? I *can't*—understand that, Julia. I can't. I'm a man—not a machine. Julia, oh my God, Julia . . .'

As he spoke his hand clasped her breast and tightened around it. He pressed his mouth, damp and warm, against the skin of her throat, and then as if he could not contain himself, as if he must hold her, touch her, explore her—all of her, now, quickly—he ran his hand down from the fullness of her breast. Over the smooth curve of her stomach, down to the tiny triangle of hair between her thighs. She cried out, lifted her arms to push him away, and then let them fall.

His hands ran down the smooth curve of her spine now, so her skin sang at the touch, down, and down further. Then he grasped her, lifting her up against him, and the hardness of his flesh against her made her heart leap.

'Let me look at you first . . . while I still have a little control left . . . Julia . . .'

His voice was thick. He held her a little away from him, just at arm's length, and Julia stood still. She felt as if she were in a dream, as if he were hypnotising her again; she felt a terrible fierceness, a desire to touch him, and at the same time the utmost lassitude. To lie back now, she thought. Oh God. Just to lie back, to let him hold me, stroke me, gently part my thighs . . .

His gaze travelled over her body. Very gently, his hand trembling a little, his breath coming hard, he reached out to touch her breasts. Lightly, oh so lightly. One finger circling each aureole, hardening the buds of her nipples to roseate points. He lowered his mouth, took first one, then the other between his lips, stroked the hard points with his tongue.

Julia shuddered. Slowly she raised her arms and she put them around him. She felt the strength of his bowed shoulders under her arm. Gently, shyly at first, she stroked the hard planes of his back, then, with a sigh, the thick black hair which brushed against her skin. She felt her whole body relax against him. She cradled his head in her arms, and he lifted his head, and, his eyes never leaving hers, moved his hand down in a slow arc. Down, over her stomach. She gasped at the pleasure of it, feeling all resistance fall away, and herself lost, quite lost.

'Not here. Come—come with me . . .' He took her by the hand, and drew her to the door. They went back into his bedroom, and he led her to the bed. He stopped then, and just looked at her. For a moment she saw that old quick dart of mockery and amusement light the dark intensity of his gaze. He reached for the fur rug, threw it across the bed, and very gently, he pushed her back on it. He bent over her and kissed her. Her mouth. Her throat. Her breasts. Her stomach.

Very tenderly, he parted her thighs, and when she gave a little cry of shame and modesty he smiled, and then bent his head. She felt his lips against the soft skin of her inner thighs; she felt his touch, there where the pleasure flamed most in her, and she knew he knew that her body was ready to make love, wanted to make love, craved to . . . She shut her eyes, and he gave a low soft laugh.

He was a stranger to her. She didn't even know his true name. She had every reason to hate him, to fear him. She turned her head to the pillow and for a second, no more, all those thoughts flashed into her mind. Yet she knew, in her heart of hearts, as women always know, that none of those things mattered a shred. Against them she could weigh other things—an unpredictable gentleness, courage, audacity . . . But none of those things mattered then, either. All she knew was that she wanted this man above all logic, and above all others . . .

She felt him move. She knew he was naked.

'Give me your hand,' he said, and Julia gave it.

His size, his strength, the fact that he knelt over her—all this suggested dominance. And yet, as Julia looked at him, she felt that was not so. His body was so strong, so powerful; but his eyes, which darkened as she looked at him, were vulnerable. She knew he could hurt her; she knew also, with an absolute certainty, that she could hurt him. In that moment, sensing his want and his need, her heart was filled with a profound tenderness for him. She knew her face softened.

As if he sensed what she felt, as if he felt it too, he lifted her in his arms, and still astride her, drew her up so she was cradled in his arms against his chest. His heart hammered in her ears; she rested her face against the warmth of his skin. Very gently he tilted her head back, and looked down into her face, lacing his fingers through her hair.

'You have never kissed me of your own free will,' he said. 'Do you know that? Maybe once—a little—but I wish—I wish you would kiss me now . . .'

His eyes searched hers. Tenderly Julia raised her hands, and held his face between them. Then, with a low sigh, she drew his mouth down to her lips.

She had not known a kiss could be like that—perhaps because when he had kissed her before, it had almost always been with anger and with passion, as if he had been trying to force her to acknowledge the same desire he felt. Now he kissed her gently, slowly, with great tenderness, his lips moving softly against her own. When he drew back a little at last, they both trembled. It was as if their lips spoke, and spoke a finer language than any words, a language in which there was no possibility of misunderstanding. That kiss, like a promise, like a bond beyond words, was for Julia like the beginning of a journey and the end of one. She looked up into his eyes then, and she knew that she loved him.

Maybe that knowledge flickered for a moment in the depths of her eyes; anyway, his dark features softened, and he smiled down at her, his expression changing utterly as he did so, so that she saw in his eyes, for a moment, concern, and gentleness, protectiveness, and pride. With a low groan he gathered her against him and rocked her gently, flesh against flesh.

Then someone knocked, loudly and insistently, at the door. For a moment he did not move. Then his arms tightened around her, and she felt his body tense with anger. He lifted his head.

'Damn you.' He swore in a low voice. 'What is it?'

'I'm sorry, sir . . .' Julia recognised the chauffeur's voice, speaking nervously in Italian. 'I'm sorry to disturb you. But the call you were waiting for has just come through. There was trouble with the lines, but we have a connection now, and we're holding.'

Raphael's eyes met Julia's for a moment, and he laughed. He kissed her gently and laid her back against the bed. 'My darling, I shall have to take this call. If it were any other I would happily tell them to go to hell and stay there, but not this one.' He raised her palm, kissed it, and then closed her fingers as if they could retain the kiss. 'This one concerns you. Concerns us. You will understand why one day.'

He lifted himself from her, and pulled on a long, white towelling bathrobe. For a moment he turned and looked back at her. 'Stay like that, my darling. Please. Just like that. This won't take long.'

But he was wrong. At first Julia did as he asked and lay still, her body pulsing with a steady, sensual lassitude, her mind lulled by his touch. But as the minutes ticked by, and the lassitude left her, her mind began to function once more. She felt afraid then, more afraid than she had ever been since all this began. She loved him; her heart sang with the knowledge. But somehow before, she had always believed herself to be, in some important sense, beyond his reach. He could dominate her, order her about, manipulate her, but he could not reach her, no matter what he did. He had broken down her resistance—not her physical resistance, that was comparatively unimportant, but her spiritual resistance. Loving him, and knowing it, immediately put her on his side.

CHAPTER NINE

WHEN Raphael returned almost half an hour had gone by, and Julia was quickly dressing herself. She heard the door of his room open, heard his soft footsteps, heard him call to her. She had shut the intercommunicating door and now, hearing his voice call to her with a note of urgency and alarm, she answered him.

'I'm here. I'm getting dressed.'

There was a silence, as if he were considering the implications of that, the fact thats he had not done as he asked. She expected him then to come into her room, but he did not. She could hear him moving about next door and quickly, feverishly, in terror that he would come in before she was clothed, she pulled on the dress she had laid out. It seemed ludicrously inappropriate, but she didn't have time to care. With trembling fingers she pulled it on, and slipped her stockinged feet into the black high-heeled slippers. A little later, she heard a servant knock at the door of his room. He called to her then.

'Julia?'

'Yes?'

He opened the door, and stood in the doorway. He was smoking one of the long black cigarettes, he was wearing black evening clothes. His expression was bland—unreadable.

'Will you join me for dinner again?' He held out his arm to her formally, as if absolutely nothing had happened. 'It's a beautiful evening. I thought we might eat outside, on the terrace.'

They sat down opposite one another, and Julia looked out over the garden. It was a clear night without cloud; above her the moon, almost full, shone across the grass and the trees, lit the surface of the sea beyond with a pale radiance. She could see lights on the masts of ships; each star, each constellation was breathtakingly clear.

The table was laid with a white cloth and the cutlery was heavy silver. In the centre of the table was a vase of white freesias, which one of the servants removed when they brought the wine for Raphael to taste. When the servant had withdrawn, Julia leaned forward quickly, before Raphael, who was watching her carefully, could speak.

'Where is Christina? Please tell me.'

An expression of faint irritation passed across his face. 'Christina is perfectly safe, quite unharmed, happy and well.'

'But where *is* she? Why can't I see her? Raphael, please—why are you keeping us apart? Couldn't she join us for dinner?'

'No, she couldn't. She was very tired. She's—resting.'

'Then let me go and look at her, just so I know she's all right. Please, Raphael. Is she over there?'

She gestured to a white cottage with the light in the windows. It was the furthest from where they sat, the closest to the sea. He followed her gesture and smiled.

'Yes . . .'

'Then let me just go and see her for a minute—please . . .' Julia half rose from her seat.

'I'm afraid you will just have to trust me. Is that so difficult?' His eyes met hers sternly. 'I give my word—and I always keep my word—that she is safe and well and happy, and that no harm will come to her. Julia . . .' He held his hand out to her across the table. 'Please—surely now, just for a little while, you will accept this?'

Julia hesitated. 'You mean I can see her tomorrow?'

'That depends.' He looked away. 'I have a suggestion to put to you tonight. If you agree, Christina can return home tomorrow.'

'*What?*' Julia stared at him; her face lit with the sudden relief and happiness she felt. 'Raphael, do you mean that? Truly? Then I agree, of course—whatever it is.'

His voice was dry. 'Wait until you hear what I have to say before you make rash promises.' He paused and his mouth gave a little twist, his eyes growing sad. 'You know how beautiful you look now?' he said. 'How your face lights up and your eyes shine at the thought of Christina's freedom? Nothing *I* say, or do, ever makes you look quite like that. It's irrational, I know, but it makes me just a little jealous.'

'Jealous?' Julia said faintly. She looked away, the colour mounting in her cheeks. 'You surprise me. And anyway, I think you know that's not quite true.'

'Ah yes. Then.' He sighed, and she knew he knew which moment she meant, that no more need be said. There was a brief silence, and then he pressed her hand and released it.

'So. We are agreed, yes? And you feel happier—now? We will discuss all this later, but now we will have dinner, I think, and just pretend that everything is quite normal. That you are a beautiful and desirable woman, and I an admiring—no, an enslaved man. And that we are having dinner together in a beautiful garden, on a most magical night. Do you agree?'

Julia smiled. 'You? Enslaved?'

'But certainly. A Samson overthrown by Delilah . . .'

'I wouldn't have said *that* . . .'

'Well, maybe not.' His eyes glinted. 'I don't feel enfeebled, quite the reverse, but I do feel enslaved. By those eyes of yours, which bewitch me, which I think are candid, but I do not quite trust . . . and by other things as well. I won't enumerate them now . . .' He paused. 'You like this dress?'

Julia smiled. 'But of course. What woman wouldn't? I've never worn anything like it in my life, and just for once, it feels wonderful. However——' she paused teasingly, 'I have to tell you that, clever as you are, brilliant though you are about sizes and colours, which most men are not . . .'

'I told you, I have a lot of sisters. All of them very frivolous and very obsessed by clothes. They educated me, no doubt.' He paused. 'You were leading up to a "but". What is this "but"? You mean there are gaps in my education, that I have made some mistakes? I see none when I look at you now.'

'There *is* a "but". You chose beautiful dresses, beautiful shoes, but I have to tell you, you know nothing about practical underclothes. Nothing at all. No tights.'

'What are you wearing now—just as a matter of interest?' he enquired lazily. As she started to reply, he lifted his hand with a smile. 'No, perhaps you had better not tell me.' He paused. 'You can always show me later on . . .'

Julia looked quickly away. How had she let that happen? Already, when they had only just sat down, the conversation was taking quite the wrong direction. It was making her heart beat faster too, and she suspected he knew that, and knew the warmth that lit in her breasts and between her thighs when he spoke like that, when he looked at her like that . . . How I could love this man, she thought silently. How I *would* love him, if we were not here, if things weren't as they are . . .

It was as if he read her thoughts. The servant brought them a first course of Greek *meze*—tiny delicate shrimps, prawns, feta cheese, olives—and as they ate, he leaned towards her.

'Tell me,' he said, 'if none of this had happened—if we had just met, in Rome say, as two perfectly ordinary people in perfectly ordinary circumstances—what do you think would have happened?'

'I think I would have liked you.' Julia raised her eyes candidly to his face. She wanted now, to be truthful to him—as truthful as she could be without acknowledging what she actually felt. 'I think I would have—been amused by you. I don't know. Maybe you would have asked me out to dinner or something, and it would have been very like this . . .'

'I think that too.' He laid down his fork, and looked at her gravely. 'I feel it so strongly that sometimes—mad though it sounds—I forget that that is not the case.' He paused. His voice became dry. 'And then what would have happened? You would have had an affair with me, maybe? Fitted me into your schedule? An hour or two in the afternoons in your apartment?'

'I don't know,' she said carefully, 'I've never exactly had an affair. I'm very ignorant, I don't know how you conduct one. Is that what you do? Is that what you think would have happened?'

He shrugged and looked away. 'It's a routine I'm not unfamiliar with, certainly. I couldn't pretend that it was. And it has certain advantages, when a man and a woman want no further involvement. It is honest, at least . . .'

'I see.' Julia looked down at her plate, her heart contracted with pain.

'You misunderstand.' His voice was crisp. 'I was not referring to you and me. I cannot imagine such a dry, businesslike arrangement between you and me. With us . . .' He shrugged, and then smiled, his voice growing lighter. 'You forget, perhaps, because I speak your language quite well, that I am not English. I am not an Englishman. I am Italian—and so all the things of which Englishwomen no doubt disapprove. Jealous. Possessive. We should certainly have quarrelled . . .'

He paused as the servant took away their plates, and then served them with grilled fish. They ate for a while in silence after that. Then Raphael talked a little, about general things, things of no consequence. But his manner was abstracted, and though she could see he was making an attempt to amuse her, to keep their conversation on a light level without danger or threat, her replies were wooden and stilted. At last, he drew back his chair, and held out his hand to her.

'Come inside,' he said. 'It is growing cold. You haven't seen very much of this house of mine, and I'm quite proud of it. I'll ask them to bring us our coffee in the drawing-room.'

His house? Julia glanced at him quickly, and then followed him. He showed her some of the other rooms in the main building—a music room, a library, an enormous dining-room that opened out into the garden. Then he led her into a large room that led off the central hall of the house. There the furniture was simple, but very beautiful. The walls were painted a pale beige, the better to show off the paintings, which were even finer than those that hung in his bedroom. Julia looked at them quietly, in awe. The jewelled colours of a Gauguin; a Cézanne still-life; a most beautiful Vuillard interior.

'My father's.' Raphael gestured to the walls. 'He was obsessed by the Impressionists, the way they captured light.' He paused. Julia sat down before the fire. 'I would like him to have seen you. You would have fascinated him. Your hair, your eyes . . . You know that there is a certain kind of skin

that transmutes light? It was a most sought-after quality in
models—particularly for the Impressionist painters. You have
that . . . Damn!'

He broke off suddenly, and Julia looked up, startled. Then
she heard what his quick ears had caught before hers: the
sound of a car drawing up on the gravel drive outside.
Raphael moved quickly to the windows and looked out, but
before he could do anything, there was the sound of a brief
but determined altercation from the hall. Julia heard one of
the servants' voices speaking in English, obviously trying to
persuade whoever it was to leave. And that person,
indisputably English and obviously in high good humour, was
having none of it.

'No, no, no,' she heard, 'I know he won't want to see me,
and I know I'm probably bursting in at a damn' inconvenient
moment, but you're jolly well not going to get rid of me. I
know he's there, I saw the lights, and I only want a quick
word . . . So just be a good fellow, will you, and tell
Raphael . . .'

Julia stood up. For a moment her gaze and Raphael's
intersected across the room. She saw the quick flare of alarm
in those dark eyes, the moment of indecision. Clearly this
arrival was totally unexpected, unplanned-for, and this time
the person was English. She saw the knowledge of that freeze
his features, just for a second. He looked at her across the
room, still listening to the argument from the hall as if hoping
that somehow the servant would win, that he would be saved
that way. He looked at her and she saw the awareness that he
was trapped, that it was over, that now he could not brazen
his way out. Then, before he could move or speak, the doors
were unceremoniously thrown back.

Raphael did not turn immediately. He kept his eyes on
Julia's face. He was very pale. He did not look afraid—he
looked oddly exultant, as if, now the moment of revelation
must come, he somehow gloried in it. Julia stepped forward,
but before she could speak Raphael turned.

A man burst into the room. A tall, dishevelled man, clad in
a crumpled suit, his tie flying across his shoulder.

Not seeing Julia, he advanced upon Raphael, arm extended, a wide smile on his face.

'Raphael! You old rogue! I've just heard the news! I was down at the taverna, having supper, in a bit of a rush as it happens, but never mind that, when who do I meet but Georgiadis, and he tells me the good news! Well, I couldn't believe it to begin with! You could have knocked me down with the proverbial feather. Raphael? I said—oh no, you must have got it wrong, Georgie old boy. Anyone else, but not Raphael. He'll never fall into the marital trap, *much* too fly, and then Georgie said no, had it on the best authority—you, no less. Well, I thought to myself, there's no arguing with that, is there? So up I jumped straight away, drove over here like the clappers. I'm off on the ferry tonight—hotfoot on a story, you know. But I just couldn't leave without shaking you by the hand and saying jolly well done and all that. Best thing that could have happened. Really.'

Julia saw Raphael give a tight, strained smile. He moved a little to one side so that Julia's presence was revealed, and the man stopped dead. A deep crimson blush spread right up his neck, and across his broad features. He gaped at Julia.

'Oh, gosh!' He raised his hand and smacked himself across the forehead. 'God, I am the most total bloody idiot. Sorry—but I was in such a lather to get here, I just didn't think, and now . . . Oh hell! I mean—oh, Raphael, I really am most frightfully sorry . . .'

'Not at all. I am delighted to see you. Have a drink.' Raphael took him by the arm. 'I must introduce you.' Slowly he turned round to face Julia. His eyes glittered at her in his pale face, and Julia took one step forward. Raphael smiled at her icily.

'This is an old friend of mine. Hugh Scott. He often stays here. He's a journalist—sorry, Hugh, Rome correspondent now, isn't it? Hugh. I want you to meet Jul——'

'Juliet.' Julia held out her hand and smiled. 'Juliet Morton. How do you do?'

'Oh God! Yes. I say. How do you do?'

Hugh was staring at her. Then, recollecting himself, he

stepped forward and shook her hand. Behind him Raphael gave a deep sigh. Julia, lifting her eyes from Hugh's face, saw the tension disappear from his body. Across the room his eyes met hers, and they danced with a wicked amusement.

Hugh was pumping her hand up and down in a very firm grip. 'Congratulations,' he said. 'Oh, many congratulations! This is the most wonderful news, you know. I'm most terribly glad. Quite by chance I ran into Georgiadis like that, another fifteen minutes and I'd have been on the night ferry back to Italy, and I'd have missed you. Oh, thank you, Raphael, yes, whisky would be lovely. I'll have to gulp it down rather. I'll have missed a berth as it is—but she doesn't sail till eleven, so I've just got time for a quick one. I say!' He was looking at Julia closely. 'Miss Morton, haven't we met somewhere before?'

'No, I don't think so.' Julia finally rescued her hand from his grip and turned away as Raphael advanced with the whisky glass in hand. She sat down, and Raphael turned to her with a wicked smile.

'Darling—I'm so sorry. What would you like?' He turned to Hugh. 'Juliet and I were just having coffee . . .'

'I'll have an Armagnac, darling. Thank you.' Julia met his eyes and just managed to stop herself laughing. She didn't know why she had done it, she couldn't justify it, and she didn't care. All she knew was that she was glad. Glad.

Hugh had seated himself opposite her, holding the whisky glass in both enormous hands. It was only then that Julia noticed that he had had a newspaper under his arm when he burst into the room. It now lay on the sofa next to him. It was an Italian newspaper. She stiffened and glanced up instinctively at Raphael, but he was pouring the Armagnac with his back to her, and she didn't think he had noticed the paper either.

'Well, when did all this happen then?' Hugh was still staring at her. 'I must say, Raphael's a bit of a dark horse. Ran into him in Rome only the other week. Never mentioned a damn' thing.'

'Oh, it was all rather sudden,' Julia said airily. 'You know how it is. Raphael and I met years ago in England, and then . . .' She raised her hands in the air—expressively, she hoped. She was not that good a liar, and she could already feel her inspiration beginning to dry up.

'Then we met again, and we both knew at once. Straight away. Didn't we, darling?' Raphael stood over her. He handed her the glass, smiled at her fondly, and sat down beside her on the sofa. He lifted her hand and twined her fingers in his. 'We were in such a rush we haven't even chosen a ring yet—let alone made any announcement. You've rather beaten us to it. Not even my mother knows yet.'

'Oh gosh, she doesn't?' Hugh looked rather grave at this.

'So if you're on your way back to Rome now, don't mention it just yet, there's a good fellow. We rather want it to be a surprise . . .' He lifted Julia's hand to his lips, and kissed it gently. Julia felt a totally mad happiness, and a great desire to laugh.

'Mum's the word.' Hugh looked solemn. 'Great shame I've got to go back—but there you are, duty calls. Bang in the middle of my well-earned holiday, too . . .'

'Some story has broken?' Raphael sounded quite casual, but Julia knew he had seen the newspaper.

'Broken? I should just say so!' Hugh laughed. 'That kidnapping case. You must have read about it—biggest thing for months. Where have you been the last week, for God's sake?'

'Oh, we haven't been in Italy. We've been on the yacht. So, we haven't seen a paper for ages.' He paused. 'Who is it, some politician?'

'No, no . . .' Hugh shook his head. 'Worse, really. The Contadelli heiress, you know, Giovanni Contadelli's daughter—and some other woman, an Englishwoman, who had some job escorting her round Rome. Julia . . . what was it?'

He picked up the paper. Across the few feet that separated them Julia could see the screaming headline. She could also see two photographs. One, the larger of the two, was of Christina, the other, much smaller, was of herself.

'Sorry—Julia, Julia Hamilton. That's it.' Hugh rustled the pages. 'Haven't had time to do much homework, so I'm not as up on the facts as I should be. But I was lying low, they only came through on the Telex this afternoon, and I had to hunt high and low to get this paper—and that's a day old. I'll have to do some fast footwork when I get back to Rome.' He sighed. 'Not that it'll do much good. I might just as well sit here—you never get a lead on these kidnapping cases, the police just clam up straight away. The families won't see you. Hopeless. Still, there you are. Mammon calls in the shape of the news editor, and who am I to disobey?'

Hugh looked up from the paper at Julia and frowned at her pallor. 'Awful thing, isn't it? Terrible country—happens all the time now, you know. Still, from our point of view it's got an English angle. I mean, they snatched both girls. Odd that—you'd think they'd just have taken the Contadelli girl and left it at that, her father's worth millions, you know, almost as much as Raphael here. You want to watch out, Raphael! You'll be next. Oh. Gosh, sorry . . .' He saw Raphael's face change. 'Shouldn't have said that, jolly bad taste. No laughing matter . . . oh well.' He raised his glass and drained it quickly. He stood up. 'I'll have to rush. If I miss that ferry, they'll have my guts for garters . . . There's another in the morning, but I daren't leave it that late. Pity—it's direct. Still—just glad I had enough time to pop in. Miss Morton . . .'

'Juliet, please.'

'Juliet.' He shook her hand warmly. 'Apologies again for bursting in on you like this. Must be off. Raphael—many congratulations. You're a very lucky man.'

'I think so.' Raphael's hand snaked down and tightened around Julia's wrist. He drew her to her feet.

Hugh bent, picked up his newspaper and tucked it back under his arm. He made an attempt to straighten his tie, which instantly went awry, then shook hands all round once more.

'I'll show you out. Drive carefully now . . .'

'Oh, I will. And when you're both back in Rome and the

announcement has been made and all that—well, maybe you'll let me take you out for a celebration dinner. Yes?'

Raphael ushered him out, and Julia stood in the room in silence. She heard the car engine fire, the sound as it disappeared gradually into the distance, then at last Raphael came back into the room. He shut the doors and stood there, tall and dark, just looking at her, his arms folded.

'Well, well, well, *Miss Morton*,' he said slowly. 'What a surprise.' He advanced across the room to her, and tilted her chin so she was forced to look him in the eyes. 'Why did you do that?' His voice was gentle; his eyes searched hers. 'You had a God-given opportunity, and you deliberately threw it away. Tell me, why did you do that?'

'I don't want you to be caught. I don't want you to go to prison.' Julia turned her head away. 'I can't help myself, I just don't.'

'I see.' His voice was quiet and he let her go. For a second she had the feeling that he had been hoping she might say something else, but if so, he did not try to prompt her.

'You're shaking . . .' He lifted his hand to her face, and stroked it. 'Do you regret now, what you did?'

'No I don't, but I know I ought to!' Julia turned to him, her eyes wide with consternation. 'Not for my own sake, but for Christina's. Raphael—oh, don't you see? You *must* let her go. They won't search nearly so energetically for me. The fuss will all die down—in a month or two you can let me go back. I'll never say anything, nothing, I promise you!'

'There is one way of assuring that.'

'You mean—kill me?' Her voice broke slightly, and he turned back to her with angry disbelief blazing in his eyes.

'Are you insane? Do you take me for a murderer?' He held out his hand, and drew her to him. He put his arms around her, and raised her face to his, and when he saw her flinch, he gently stroked her cheek.

'Marry me,' he said.

There was silence. Julia stared into his face, into those dark unfathomable eyes, and she felt tears of pain and anger mist her eyes.

'*Marry* you? That would assure my silence? You mean I couldn't give evidence against you?'

'That is certainly the case.'

His voice was flat and unemotional. With a low cry of despair Julia broke from his arms.

'Why?' she cried passionately. 'Why do you go out of your way to try and hurt and humiliate me? When there's no *need*, when I've told you, promised you—when you've just *seen* that I mean what I say . . .'

'Is it so humiliating to be asked to marry me?' he said stiffly, and she saw his eyes darken in anger.

'Of course it is, on those terms! When you're only asking me out of self-preservation. When there's no love between us—how can you do such a thing?'

'Marry me,' he said. 'Marry me, and I'll give you a wedding present . . .'

'There's nothing you could give me that I want. Nothing!'

'Isn't there? I think you're forgetting something. Marry me, and Christina can go free. In fact . . .' He stepped forward. 'Marry me tonight, and she can go free in the morning.'

'No!' Julia stared at him in horror. 'It's you who must be mad even to suggest such a thing. And how can I marry you tonight? It's past eleven—you're out of your senses.'

'Not at all.' He smiled and sat down, crossing his legs and regarding her calmly. 'It's only too simple. You may have gathered I have a certain influence on this island. I own it, so it's hardly surprising, and occasionally, just occasionally, such ownership can be useful. Besides, I have had this idea for some while—I mentioned I had a proposition earlier, you recall? So—the arrangements have already been made. They can be put into effect with one telephone call.' He smiled. 'There is a small chapel, not far from here. There, there is a Greek Orthodox priest only too delighted to marry me, and a civil licence which requires only the signature of two witnesses of our marriage to make it binding. It will be a religious and civil ceremony, perfectly legal. It shouldn't take more than . . .' he glanced at his watch, 'forty minutes. You might need to change, perhaps—I don't think black is quite appropriate for a wedding.'

'It would damned well be appropriate for this one!' Julia rounded on him in fury, but he continued as if she had not spoken.

'We can return here from the wedding, and I will order Christina's release for the morning. The servants will leave some champagne and so on, and then we can return to my room, and continue where we left off. It seems an excellent plan to me, and everyone quite understands, I assure you, my preferring to keep the ceremony secret.'

There was a little silence.

'How long have you been planning this?' Julia said eventually.

'Since yesterday. You will recall I was busy this afternoon. That was one of the things I had to attend to.'

'Oh, *one* of the things!' Julia's voice rose in scorn. 'I suppose I should be grateful you found time to fit it in. Well, you can just unarrange it—when you have time. Because I won't do it.'

'Then Christina will stay right where she is.' He smiled at her calmly.

'But why? What do you gain from it?'

'Why, the pleasure of your company,' he said. 'Since I can't have it legally of your own free will, I'll have it illegally.'

'Of my own free will? You think I'd marry you of my own free will?'

'Obviously not.' He shrugged. 'Upon compulsion then.' He paused. 'I should tell you, though, that one of the reasons for coming here is that there are no extradition agreements between Italy and Greece. I can stay here, in perfect safety, for as long as I like.'

'But you can't keep *us* here!'

'If you're traced, I agree, it might be difficult.' His voice was silky smooth, perfectly assured. 'But I think you might not be traced. We can move again, if need be. And again . . . It could go on for a long time. Months. I should be perfectly happy, but I wonder about you and Christina? She might miss her family. Her little brother Carlo, his well-publicised wedding—always supposing that ever takes place.'

Julia stared at him, and suddenly, with a horrible perfection, everything fell into place. She had been right, she thought suddenly, her theories had been at least partly right. The antagonism when he spoke of Carlo was transparent. It *was* Carlo he aimed to injure, and Carlo's life he aimed to wreck. And that was the reason for this insane proposal. Of course. He still believed Carlo loved her, he thought Carlo meant to marry her, and that she would go along with it. And he didn't want that. What surer way of preventing it than marrying her himself?

She stared at him in silence, her heart burning. He *was* using her; he had been using her unscrupulously all the time, when he made love to her and now, above all, when he asked her to marry him. She was nothing to him, nothing; the means to revenge himself on Carlo—that was all. Very slowly she turned back to him, her mind racing.

'Supposing . . . supposing I offered you a bargain,' she said hesitantly.

'Go ahead.' His eyes narrowed slightly. 'You're not in a position to bargain very much, but by all means try.'

'Then suppose I said yes—to part of your plan?' Julia watched him closely. 'If I said I would go through with this ceremony you propose you would let Christina go then, at once?'

'I've already said as much.'

'You swear to me?'

'I swear.' He smiled. She caught the light of triumph in his eyes.

'Because then I couldn't ever testify against you.' She hesitated. 'I would be married to you. You'd have what you want?'

'I would have what I want. Yes.'

She would never forgive him for this, she thought, and this time, wanting revenge, she knew exactly how she would get it. This time, just for once, she would outwit him.

'Then I agree.' She turned to the door. 'I'll go and change. You can make your telephone call.'

'Julia . . .' He had risen to his feet, and she heard the sudden note of entreaty in his voice. She ignored it, and swept out of the room.

CHAPTER TEN

SHE had thought with one part of her mind that he was lying, that he had made up this fantastic story of a chapel and a priest, and that if they existed he would not, could not, go through with it.

It wasn't until he halted the car under a clump of cypress trees, and she saw the tiny chapel close to the shoreline, saw the candles, saw through the lighted doorway the figure of the priest, that she realised he meant it all; that all of it, every word, was true.

Raphael paused a moment, looking down into her face, and his eyes were troubled. 'Julia . . .' The pressure on her hand tightened.

'Don't say anything. If you speak to me now, I know I won't be able to go through with it.'

'Very well.' His mouth set in a hard line, and he led her into the doorway.

The priest was standing in front of a simple altar. At the back of the church were two people, a man and a woman, wearing simple peasant clothes; the woman's head was covered in a dark shawl. As she and Raphael came in they turned, their faces smiling with happiness. Shyly the woman approached, and lifted a circlet of flowers, and rested them on Julia's head. Raphael pressed the woman's hands, and Julia saw that the woman—she must have been sixty or more—had tears in her eyes.

If she had not seen that, if she had not guessed at once that these people knew Raphael and rejoiced in what they thought was his happiness, Julia thought she might have been able to harden her own heart. But the woman's tears released her own, and broke her resistance. Then, when she least expected it, she felt a rush of pity and love for the man by her side. If this cost her pain, she thought, it would cost him pain too.

152

Not now, maybe, but inevitably after.

There were two rings, and they had to be exchanged. First the priest held them, and raised them so they caught the light, then Raphael took one. She held out her hand, and his shook as he placed it upon her finger. The priest held out the second ring to her, and Julia took it. She held its weight for a moment in the palm of her hand, and then for the first time Raphael looked at her.

She saw then, deep into his eyes, and saw that there was no mockery, no pride there, but only a pain, a fear. It was like looking into the heart of a storm, and she knew that even then, especially then, he expected her to draw back, to fling the ring on to the floor. He did not know, could never know, how joined she felt to him; as if they were bound together already, and this strange ceremony was but a confirmation of that.

Slowly, gently, she lifted his hand. It felt as cold as ice. She slipped the ring on to his finger, and at once his fingers closed over hers in a grip so tight she thought they should never let each other go.

After that, the rest of the brief service seemed to pass by like a dream. Dimly she was conscious of the priest's voice, and of his blessing. Vaguely she was aware that she put her signature to something, and that Raphael, gently laughing, had to correct her.

'My darling, no—you must write your new name, your married name—see, there, under mine.'

She looked down blankly at the piece of paper. His signature seemed very long, scrawled, illegible. She hesitated, and then wrote *Julia Pierangeli*. She saw Raphael glance up at the priest. He smiled, and said something, and Raphael touched her hand.

'He says that is sufficient. It is done.'

The old woman and the old man added their signatures. The old man signed, Julia saw, with a cross. Then the old woman broke down and burst into tears, and embraced Raphael, and then Julia. The old man made a short speech in Greek and pressed their hands together, and then they left, and she and Raphael were alone under the stars.

'She was my nurse, the old woman.' He spoke stiffly. 'We are very close. When I was a child I came here often, and she was like a mother to me. She has waited a long time for this moment. She said . . .' He hesitated. 'She said she wants to see our children, then her old age will be a contented one . . .' He stopped, and with a quick anguished gesture he pulled her against his heart, and kissed the tears from her eyes.

'What have we done?' Julia drew back from him and gazed up into his face. 'To have deceived that woman—you could see how happy she was for you! It's cruel. It's wrong.'

'She rejoiced at my marriage,' he said, his voice suddenly cold. 'We *were* married. What deception is involved?'

Julia turned back to the car without answering him. She wasn't going to argue with him, she thought. He knew as well as she did what a black farce it was—however differently she might have felt at the moment it actually took place. Well, she had done it; and now she just had to fight to keep calm and cold and unmoved. It was a bargain, she had fulfilled her part. Now he should fulfill his . . .

He tried to talk to her in the car, but she answered him only with monosyllables. When they got back to the house, and he said he would ring for the champagne, Julia shook her head.

'No, thank you,' she said coolly, 'I'm very tired. I shall go to bed.'

She brushed past him, through the door of his room, across the room and into her own. He followed her. As she raised her hand to close the intercommunicating doors he moved, quickly, so his shoulder was against the jamb. For a moment they looked at each other.

'Just what do you think you're doing?' She saw the anger flare in his eyes, but he attempted to control it. He took up an indolent pose, leaning against the frame, but she could see the tension in every line of his body.

'I'm going to bed. I should like to sleep.' She paused. 'Alone. I'd be grateful if you'd move so I can close the door.'

He didn't move a muscle, but stood still, regarding her, his eyes darkening.

'You are my wife. This is our wedding night.'

Julia swallowed. She had had her next speech in mind all the way back in the car; she had been rehearsing it, but now the moment came it wasn't easy to say.

'We made an agreement. A bargain.' She spoke as coolly as she was able. 'If I married you, you swore you would let Christina go in the morning.'

'So I shall. Meanwhile, it's still night . . .'

He took a pace forward, and Julia held up her hand.

'That was the extent of the agreement. Marriage. A marriage service, nothing more. Are you going to break your promise?'

His mouth tightened. 'How very clever of you. And how very cold-blooded. It reminds me of something—as I'm sure it reminds you. I am to play Shylock, is that it? And you, Portia, with your neat legal mind, will ensure I keep to the letter of the bargain. A few words, a signature on a piece of paper—is that what marriage means to you? Is that what you thought I meant?'

'No, of course it isn't. I knew exactly what you meant. That doesn't mean I have to go along with it.' Julia turned away from him angrily.

'Why are you doing this?' With a swift gesture he was across the space that divided them, and took her by the arm, wrenching her round so she had to meet his eyes. '*Why?* It doesn't make you happy any more than it does me—you're fighting yourself and your own feelings every time you speak, I can see it. I thought you understood—that you understood with your heart, which is all that matters.'

'Oh, I do understand. I understand very well.' The taunt cut her, and Julia's eyes blazed at him. 'I understand that ever since you pulled me into that car in Rome you've set out deliberately to humiliate me—to use me. Do this? Do that! Write to your stepfather. Leave this place and go to another one. Listen to all the lies I'm going to read you about yourself! Tell me about your private letters! Come to bed with me! Marry me! Well, all right, so help me, I've done all those things—most of those things—and now it's your turn. Let Christina go in the morning. Let me go when you finally decide you're bored with all this. And then let me get an annulment for this farce of a marriage—it seems to me pretty little in return for what you've made me do.'

'*Made* you do? Are you sure of that?' His face hardened, and the grip on her arm tightened. 'Did I make you get into bed with me this evening? Did I make you lie—tonight—when Hugh turned up, and you had a chance to go free? Did I?'

'No——' She hesitated, and his face softened. His hands slipped up to cradle her face.

'Don't you see, Julia? Don't you understand?' His voice was husky, as if he were genuinely moved by what he said. 'We are both operating on two levels. Your actions, my actions—they can both be examined and judged on a rational level. But that argument is unimportant—I know, you know, that something else is happening. It is not what we said, or even did. It is what we both felt, for each other . . .'

'I feel *nothing* for you!' With a cry of desperation, Julia broke from him. She knew if she stayed there, close to him, if she went on listening he would convince her, with his soft words, with the tenderness he could act so well. And that was something she dared not risk, because she knew the pain afterwards would be so great.

'Is that true?' He hadn't moved, and he spoke very quietly, so she stopped, held by his voice. When she did not answer him, he sighed. 'Julia—turn around and face me. Look me in the eyes, and tell me that's true. You can't do it. On my soul, I don't believe you could tell such a lie.'

She kept her face averted from his. 'I . . . I feel nothing for you. I feel pity perhaps—I don't want you to have to go to prison—but that's all, do you understand? Apart from that . . .' She hesitated, and the words choked in her throat. 'I want nothing more than to be free—never to have to see you again.'

He swore softly, and held out his hand to her. 'Look me in the face and say that, and I give you my word yet again. I will leave you now, and I will never ask you again, so help me. You can go to hell with your frigid English lies.'

Julia thought of Christina; she thought of this man's

embrace. Images eddied in her mind, and all she knew just
then was that she had to make one last effort to free herself
from this man, before it was too late. She set her mouth, and
very deliberately she turned to him and looked him in the
eyes. At that moment she wanted nothing so much as to run
into his arms, but she hardened her heart.

'I feel nothing for you,' she said flatly. 'Nothing. I wish—I
just wish, dear God, that you would leave me alone!'

'*Certamente.*'

Very slowly then, he reached a hand up to her face and
tilted it, and looked deep into her eyes. She knew they filled
with tears; she knew her body trembled at his touch. Slowly
he lowered his face, and kissed her on the lips.

'Julia, good night,' he said.

Then he turned and left the room, and closed the door
behind him.

Julia looked at her watch. It was five-thirty; she had slept for
perhaps two hours. The night before, she had not really
believed Raphael would leave her and not return. For what
had seemed like hours she had just sat there in her white lace
dress on the edge of the bed, waiting for the sound of the
door-handle.

Waiting for what? Waiting for him to come back and take
her in his arms and kiss her, and tell her he knew she had lied,
and he understood why and it didn't matter, because he knew
she loved him, and he loved her . . . When he did not come,
and the hours passed, she grew numb with cold and
exhaustion and despair.

He was more truthful than she was, she thought; he would
not do that, because unlike her, when it mattered, he didn't
lie. Now, she must try and find Christina before she was
released. She didn't know what she would say to her, but she
must try and persuade her not to identify Raphael.

She was wearing trousers, flat shoes, a shirt and a warm
sweater. Now, very carefully, she tried the door that led from
her room to the corridor. As she had expected, it was locked.
She drew in a deep breath, and stole across to the doors that

led into Raphael's room. Silently she turned the handle, her hand shaking, and the door opened. She looked across the room.

Raphael slept naked. One bare arm was thrown out across the pillows as if he, as she had done, had slept only out of exhaustion, and a mind that had refused to rest. For a moment she looked at him, her heart full within her, then very quietly she stole across the room. The door opened, and she was out in the corridor that led off the hallway.

She tensed then, afraid of encountering some of the servants, but the house was silent. She listened intently, then tiptoed through to the wide marble-floored hall. The doors were bolted there, but she didn't dare to try and search for another way out. Standing on her toes she carefully eased one bolt back, then the other. They squeaked; she froze, listening intently, but there was no answering sound. She turned the handle, opened the doors and looked out at the dawn.

The gardens were deserted. The first rays of the sun lit the grass, the shrubs and the trees with a low, slanting light; scents of plants and freshly watered earth rose up to meet her. Silently she sped across the grass; her footsteps left a silver trail in the dew behind her, but she didn't care. The cottage, she thought. The furthest one from the house, where the light had been burning: she had to talk to Christina.

She stopped short, her breath coming fast. The shutters were open. Could Christina be up so early?

When she tried the handle the door opened, and Julia stared around the room before her. It was a guest room, not unlike the one she had been given; it was prettily furnished, and it was empty. She stared at it uncertainly. On the bed some clothes had been left neatly folded—Christina's clothes. Julia gave a low moan of disbelief.

Feverishly, not knowing what she was looking for, she began to search the room and its adjoining bathroom. The bed had not been slept in; its linen was uncreased. In the bathroom wastepaper basket was an empty canister of *Rive Gauche* scent—the make Christina always used. Apart from that and the discarded clothes, there was no evidence of her occupation.

Frantically, Julia ran out of the little house and stood looking around her. There were three other guest cottages, apart from the main house, and she was certain Christina had not been kept there. Quickly she ran to them, peering in through their unshuttered windows. All three were empty, and it was obvious none had been recently used. She closed the door of the last cottage and leaned back against its wall, sick fear and despair rising up in her.

Christina had been moved somewhere else already. Raphael had lied. He had had no intention of keeping his word. Cold-bloodedly he had tricked her yet again, in the full knowledge that he was lying. And he had done it, moreover, a few minutes after his journalist friend had left, when she—so weakly and so foolishly—had failed to give him away.

She felt nothing but hatred for him then, a hatred so intense that it made her tremble. The scorn he had shown her, the ease with which he had duped her—these things she could never forgive. She stood for a moment thinking. Both house and garden were silent; there was no sign of movement from the house. Then Hugh's words from the night before suddenly came back into her memory, and she straightened: *I could have waited for the morning ferry, it's direct.* She looked at her watch. It was still not six—surely the ferry couldn't have left?

She began to run then, weaving and ducking between the shrubbery, keeping to footpaths so she would leave no tell-tale tracks on the grass, and keeping well out of view of the house. On the other side of the garden wall was the road that led back to the town and the port . . . She ducked under a tall bush, its wet branches scratching at her face, and stopped. The garden wall was directly in front of her now, and growing close to it, its gnarled branches bent low, was an ancient olive tree with a low forked trunk. A child could have climbed it: it was simple.

Julia felt a mad rush of exhilaration as she hauled herself easily up into the tree and on to the top of the wall. She knew—she felt absolutely certain—that this time it was going to work. She was going to get away.

It was a high wall—over ten feet—but in her present mood

nothing could have daunted her. She let herself drop down on the other side into a low, grassy ditch. She lay there for a moment, listening. She could hear an engine—something coming that way—not a car, a lorry, she thought. Quickly she pulled herself out of the ditch, stood by the roadside, and, as she saw the lorry materialise over the brow of a low hill, its wheels sending up clouds of white dust, she lifted her hand. She knew it would stop, and it did. She knew that somehow, with a combination of words and gestures, she would make its driver understand where she wanted to go, and she did.

He was going to the port anyway. In the back of the truck were two sheep and several crates of chickens, of which he seemed very proud. Clearly they had to catch the ferry, and clearly he intended to get them there on time. Once they narrowly missed a donkey with laden panniers; another time they accelerated through a flock of goats, all of which leaped nimbly out of the way of his thundering wheels at the last possible second. Julia looked up at the plastic flowers and saints' portraits that decorated the windshield, and offered up a silent prayer of thanks to the gods. The man might drive like a madman, but just then that was just what she needed. When they reached the port, and she saw the familiar quay once more, it was bustling with people. The ferry was there, its gangplank still down, and a crowd of islanders and some tourists were pushing and shoving to get on.

The driver pulled the lorry up in a screech of brakes. He held out one massive hand.

'*Efharisto...*' Julia said; it was the only Greek word she knew. His features broadened into a delighted grin.

'*Kalimera sas*—beautiful lady...' He lifted his hand in a salute, and then jumped down and began to unload the crates of chickens on to the quay.

Desperately Julia felt in her pockets. She had a few thousand lire there—about four or five pounds. Would it be enough? Would they change it? She didn't want to cause any delay or confusion. In front of her there were two young hitch-hikers—Americans by their accents. Both women were carrying laden rucksacks. Carefully Julia attached herself to them and followed them up the gangplank. No one stopped them. No one asked for a ticket.

When they were safely on deck, she drew in her breath.

'Excuse me . . .' She tapped one of the two women on the arm, and she turned with a smile. 'This is the ferry for Italy?'

'For Brindisi? Sure.'

'I wonder . . .' Julia hesitated. 'You don't know what the fare is? I'm not sure I've got enough, and I've only got lire.'

The American glanced down at the bundle of notes Julia held in her hand.

'No problem—that'll be more than enough. We've just come all the way from Athens for less than that, and they'll take lire. There's no banks on Kithiras—right? On these ferries they'll take anything—lire, pounds, Deutschmarks—yen, probably!' She smiled up at Julia.

'And does the crossing take very long?'

The girl frowned. Her gaze became slightly curious.

'Long? About three hours, I guess.' She hesitated. 'Lovely place, huh?'

'I'm sorry?' Julia stared at her blankly.

'Kithiras—this island. Great, isn't it?'

'Oh, yes. Very beautiful . . .'

'Imagine owning an island like this!' The girl gestured around her at the beautiful azure bay, the promontory with its dark cypresses. 'He must be some guy . . .'

'Who?'

'Why, Raphael di Montesole, of course . . . You came here without a guide-book, or what? He owns it. His father bought it back in the 'thirties or something. *You* know—*Montesole*: wine, petro-chemicals, cars, banking . . .' She raised her eyes to Julia's face, and shielded them from the sun. 'You must have heard of him—biggest company in Italy.'

'Oh yes, of course, that Montesole. I hadn't thought.' Julia turned away.

The girl stared after her, then shrugged, and went back to her friend. Julia gripped the rail of the ship very tightly; for a moment she felt as if she might faint. *That* Montesole. How many times had she drunk Montesole wine? Cashed cheques at a Montesole bank? Seen cars filling up at Montesole petrol stations? She remembered Christina's words—'Pierangeli. There's the Marchesa di Montesole—she's great mates with Lucky's family. She's her godmother or something . . .'

Could it be? Julia stared out across the blue water. Surely not? It was impossible, unthinkable. How could such a man be involved in a kidnapping operation? But if it wasn't he, then who was it? Some impostor? But even that made no sense. He had been recognised—clearly Raphael was his real name. And Hugh had made that remark about his wealth which she had taken as a joke . . .

She frowned. She didn't understand any of it. Nothing made sense. How could you calmly kidnap someone, whatever your motives, and tell them your real name—particularly when that name happened to be one of the most famous in Italy?

The gangplank was being lowered, the ship's engines were starting up. Looking down over the side she saw the water begin to churn. On the quay, men were untying the hawsers; children were waving. An old woman, wreathed in black, called last messages in Greek to someone on deck . . . Julia looked back at the quay, and froze.

A large black Mercedes was approaching the market square fast. Even as she looked she saw it screech to a halt, and a flock of chickens scattered. The ship inched away from the quay another yard; Julia ducked back behind one of the lifeboats, her nails cutting into the palm of her hand. *Oh, hurry*, she prayed silently. *Don't stop now. Please God, hurry*.

The door of the Mercedes opened, and she saw him leap out. A tall, dark figure, dressed in black. Across the distance that separated them his figure drew her eyes like a magnet. His driver was also out of the car, was running forward, shouting something, but the ship wasn't stopping. It was gathering speed now, it was out in the channel . . . Raphael stood still, she saw. Then he lifted one hand to shade his eyes from the sun and she felt his gaze burn her, though she knew, logically, that at this distance it must be impossible for him to pick her out. Then his hand dropped. The ship veered round.

Raphael was getting back into the car, and they were making for the open sea.

She was safe, she told herself silently, over and over again. He couldn't stop her now, it was impossible. It was what she had wanted. She had escaped from him at last. So why did she feel no relief? Why did her heart feel broken?

'I must speak to Signor Contadelli himself. Now, at once. It's terribly urgent. This is Julia—Julia Hamilton . . .'

Julia spoke rapidly into the receiver. The line was bad, and at the other end the manservant who had answered her call seemed maddeningly slow. She had had to reverse the charges, and that seemed to be causing suspicion and uncertainty.

'Please . . . please. It's Julia—I must speak to him. Quickly . . .'

'*Momento . . .*'

There came a long buzzing silence. Julia looked around the small office in which she sat, and the three men there looked back at her grimly. The immigration office at Brindisi was small and shabby; she had no passport, no money, and no proof of identity. It had taken her half an hour to persuade these dour men to let her make this call. They had listened to her story, and it was transparently obvious that they didn't believe a word of it.

'He's coming. The servant's gone to get him. Please—just a moment longer . . .'

She raised her eyes pleadingly to the men's impassive faces. She couldn't understand it—why weren't they reacting? They must have read the stories in the newspapers. Surely they had recognised her, or if not, they knew who she was, what had happened to her? Yet they showed no sign of doing so. They sat there now, watching her with their faces closed, their hands resting on their laps. It was like facing the Inquisition!

Someone was coming. Through the buzzes and clicks on the line she heard first the receiver being picked up, and then at last the familiar voice. She almost sobbed with relief.

'Signor Contadelli? Giovanni? It's me, it's Julia. I'm in

Italy. I'm free—I got away from them. Giovanni, please, you've got to help me. I'm in the immigration office at Brindisi. They don't believe me—please—you've got to do something fast. Christina's not with me—I don't know where she is—they moved her, but she can't be far away. If we move quickly . . .'

It all poured out in an incoherent torrent—partly in English, partly in Italian. She saw the three officials exchange glances. Her hands were sweating; she was shaking so much she could hardly hold the receiver. Eventually she stopped speaking, and there was a silence. Then Giovanni spoke. His voice, as it always did, sounded businesslike, efficient, masterful, and she gave a sob of relief.

'You're in Brindisi? I see. Right. Now, Julia, listen to me carefully. I want you to do exactly what I say, do you understand? Can you hear me? You're to wait where you are. Stay there. Don't leave, and don't talk to anyone. I'll arrange a plane. It will bring you straight back to Rome. I'll meet you at the airport—on the runway. I'll have a car to meet the aircraft. Meantime, remember, talk to no one—do you understand? Not even the men with you. Now—which is the senior of them? Put him on the line.'

Julia stared at the receiver in her hand. Then, silently, she held it out and one of the men got up and took it from her.

Wearily she sat down. At the back of her mind she could hear the man speaking, his voice respectful, obedient. She stared at him unseeingly. What was happening? she thought confusedly. Why hadn't Giovanni asked about Christina? Why hadn't he seemed more surprised, more relieved? Why wasn't he calling the police? Why mustn't she speak to anyone?

'Si, Signor Contadelli. Certamente—si, comprendo . . .' The man on the telephone was nodding energetically. He hung up, and turned and looked at her. He looked at the two other men.

Then, more kindly, he gestured to her to follow him. He led her into a small room that led off the office. It contained a desk, a chair, and a small bed.

'You will wait here.' He frowned. 'A car will come to take you to the plane. Meanwhile, I think it is better if you rest. You are not well, I think. You look very tired ...' He hesitated, shouted to one of the other men to bring him something, and then turned back to her, his face more gentle. 'Perhaps ...' He hesitated. 'Perhaps while you wait you would like something to read? Here we are.' He thrust a newspaper into her hands. 'Rest, signorina, yes? I will call you when the car arrives.'

Julia stared after him, puzzled by his manner. Then, slowly, she opened the newspaper. It was that morning's edition; she stared at it in disbelief. On the front of it was a huge photograph of Christina, and a two-inch headline *Christina is safe!* Christina is safe—the letters jumped and leaped before her eyes. She stared at them in stupefaction, and sank down on the chair.

According to the newspaper, both Christina Contadelli and her English friend, Julia Hamilton, had been released the previous night. They were safe and they were in good health; they were unharmed. The identity of their kidnappers was not known and, naturally, after their ordeal, neither girl was prepared to talk to reporters ...

'I want an explanation.'

It was mid-afternoon, and very hot. They were sitting in a small room at Rome airport, which Giovanni said had been put at his disposal by the airport authorities: Julia in her crumpled and travel-stained clothes, her face wan with exhaustion; Giovanni in his beautiful, three-piece grey suit, his silk shirt, his hand-made shoes.

Giovanni sighed, took out a packet of cigarettes and lit one. His eyes met hers.

'Christina is safe. You have obviously seen a newspaper, which I regret, I wanted to tell you myself—to try to explain.' He paused. 'What you read is partly true. Christina was released yesterday. I met her last night. She is at home, sleeping. She is quite well, and quite unharmed.'

Julia let out a low sigh of relief, and all the tension seemed to ebb out of her body. She leaned back in exhaustion against her chair.

'I see . . . So you mean that was some kind of ploy on the part of the police, pretending I was released at the same time? They had a reason for it?'

'Not exactly, no. It is a little more complicated than that.' Giovanni hesitated. He reached for the coffee-pot on the tray between them. 'Please, Julia, take something. You look exhausted. If you don't want coffee, let me send for something else. Brandy? A glass of wine?'

'I just want an explanation! I want to understand what's happened——'

'Christina is safe. You have returned safely. That is what has happened.' Giovanni lowered his eyes and spoke flatly.

'But *how*? How did Christina get away? Did she escape? Did he—did they let her go? They separated us, I had no idea what had happened. We were on an island, and . . .'

'I know all this.' Slowly Giovanni inhaled on his cigarette.

Julia stared at him.

'You *know* all this?'

'I know where you were being held, yes. And—since I think you have a right to know—Christina did not escape, she was released. The yacht that took you to—to the island—brought her back to Italy yesterday evening.'

'Yesterday evening?' Julia's eyes widened. 'What is this? I don't believe it! I just don't believe it!' She sprang to her feet and stared down at him angrily.

'Julia, please, sit down.' Giovanni looked up at her, and something in his expression made Julia hesitate. She stared at him, and then slowly she sat down again. He looked at her quietly.

'You must know where you were, yes? The name of the Greek island—you know that?'

'Yes.'

'And you know who took you there? There was a group of men, I understand that—but their leader, the man who gave the orders, made the decisions—do you know who he was?'

'I . . .' Julia swallowed. 'No, I don't,' she said at last. 'He gave a name. It was a false one, obviously.'

There was a silence. Giovanni tried to disguise it, but she thought she saw something like relief mark his face for a second.

'*You* know who he was, don't you?' She stared at him. 'You know, and yet you're asking *me*. Why? Why, Giovanni?'

Giovanni met her eyes for a long moment, then he stubbed out his cigarette with a brisk gesture, as if he had just come to a decision. He bent forward, and opened the briefcase that lay on the table before him. His manner had now changed; he was brisk, decisive, matter-of-fact.

He held out a package to her. 'I want you to take this. Inside . . ' He paused, looking faintly embarrassed. 'Inside you will find a first-class air ticket in your name on the first flight back to London tomorrow morning. You will also find some money. Ready money, in cash, which you will need for your journey, and a cheque from me. It is to cover your salary for the rest of this year. It is in lieu of notice, you understand?' He paused as Julia silently opened the envelope, then he cleared his throat and continued. 'I have reserved a suite for you at the hotel just outside the airport here. My car will take you there in a few minutes. I would like you to rest there until your flight tomorrow morning. The bill will be settled by me, naturally. I regret this—that your employment with my family must end in this way, and . . .'

Julia slowly raised her face to his. 'This cheque. It's for twenty thousand pounds.'

There was a little silence, and Giovanni looked away.

'I take it you want my silence, as well as my co-operation,' Julia said in a tight voice. 'Is twenty thousand the price you put on it?'

Giovanni flushed. 'Please . . . I understand, of course, this termination of your employment places you in a difficult position. If I have been insufficiently generous, please . . .' He was drawing a cheque-book and pen from his briefcase.

Julia took the cheque between her hands and tore it into quarters. 'I want an explanation.' She set her mouth and looked at him. Her heart was raging with pain and humiliation, with anger that Giovanni, whom she had liked, who had been her father's friend, could treat her like this. Giovanni slowly shook his head.

'I expected as much. I apologise, Julia, but I can and will explain nothing. This is a difficult matter, a sensitive matter. It involves my family. And it involves my—friends. Since I cannot order you, I can only ask you. Do as I say.'

Julia stood up. 'I shall go to the police.'

'I wouldn't advise that.' Giovanni cut her off with a wave of his hand. 'It would get you nowhere. I think you would find they had suddenly become very deaf, and very slow. You could go to the press, of course. There my influence is considerable, naturally, but less extensive. You *might* find people who were willing to listen to you . . .'

'I think I might. Hugh Scott, for one. He's the English correspondent in Rome, for . . .'

His face grew stern. 'I think you should remind yourself of the consequences if you speak to Mr Scott or any other journalist. They will want, naturally, some confirmation of your story, and I rather think that would involve your revealing a certain name, don't you? A name you seemed reluctant—for reasons of your own, into which I will not enquire—to reveal to me. Had that occurred to you?'

It had not. Julia stared at him, and Giovanni looked at his watch, then stood up.

'Julia, please. We were friends, and I should like to think we could part that way. Believe me—I am grateful, more than grateful, for what you have done—and one day I would like to think it could be explained to you, and that you would understand, and we could laugh about it together. But not now. Now I want you to go to that hotel room, and then take that flight tomorrow morning. If, at any time in the future, there is anything you need of me—you must know you have only to ask. I am in your debt, more than you know.'

He paused, and held out his hand to her. 'Please, Julia, it is all arranged. In the hotel suite you will find your passport, all your belongings from your apartment, safely packed up. Your rent has been paid to Mr Fletcher for the rest of the year. There is nothing for you to worry about. You can return to

England and forget this whole episode. Believe me—it will come to seem very unreal.'

An image of Raphael's face as he had held her in his arms, as he had looked at her in the little chapel the night before, swam into Julia's mind. She blinked back her tears and turned to the door.

'You're quite wrong, Signor Contadelli,' she said flatly, 'but I will do as you say.'

CHAPTER ELEVEN

SHE waited half an hour in the hotel suite, and then she rang Hardy's number. It rang and rang; there was no answer, and carefully she replaced the receiver. She sat for a moment, staring straight ahead of her. Giovanni was right, she was tired, terribly tired, but with a mental rather than a physical exhaustion. Desperately she tried all the pieces of the jigsaw this way and that, but no matter how she rearranged them, they refused to fit. Only some things were clear. Giovanni knew a lot—she suspected he knew that it was Raphael who had kidnapped them, and she suspected he knew why.

But there were some things he did not know. He did not know about the marriage—of that she was certain. If he had, no doubt he would have briskly undertaken to arrange a divorce, she thought with a curl of her lip. And he had been wrong about one other thing. If he thought she was going to sit quietly here and get on a plane like a docile child, he was an idiot. No way.

If only there was someone she could talk to! She would have liked to try and contact Christina, but she knew that would be fruitless—they wouldn't accept her calls, and if she went to the house obviously they wouldn't admit her. She would like to talk to Hardy—where could he be? Impatiently, she tried Hardy's apartment again. Again the phone rang unanswered.

She stared at the table on which the telephone stood. On a shelf beneath it there was a bulky Rome telephone directory. Slowly she picked it up, and began to riffle quickly through the pages. First under the letter 'P', then under 'M'. Her finger ran down the list, then stopped. There: it was listed. *Montesole*. Marchesa di . . . an address in one of the oldest and most exclusive districts of Rome; and a number. She paused. There was no other listing under that name, no listing for a Raphael Pierangeli . . .

Carefully, her hands shaking a little, she picked up the receiver and dialled the number.

It rang for a long time. Then at last, just when Julia was about to hang up, it was answered; a woman's voice. Julia could almost see her as she listened. She could hear the age in the voice, and also a slight tremor, as if the woman were frail or unwell. But she spoke with a slight haughtiness and an authority that Julia at once recognised: his mother's voice. She did not doubt it for a second.

'I should like to speak to the Marchesa di Montesole . . .' she began, speaking in Italian.

'This is she.'

'Donna . . .' Julia hesitated. Then, still speaking in Italian, she went on, 'I am a friend of your son, Raphael . . .'

'Raphael? My son? He is not here . . .'

'I . . . I want only to leave a brief message for him.' She swallowed.

'Who is this? You are English?'

For a moment Julia had an image of the woman, stiff-backed, proud like her son, and her heart relented. She knew she could say nothing to alarm her; there was no point in causing more trouble now. She sighed.

'Donna, please. When you see your son, would you say that I telephoned him? To say goodbye.'

There was silence on the other end of the line. Then, to Julia's astonishment, there came a deep and throaty chuckle, a rich laugh.

'To say goodbye? That is all? That is not very much of a message for a young woman to leave a young man.'

'That is the message. That is all.'

The woman laughed again. Suddenly she switched to English—less perfectly accented than her son's, but none the less startlingly like his.

'And who shall I tell him left this little message?'

The voice sounded amused, much more confident. Julia stared at the receiver; she could hardly say 'Pierangeli'. 'Just say, "Julia",' she said. And she hung up.

She pressed her hand against her eyes. It was terrible,

terrible how much it hurt. His mother's voice had brought her a sense of Raphael, so intense it was as if for a moment he were in the same room with her. And the fact that he was hundreds of miles away, that she would never see him again—the pain of it cut into her heart like a knife.

Slowly she stood up and went to the desk. She would write a note and take it round to Hardy, and ask him to deliver it safely for her, so she knew for certain it could not go astray. Then she would come back to the hotel and take the plane in the morning, just as Giovanni had asked. Perhaps he was cleverer than she had thought. Perhaps he wanted, quite simply, to spare her further hurt.

She chose a piece of plain paper, without heading. On it, she wrote the date. Then, after much thought, she simply wrote: *Raphael—I told you one lie. It was the night we were married. I am sorry now.*

She signed it, simply, *Julia,* and then, as an afterthought, because her heart ached so, and it comforted her, she added his surname. She looked at the piece of paper. *Julia Pierangeli.*

Slowly she put the piece of paper in an envelope. She knew what she hoped, though she did not dare spell it out to herself.

She hoped it would bring him back to her.

She left the hotel by a side door half an hour later, having quickly showered and changed. Then she took two taxis before she continued her journey to Hardy's apartment on foot.

She wasn't certain, but she wouldn't have put it past Giovanni to have her watched—if only to ensure she did not go to the newspapers, and that she did take the flight the next morning. But by the time she reached the Via Bocca di Leone she felt more relaxed, and certain she was not being followed.

It was early evening now, and the light was failing. Julia felt desperately tired, but as she neared the familiar house, her spirits rose. She was almost certain Hardy would be there. He rarely left Rome; he was always at home at this time of day. With Hardy she knew she could confide safely; he would not judge or censure or reprove. And she could give him the letter—she knew she could depend on his delivering it.

She glanced up at the tall house, and her heart leapt. His light was on: it was all right, he was there. Quickly she ran across the shadowed silent courtyard, and began to mount the stairs. It was less than a week since she had last been here. She paused on the landing, counting up the days in a second of disbelief. But yes, it was true—less than a week. It felt like years rather than days.

Breathlessly, she came to a halt outside Hardy's door, and tapped on the panels. 'Hardy? Hardy?' she called. 'It's me. It's Julia . . .'

She hesitated, and then turned the handle. The door opened. The room beyond was in darkness, but a window was open. The curtains fluttered in the breeze. She stared into the shadows of the room uncertainly. That was odd. She knew she had seen a light just a moment ago. He couldn't have left—she would have passed him on the stairs.

Of course! He must have gone up then, to her old apartment—to his old studio. Maybe there was something up there he wanted . . .

She began to run up the stairs to the attic floor, calling ahead of her.

'Hardy? I saw your light! It's me—it's Julia . . .'

The door to her apartment was open, and from the landing she could see that one of the lamps was on. She ran forward eagerly, pushing back the door.

'Hardy . . . Hardy? Where are you?'

She stared across the empty room, ceasing to call, some sixth sense alerting her at the last instant. She felt the skin on the back of her neck prickle with alarm. She half-turned, and the door behind her slammed. A man's hand came around her throat, and over her mouth as she opened it to scream.

She heard his intake of breath, smelt his sweat, then he twisted her arm up behind her back so sharply she cried out in pain, and wrenched her round to face him. Julia felt her skin go cold. She stared at his face in the dim light, and Pietro smiled. A long, slow, nasty smile.

'Yes, it's me. You weren't expecting that, were you?' He spoke in Italian, his voice pitched low, his eyes burning into hers. 'Thought you'd seen the last of me, did you? Little bitch! Look at this—go on—take a good look!' He turned his face to the light, and she saw the mark on his face. A cut; a black bruise, still swollen around the eye.

'You know who did that?' His fingers tightened over her mouth. 'Raphael—precious Raphael, that's who did it. Knocked me down and kicked me out—did you know that? And why—because of Christina, is that what you think? Because I roughed her up a bit? Oh no. You're wrong, my sweet. Because of you.'

Julia stared at him, feeling the sweat start to break out on her brow. She caught the fresh, sweet smell of alcohol on his breath, and tried to wrench her head away in disgust.

'Oh no.' He wrenched it back again viciously. 'You'll listen, and you'll listen good. Because you want an explanation for a lot of things, don't you? And I'm going to give it you.' He paused and grinned. 'He knocked me down and he kicked me out—because of you. And not because I nearly let you get away, you stupid little bitch. Oh no. Because of what I'd said about you—what I said again that day. I'd seen you, I'd been watching you for weeks. Months, long before he came on the scene. I knew what you liked, what you wanted. I'd seen you with all those men—and I told him. He believed it at first—lapped it up. You should have seen his face when he first read that letter of little Carlo's! I thought—right, that's good—now he knows what she is—and then what happened? You got to him somehow, didn't you, with those innocent eyes of yours—and he was taken in, just like all the others—all of them except me. Suddenly he's not so sure I've been telling him the truth. So I tell him to his face what you are. And you know what he does? He knocks me down. Half kills me—kicks me out. I'd like to slit his throat for him—stupid arrogant fool. But I knew a better way of getting at him. So I came back to Rome, and I waited. I saw the newspaper today. I knew you'd come back here sooner or later, and when you did, I'd be waiting. Just the way I am now.'

Slowly he lifted his hard hand from her mouth. Julia stared at him in silence.

'Scream—go on. Why don't you scream? No one will hear

you. Your old scarecrow of a lover is away—that was me in
his apartment just now. The building's empty. There's just the
old woman on the ground floor and she's deafer than a post.
So—go on, why don't you? I'd like to hear you scream . . .'

'Then you're going to be disappointed.' Julia was shaking, but
she gazed at him with contempt. 'You think I'm afraid of you?'

'Oh, not yet. Don't let's rush things—I'm in no hurry.
There's plenty I want to say. And plenty I want to do, too.
You've caused me a lot of trouble. I don't intend to hurry
now . . .' He paused, and then very slowly, with one last
vicious little twist, he let go of her arm. Julia backed away
from him, and he moved in front of the door.

She stood still, looking at him, trying to calm herself, trying
to think. He watched her, as he lounged against the door,
then he took out a packet of cigarettes and lit one.

'You think Raphael hired me, don't you? And you couldn't
be more wrong.' He flicked his ash on the floor. 'It's very
simple, really. The Ricioni family hired me, Lucrezia's
parents, because they got to hear about you and Carlo
Contadelli.'

He smiled lazily at her. Julia stared at him. Whatever she
had been expecting, it was not this. Slowly she backed away
from him.

'Why did you think I took Carlo's letter? That marriage
between Carlo and Lucretia—that's a big deal, you know. It's
been planned a long time; there's a whole lot of business deals
hanging on a little thread, just waiting for that marriage to
take place. The Ricionis wanted it; Giovanni wanted it—and
when they found out little Carlo had the hots for some stupid
English bitch with no family and no money—well, they
weren't too pleased. And when Carlo, the stupid bastard,
starts telling everyone who'll listen that he's going to break off
with Lucretia, that he wants to marry you, for God's sake . . .
well, it stands to reason, my sweet. They wanted you out of
the way, and fast. So who do they call in? Mr Big Shot, the
old family friend. I told them not to—I told them to leave it
to me, but no. Maybe they thought I was getting a bit too
involved, you know what I mean?'

He paused, and Julia pressed her shaking hand against her forehead.

'You mean—all this—*was* because of Carlo? To get me away from Carlo? But there was no *need* . . .'

'Oh no?' He sneered at her. 'I wouldn't have said that, not the way he was carrying on. They wanted you out of the way—for a nice long time. Till after the wedding, for instance. Once Carlo was married they reckoned he'd come to his senses . . . and meanwhile, it had to look convincing. I mean you couldn't just disappear, could you? And you couldn't be snatched—what sense would that make? Oh, I know Raphael told you some cock-and-bull story about your stepfather, and you're so dumb you bought it—but no one else would have done. So they took Christina as well, just to make it look real.'

'But what about Giovanni? They wouldn't have done that—Christina's his daughter! Raphael would never have agreed . . .'

'It was Raphael's idea, baby. From the word go. I had a much simpler solution, but no one would listen to me. And don't break your heart over Giovanni Contadelli—he knew. Not before it happened, I give you that, but the day you tried to get away and Raphael caught you—you remember? He'd been down to the nearest village to call Giovanni personally. And you know what? By the time Raphael had talked to him and the Ricionis had talked to him, Giovanni was ready and willing to go along with the whole thing. Because he didn't reckon his son and heir getting mixed up with a nobody like you either . . .'

'I don't believe you. Giovanni wouldn't put Christina through all that . . . he couldn't.'

He laughed. 'Why not? They want to stay on the right side of Raphael. He's eligible, for one thing, and richer than both families together, stinking snobs! Little Christina will have to marry one day, and Lucretia has a younger sister coming up fast. They'd both give a lot to fix a marriage with him—so when he proposes, they don't argue, believe me.'

'Well, they're going to be unlucky then.' Julia's eyes flashed. 'That won't be happening. Because he's married me.'

For a second his handsome face fell, then he recovered himself.

'Has he, now? Really? Well, you have to give him credit. He moves fast. Of course, you know why he did that, don't you?' He caught the momentary uncertainty in her eyes, and he began to laugh. 'Oh, come on, come on, it's obvious enough. He played you like a fish from the very first. I knew why he was doing it, but even I had to admit he did it well. After all, if he was going to keep you there and keep you quiet long enough to get Carlo's marriage over and done with, he had to do something, didn't he? And besides—even I wouldn't deny there was probably some pleasure involved. You look OK. You've got a good body.' He reached out his hand and lightly caressed her breast. Julia recoiled. 'So—he married you to shut you up. I have to admit that's clever. I mean, Carlo can't exactly marry you when you're already married to someone else, can he? *Can he?*'

He caught hold of her by the arm, wrenching her against him. His body felt hot and hard, and with a sickening lurch of fear Julia realised that all the time he had been talking he had been growing more and more aroused. He pressed her against him, grinding his hips against hers, as she struggled, and Julia, in spite of herself, cried out in pain. He laughed.

'Come on, come on,' he said thickly. 'You don't need to lie to me. Come on . . . Damn you. Come on . . .'

Julia kicked him. She brought her foot up against his shin as hard as she could, and then she raised her knee, hard. He gave a grunt of pain, and half doubled up, and in a second Julia was past him and running for the door. She wrenched it open, and burst out on to the darkness of the landing. She screamed loudly then, as loudly as she could. She could hear him coming after her, heard his footsteps; terrified, almost falling, she felt for the banisters, and then Pietro was on her again. She fell under his weight, and all she could hear was the sound of his breathing, his voice against her ear.

'You little bitch—you had this coming to you—I'll kill you for that . . .'

Julia screamed once, the sound terrifyingly loud, into the

blackness, and then suddenly she felt Pietro's body go limp. There was a horrible gagging sound, a choking groan, and then his weight was gone. She lay there on the hard marble floor, staring up into the blackness. Dimly now, she could see two shapes, two figures; she heard the sound of a body slammed against a wall.

And then she heard Raphael's voice, very low, speaking in Italian. A stream of oaths; the smack of a fist. Pietro groaned—she saw a black shape stagger back against the banisters, slip, start to slither. There was a dull thump, then silence, then a moan.

She screamed. 'Raphael . . .'

She felt a hand come down out of the darkness and grasp hers, then two arms came around her and lifted her to her feet. She stood up, shaking, and clung to him. He held her very tight, his breath coming fast, pressing her against his heart.

From below there was a long groan, then the sound of a man lurching to his feet. Raphael smiled down at her grimly; as her eyes grew accustomed to the shadows, she could just see the hard familiar planes of his face. He led her slowly back into her old room, and closed the door.

Julia stepped away from him, her face strained and white, quite mute.

'He's all right.' Raphael read the fear in her eyes. 'He'll be able to get home, after a fashion. If he ever comes back, if he ever touches you again—so help me God, I'll kill him.'

He sat her down gently on the bed, and bathed her face where Pietro had scratched her, and bathed and dried the cuts on her hands and arm. Then he went back into the kitchen, rummaged around on the shelves, and returned with a bottle of brandy Hardy had once given her. He poured two glasses and gave her one. 'Drink it,' he said gently. 'It will make you feel better.'

Julia did as he bade her. The brandy scalded her throat; then she felt it course down and warm her stomach. Her nerves relaxed a little. She looked up at him. Slowly Raphael drew up a chair, and sat down in front of her. On the floor between them lay her letter to him, face up. It bore his name on the front. At last, after a little silence, he bent down, picked it up, hesitated and then handed it back to her. Julia clasped it tightly in her hand, and Raphael smiled.

'It's all right. I shall never take your letters again—even those addressed to me—without your permission.'

He paused, and she realised that he too looked very tired. There were dark shadows under his eyes; the lines from nose to mouth looked deeper than she remembered. As she looked at him he sighed, and pressed his hand for a moment against his eyes.

'I saw you on the ferry,' he said. 'Even among those people. I could see you, Julia, among ten thousand. Among a million. I knew where you would be going, and why. I left myself, almost immediately.'

'There was another ferry? You took the yacht?' She stared at him, still hardly able to believe he was there, and he smiled.

'No, I took a helicopter. There's a heliport not far from the house. I must have been at Brindisi while you were there, but those idiots, those mules, they denied all knowledge of you. By the time I got hold of Giovanni, you'd left for Rome. I've been looking for you ever since.'

He paused. 'I think Giovanni has cold feet about the whole thing. All he wanted was to get you on a plane and out of the country—God knows how many people he's had to bribe to pull this off. When I finally tracked him down, and made him tell me where you were, it was too late. I went straight round to the hotel, and you'd disappeared. They thought you were still in your room; the tail Giovanni had on you hadn't seen you leave. I was frantic—like a madman. I phoned my mother—I had some crazy idea you might have gone to our house. She told me you had rung to say goodbye . . .'

He hesitated. 'At that point I nearly cut my throat. And then I realised how stupid I'd been—that there was one obvious place you would go. To your friend's. I came straight here, and I was almost too late.' She saw the bitterness in his mouth, the dejected slump of his proud body, and somehow, suddenly, her heart started to race.

'Do you think I could have another glass of that brandy?' she said distinctly. 'I think it's doing me some good. *Something's* doing me good . . .'

He glanced up at her, and she saw a little light come back into his eyes. Solemnly he handed her another glass, hesitated, then poured himself one too and downed it in one swallow, making her smile faintly.

She paused. 'That man—Pietro—he talked and talked. He wouldn't stop. He got some kind of kick out of it, I think. So you don't have to explain. He did it quite efficiently.'

'Don't say that—he can't have done!' He swung round to her impulsively and she saw the pleading in his eyes. 'Or maybe he did, I don't know. Nothing I say will be very defensible either—except—except—mad though it all was, insane though it was—it was done from the best of motives. For Lucretia's sake. I genuinely believed that . . .'

He paused, and looked down at his hands. 'My mother is very fond of Lucretia—so am I come to that. I admire her and I like her, and as a matter of fact I think she deserves a far better husband than Carlo. But it's Carlo she loves, and, who knows? Maybe he'll grow up eventually. If their marriage hadn't taken place, it would have broken her. More than that, it would have caused a rupture between those two families, and the ramifications of *that*—commercial and personal— well, they would have been considerable.'

'I know all that,' she agreed, a little bitterly. 'I can quite understand how important it was to both families, to you—to all your business empires. But you were really very stupid. If Giovanni had simply come to me and explained the position, I would quietly have gone away, like the amenable English girl I am, until Carlo was safely married. Did that idea occur to no one?'

'Amenable?' He smiled. 'That's your idea of yourself, is it? Well, it's not the first word that springs to my mind. No.' He shook his head. 'In the first place we are in Italy, and not in England, and as you may have noticed, the Italians lack your cold northern logic—we thrive on complication, on intrigue and drama and passion—it's our greatest strength.' He smiled. 'Also, I should point out that according to Pietro you had been encouraging Carlo . . .'

'And everyone else,' Julia put in bitterly.

'Oh yes—but everyone,' he agreed, with a cheerfulness that made her heart beat faster. 'Though I must say I was considerably set down when I discovered this complaisance did not extend to me—however, there was then Carlo's letter. As far as the Ricionis were concerned, that removed all doubts. Signora Ricioni became hysterical, and this plot was born.

'To begin with it was, as Italian plots go, a nice simple, uncomplicated one. I, the dependable family friend, would stage a kidnapping, taking Christina as well as you initially, for credibility. Almost immediately Christina would either be allowed to escape, or would be released. Giovanni—by then he was involved—would use his influence to quieten everything down. After a bit everyone would forget about you. I would keep you out of the way, somewhere quiet and pleasant, until Carlo's marriage was over and Carlo was judged to have come to his senses—which no one doubted would be quickly. And then you would be released. Giovanni would encourage you to return to England—give you money and so on—and I would go back to being a hard-working man and valued family friend. End of story. The only trouble was——' he paused. 'It didn't quite work out like that.'

'Why not?' Julia prompted, keeping her own voice quite calm. 'Why didn't it work out?'

'Well, in the first place, no one had had the intelligence to foresee Carlo's reaction—which was dramatic to say the least. Carlo played the whole thing to the hilt. He announced he was prostrate with grief, that the woman he loved had been stolen, was possibly in danger—even dead. His marriage to Lucretia was therefore out of the question. He was either going to pine away of a broken heart or personally deliver you with fire and the sword—he wasn't quite certain which. It depended on the time of day, and who he was talking to.'

'I see.' Julia gave a little smile, and Raphael's eyes flashed.

'That pleases you? That kind of tribute—from a clown like Carlo?'

'Maybe my confidence is a bit low.' Julia smiled wryly. 'Just now any kind of tribute is quite welcome.'

'Well, I'm sorry to say his emotions did not last,' Raphael said sharply. 'Christina was returned, and Giovanni told Carlo—and the police, incidentally—that the whole thing was a mistake. That you had taken off with a lover, that Christina had gone along out of devilry, and had then got bored and returned. You were still sunning yourself somewhere in another man's arms, and the whole story, the whole investigation had better be quietly dropped to save face. The police played ball, and Carlo had a change of heart. He suddenly discovered you were a faithless, worthless woman who had been stringing him along, whom he didn't care very much about anyway, and the whole idea of marrying Lucretia was suddenly on again. Which was interesting, of course.' He paused. 'Not so much because of Carlo's reaction, that was fairly predictable, but because, as it happens, there was just a little truth in that version of the story.'

'There was?' Julia raised her eyes slowly to his.

'God damn it, don't look at me like that—you know there was!' His face darkened momentarily; then, arrogantly, he held out his hand.

'May I see that letter now?'

Julia hesitated, and suddenly he moved. He was beside her on the bed, and his arms came around her tightly. He lifted her face to his so she was forced to look into his eyes; he looked into hers for a long time, and Julia had the distinct impression that whatever it was he saw there was making him forget what he meant to say next, but eventually, with a gesture of exasperation, he tore his eyes away.

'I knew it! I knew it all along. I know what you want—a declaration. Very well, you shall have one.' He paused, and glanced at her sideways. 'It's very English of you, you know, to want one at all, and quite unnecessary. I know you know, and I know you understand, damn you, but still . . .' He paused, and gritted his teeth. 'I love you.'

Julia's heart gave a great leap of joy, but she managed to hide it.

'You do?' She opened her eyes innocently wide, and Raphael swore.

'Damn you—yes, I do—*and* you know it! I loved you from before I even met you, when I watched you in Rome. I loved you in that car, when I kissed you. I loved you from the moment I set eyes on you. That's why I agreed to take this on—though I didn't admit it to myself, certainly not! I loved you and I wanted you, and I wanted to marry you—and I knew damn well that nothing on God's earth was going to stop me doing that. No matter how you fought me, or disdained me, or—lied to me. Now.' He held out his hand. 'Give me that letter.'

Julia hesitated for one last moment.

'Pietro said . . . he said you married me to ensure my separation from Carlo.'

'And did you believe him?' He lifted her face tenderly to his.

'Perhaps, for a moment.'

'Never believe it again—or anything like it.' His face softened, and he kissed her very gently on the lips. 'I love you, my darling Julia, with my heart and my mind, and my body and my soul. Always. Something like that cannot change—I think you know that.' He lifted her hand and touched the gold ring upon it. 'You knew then,' he said, 'at the church. You must have done. And when I held you in my arms, when I felt like a man standing on the edge of a new world—a place he never thought he would reach, never attain. I believe you knew then, as I did. If you did not, then I believe in nothing. Nothing.' He paused. 'Now may I read that letter?'

Silently Julia handed it to him, and he opened it.

When he looked up at last she saw his eyes light with happiness. He clasped her hand. The mockery, the instinct to protect himself and what he felt—all that had gone from his eyes; the harshness and the occasional bitterness that could mark his mouth, that had gone too. He looked at her with a desperate candour, and Julia felt her heart contract with love for him. Like a current she felt again that electric awareness of him, that ache for his touch. His eyes held hers for a moment, an eternity.

'I thought . . .' He hesitated. 'I thought this would never happen to me, you know? I'd given up hope.' He gave a sudden angry gesture, a quick movement of the hand. 'It began when I was very young. It was dinned into me by my father; by my mother; by my younger brothers and sisters, servants—everyone. I was my father's son, his heir. Can you imagine what that is like never to feel you have an identity of your own? My father had one maxim: *learn, respect—but never trust.* I thought it worked for him until I was twenty and he was dying, and I saw how alone he was, how even my mother, who loved him, could not reach him.' He paused. 'I swore then, for the first time in my life, I would not be like my father. But I thought it was too late until I met you.'

Julia looked at him, at the vulnerability which even his pride could no longer disguise, and she felt herself grow gentle and peaceful and still with the love she felt for him.

'Why then, Raphael?'

'Because my heart spoke,' he answered simply. 'Not my mind, not even my imagination, my heart. And because when that happened, everything else followed. It was as if some great dam broke in my soul. I trusted you. When all the evidence of my eyes, Carlo's letter, those reports the Ricionis commissioned on you—all those things indicated one thing, and you denied them. You looked at me, and I looked into those eyes of yours—your amber eyes, your topaz eyes—and I knew I believed you. That was all. I loved you and I trusted you.' He gave an odd, angry little gesture of the hand.

'It was ironic. I—who had never learned to trust, who had been trained from the cradle to dissemble, to disguise—I was with the only woman I would ever love, and I could not tell her the truth. I had to lie for the sake of my friends. For the sake of a stupid promise.' He looked away. 'I have never hated myself so much. All I could hope—all I could pray was that what I felt was so strong, so intense, that you must sense it. I prayed too, of course, that you would feel as I felt. Because if there were no answer now, no response—there was *nothing.* If I saw a future without you, I saw a wasteland . . . my darling. My sweet Julia . . .' His voice broke. 'Tell me you understand.'

'I understand. I understand because I felt exactly the same. And because—well, I too had to lie.' She smiled gently. 'For Christina's sake, but also for my own. Could I say to a kidnapper, one day after I had first spoken to him, that I loved him?' Her lips rose at the corners. 'I thought it might be prudent not to . . .'

'I hate prudence!' He laughed, and his arms tightened around her joyfully. 'I hate and loathe and distrust it. The first imprudent thing I ever did in my well-organised regimen of a life was to agree to this plan. The second was to kiss you. The third was to love you. The fourth was to marry you—and that is only the beginning.' His eyes darkened; he hesitated. 'After what has just happened to you, I feel I should not say this now—but the next time you tell me you love me, I shall become very imprudent. I cannot look at you without wanting you, and I think . . .' Carefully he loosened Julia's fingers as they tightened against his arm, stood up and drew her gently to her feet. 'I definitely think that now is not the time nor place. I want to take you away from here. I would like to take you back to Kithiras, and then . . .'

Julia smiled at him. She rested her head against his shoulder. With a low groan, he gathered her in his arms, and kissed her on the lips.

'If we take my plane now, we can be there in time for dinner. And then you will sleep—yes, my darling, sleep. And then, in the morning we will begin the honeymoon I planned for us. And this time, there will be no interruptions. And no running away.'

She slept in his arms in his room at Kithiras, and although his body stirred against hers and her own pulsed with desire for him, he did not make love to her. Instead they talked a little, softly, and he stroked her hair until—exhausted but at peace—she fell asleep against his shoulder.

In the morning, when she woke, he fastened around her throat a necklace of gold and topaz.

'They are the colour of your eyes,' he said. 'I want you to wear them and nothing else.'

Then, naked himself, he undid the fastenings of the nightdress she wore and took her in his arms, skin against skin, flesh against flesh. He kissed her eyes, her lips, her throat, her breasts, her hair. Then, when her skin was moist and soft, when the blood in her veins felt sweet and thick, like honey, he slipped his hands under her, and lifted her up to him. When he entered her, she felt no pain, only a great building sense of peace, black shot through with scarlet, gentleness and urgency all at once. It was like a wing beating over her, beating in her, high at the neck of her womb, a pulse that beat with his thrust, and beat faster, so when he slowed, and then moved again, and she sensed the control was going, her body quickened with his.

'Wait,' he said. 'Wait, Julia . . .'

He held her, there on the edge, held himself there.

'Now,' he said, and moved, and took her over.

They stayed in his room all that day, and all the next night. When they emerged the day after that, for breakfast, the servants' expressions were bland. Raphael took her out into the garden, and he smiled.

'Damn them,' he said. 'You saw their faces? They know, of course. They know I no sooner have made love to you than I want to make love to you again . . . you've bewitched me with those topaz eyes of yours, do you know that, Julia?'

She smiled. Had he not bewitched her, she thought, with his eyes, as dark as water at night, with his power, and his strength and his gentleness?

He took her hand, and they walked down the same path she had taken the morning she had run away. Past the oleander trees, and the gardenia bushes, through the scent of the first roses and carnations. They went on further, where the garden grew wilder, until they came to the cliffs that overlooked the sea. There the hillside was warm; there was the scent of rosemary and wild thyme. In the shade of one of the cypress trees, he put his arm around her waist, and together they stood and looked out over the waters of the Mediterranean. Raphael looked down at her, his dark hair falling forward across his forehead. He pretended to scowl.

'You know what is across that water? Italy. Rome. Shall you mind going back there? Being a wife? The Ricionis, the Contadellis—Carlo's marriage—it seems very far away to me, and entirely unimportant, but we shall have to go back there eventually.'

She caught the second of doubt, of hesitation, in his voice, and turned to him sternly. 'Wherever you are, I am,' she said simply. 'You know that.'

His arms tightened around her. 'It is the only thing I truly know. The only thing I care about.'

Julia smiled. 'We can be imprudent in Rome as well as here, you know. We can live in an imprudent house. Hardy can come to dinner. You'll like Hardy—he's been imprudent all his life. We can have imprudent meals . . .'

'Drink imprudent wine—the best kind.'

'Make imprudent love . . .' Julia laughed, as his face grew intent. 'Have imprudent children in imprudent numbers . . .'

'I should like that.' He rested his hand gently over the soft curve of her stomach. 'To feel my child move in your body—I want that, Julia.'

'I want it too.' She laced her arms around his neck, and lifted her face to his. 'I love you, Raphael . . .'

He moved with a swiftness that took her by surprise, pulling her down on to the grass, rolling over so she lay beneath the weight of his body. She gasped, and leaning on his elbows he looked laughingly down into her face.

'I warned you,' he said. 'I warned you what would happen whenever you said that.'

'Here? But someone might . . .'

'I couldn't give a damn.' He began to unbutton her blouse. 'And neither could you . . . Tell me something.' He paused for a moment, fingers warm against her skin, his mouth very close to hers, his eyes dancing. 'Who the hell is this Juliet Morton woman anyway?'

Julia smiled. 'Oh, I don't know—it's a long story . . .'

'Then tell me some other time,' he said grimly. 'We have the rest of our lives, after all. And just now . . .' He bent his head. 'Just now, I don't think I want to hear it.'

'Nor do I,' said Julia, as that golden languor built and grew and flowered in her body, pulsing, keeping time with his touch.

'Good,' said Raphael, and kissed her.

Harlequin Presents

Coming Next Month

Here's how to get this special offer from Harlequin!
As simple as 1...2...3!

December
BETTY NEELS
TREASURY EDITION
COUPON

1. Each month, save one Treasury Edition coupon from your favorite Romance or Presents novel.
2. In four months you'll have saved four Treasury Edition coupons (only one coupon per month allowed).
3. Then all you have to do is fill out and return the order form provided, along with the four Treasury Edition coupons required and $2.95 for postage and handling.

Don't miss a single title from this great collection. The first eight titles have already been published. Complete and mail this coupon today to order books you may have missed.

Harlequin Reader Service
In U.S.A.
901 Fuhrmann Blvd.
P.O. Box 1397
Buffalo, N.Y. 14140

In Canada
P.O. Box 2800
Postal Station A
5170 Yonge Street
Willowdale, Ont. M2N 6J3

Please send me the following titles from the Janet Dailey Americana Collection. I am enclosing a check or money order for $2.75 for each book ordered, plus 75¢ for postage and handling.

_____	ALABAMA	Dangerous Masquerade
_____	ALASKA	Northern Magic
_____	ARIZONA	Sonora Sundown
_____	ARKANSAS	Valley of the Vapours
_____	CALIFORNIA	Fire and Ice
_____	COLORADO	After the Storm
_____	CONNECTICUT	Difficult Decision
_____	DELAWARE	The Matchmakers

Number of titles checked @ $2.75 each = $_____

N.Y. RESIDENTS ADD
   APPROPRIATE SALES TAX $_____

Postage and Handling $___.75____

                                    TOTAL $_____

I enclose _____

(Please send check or money order. We cannot be responsible for cash sent through the mail.)

PLEASE PRINT

NAME _____

ADDRESS _____

CITY _____

STATE/PROV. _____